A Person of Letters

To Hugh, my old friend, best wishes!

RON THOMPSON

Ron Thompson

Martin Scribler Media
Toronto

This is a work of fiction. Any references to historical events, real people, or real places are used fictitiously. Other names, characters, places, and events are products of the author's imagination, and any resemblance to actual events or places or persons, living or dead, is entirely coincidental.

Copyright © 2015 by Ron Thompson

All rights reserved. No part of this work may be reproduced or transmitted in any form or by any means – graphic, electronic, or mechanical, including photocopying, recording, taping, or information storage and retrieval systems – without the prior written permission of the publisher, or in the case of photocopying or other reprographic copying, a license from the Canadian Copyright Licensing Agency.

Permission is provided for the use of brief quotations embodied in reviews. For information or queries, contact info@martinscribler.com.

Martin Scribler Media trade paperback first edition, September 2015

Cover design by Jana Pavlasek
Illustration by Andrew Judd

ISBN: 0994796102
ISBN-13: 978-0-9947961-0-3

To Jacquie and Kaitlin, for their patience.

Unprovided with original learning, unformed in the habits of thinking, unskilled in the arts of composition, I resolved to write a book.

Edward Gibbon

CHAPTER ONE

If you can't annoy somebody, there's little point in writing.

Kingsley Amis

I deal with writer's block by lowering my expectations.

Malcolm Gladwell

In this city, you are forever accosted by nuts. To look them in the eye, as I was raised to do, invites an unwelcome dialogue with a deranged *philosophe*. Careful breaking off contact. It is best to endure a few moments of one-sided discourse, an exposition on how that man over there is a Martian; how the swine flu is a government plot; or how Jesus could save us all if only the government would grant Him refugee status. Give no offense but move away at the first opportunity. Otherwise, things may spiral. At the very least you will be asked for a smoke or a few coins for a coffee. These are mere gambits to hit you up for some real money; or the prelude to more wobbly facts about that goggle-eyed Martian, the swine flu cover-up, or the lamentable state of Our Lord and Saviour's refugee claim.

The wild-eyed man who sermonizes to passersby from his

perch atop a fire hydrant is easy to avoid, but others sneak up on you. You need a strategy to fend them off.

Assumed oblivion is the usual tack. Keep your head down, hurry like you need to be somewhere, and look no one in the eye lest you be mistaken for a rube or a crazy yourself.

Now there's a thought: a crazy yourself. Turn everything on its head and act like one of them. Unconventional, but it can work, so long as you don't hold back. Look *everyone* in the eye, be careful not to dress too well, and mumble to an invisible companion. Stay in character, and you may walk freely amongst street loons and hucksters, the sanity of your thoughts undetected, your pockets jingling with change—

I started at a *CLANG*, looked up and saw a crowd of disembarking passengers scatter before a man on a bike. The streetcar driver dinged him again but the man rode on, a study in poise. At the third ding he finally acknowledged the rebuke, sort of, by extending a finger, the middle one, over his shoulder, without deigning to look back.

Here, I reflected, was ballsy rudeness, another viable strategy for urban survival.

We were at Spadina, almost at my stop. I stood and edged towards the rear exit, glancing at those I passed, wondering what they saw when they glanced at me. Perhaps nothing out of the ordinary: a normal-looking person within the usual range, nineteen times out of twenty. These days the concept of "normal" is inclusive and forgiving, and rightly so, for everyone is different, everyone's unique—"exceptional" in the modern parlance; and that is surely something to celebrate.

I cast my eyes down, away from others' gaze, knowing *I* was nothing to celebrate. How could anyone celebrate an empty vessel, a cipher, a lifelong piece of flotsam now sinking inexorably, no bottom in sight.

I got off at McCaul and crossed College at the lights. At the curb I stopped, feeling a presence, a flit of light in the gathering dusk. I turned around to look.

No one. College Street was quiet. The streetcar was

already at University, pouring passengers into the subway. Many blocks to the south, the towers of Bay Street shone brightly in the autumn dusk. They were what had caught my eye. They were the weight I'd suddenly felt. Within them, and in towers just like them in London, in Frankfurt and New York, traders and moneymen sat at their desks, hunched before screens; or huddled in boardrooms, caffeinated, enervated, stomachs churning, waiting. The Asian markets were just about to open and Lehman was dead, the banks in Europe on life support. Trillions in value had already evaporated. Uncle Sam had just grabbed Fannie Mae and Freddie Mac and bailed out AIG. A world the financiers had thought predictable was crumbling, and they were scrambling, running scenarios, unwinding positions, dumping what they could before it was too late. Houses of cards, those glimmering towers, teetering now, undermined by Rolexed jokers.

You take the risk, you wear it. Guilty is as guilty does. I glanced at my own watch, turned my back and walked away, up Kings College Road and onto campus.

*

A few minutes later I stood in the rear of a wood-panelled teaching theatre, propping the heavy door open with my shoulder and eavesdropping. I was early and Farley was in full flight.

". . . situational ethics . . . moral relativism . . . subjectivism a cover for . . ."

I considered slipping back out. I could just meet him at the bar.

". . . frankly, criticisms like these miss the point. In postmodernism 'Truth' does not exist in an objective sense. Truth is *created*. And there, in a nutshell, is the crux of its appeal."

Laptop keys clattered like falling rain. He paused to consult his notes.

"Postmodernists recognize the fragmentation of existence, the futility of the grand narrative. They respond with irony and black humour. Case in point: Joseph Heller's *Catch-22*. Or Thomas Pynchon's *Gravity's Rainbow*. There's a dose of paranoia in that one. Other examples. Anyone?"

The click of keys ceased abruptly. Farley stood at the podium and waited. A delicate hand rose from the front row but he seemed not to notice it. His eyes roamed the big amphitheatre's middle tier.

The hand began to wave. Farley's gaze rose higher, away from it, towards me.

"LOLITA!"

The hand's owner had spoken louder than she'd intended, and her answer drew a laugh, but Farley merely nodded. "Yes. Nabokov's *Lolita*. It's told by an unreliable narrator, which is a common device in postmodern literature. Others?"

Another flurry of tapping was followed by glacial stillness. Someone coughed. Farley acknowledged a hand. It belonged to a bearded youth in a lumberjack shirt.

"*Slaughterhouse-Five*, by Kurt Vonnegut."

From where I stood resisting the weight of the door, I could see the lumberjack's screen. It was on Wikipedia.

"Sure. That one's a good example of the writer placing himself in his own work. Fiction reflecting upon itself. The device has been around for a long time—Cervantes did it with *Don Quixote*—but the postmodernists really embraced it as their own."

Amazing how classrooms had changed since Farley and I were in first year. The rustle of paper was almost lost in the rattle of keys. Half the students were on laptops. Most were earnestly inputting notes, but there were two scrolling on Facebook and one watching YouTube; and Paul Bunyan on Wikipedia. In the front row, Lolita pensively twirled a tress around her finger and pulled it taut.

". . . what it stands for, if anything. They parodize convention yet tip their hats to what's gone before. And that's possibly postmodernism's only unifying thread, the notion that nothing is new, that everything's been tried, that there are no originals left to discover. And if that's the case, is postmodernism unoriginal and derivative, soulless and clichéd? 'Simulacran', if you will, to adjectivize Baudrillard?" He paused and smiled vaguely. I glanced at the time, feeling fidgety, thinking he must be almost done. "Or is the cliché intentional, and thus darkly subversive?"

A hand shot up from the front row. It was Lolita again, still winding that tress with the fingers of her free hand. Farley scanned a far horizon well beyond her reach. "A realist might say that the postmodernist is childish, that he never grew up. And the postmodernist would offer no defence. In fact, he'd testify for the prosecution. John Barth, for example, once described his own books as novels imitating the form of a novel, by an author imitating the role of an author."

Only I saw his face fall at the bare murmur this drew. He covered his disappointment by glancing down at his watch. "Any questions? Comments?" He looked up and noticed Lolita. "Yes?"

"Professor Lictor, what's the difference between postmodernism and modernism? They seem similar in many ways."

There was a sudden commotion in the corridor behind me, shouts and scuffling, some echoing laughter. I worried Farley would get distracted so I stepped away from the door and gave it a tug. It began to close, but slowly. I gave it another tug and headed for a seat in the back row.

". . . solved through art—through the work of the artist." The door clanged shut and Farley looked up. I waved and sank into a chair. His eyes lingered on me for a moment before he continued. "Postmodernists also perceive a world in crisis, but in their case it's not solvable. Think of the futility, the powerlessness and disconnectedness this causes. Think Man-as-Failure and hold that thought . . . Now give a giant wink. *That's* postmodernism."

Two students chuckled appreciatively a few rows down. Farley acknowledged them with a slight tilt of his head. He could not see the screen they were watching: YouTube, a dog in a casket.

"Another major distinction relates to endings but . . ." He gathered his notes and tapped them on the lectern. ". . . in the spirit of postmodernism I'll start there next time."

I jostled against the flow of departure to get down to where he stood amid a cluster of students. When I got there only one remained, and he was addressing her. ". . . an unconventional arc, a disjointed narrative with many voices or a single flawed and undependable narrator." He looked up, saw me and nodded. "Look, I have a meeting now, but if you'd like to discuss it further I have office hours tomorrow. Come by any time after three." She smiled and turned to go and I realized it was Lolita.

He watched her climb the stairs towards the exit and I did too. "It's Henry Miller time, pal," he said softly, punching me lightly on the shoulder.

"That's why I'm here. But not for Miller. Tankhouse. Let's go."

His grin faded and he seemed to study my face. The scrutiny made me uncomfortable. When he turned his attention to packing up I gave my nose a furtive swipe.

We walked to a student dive on College and ordered vodka shooters, and when they came he downed his straight. To be sociable I did the same. "So," I said when I'd caught my breath. "Postmodernism."

"It's a survey course. The history of modern literature." He signalled the waitress.

"Ah."

I switched to beer and he ordered another shot. He was on a post-performance high.

"So how's it going," he asked when the drinks arrived, "on the new project? Are you—"

"Pretty good. What about you?"

"What?"

"How's everything? Good?"

"Yeah."

"Fantastic." He opened his mouth to speak but I beat him to it. "And Paola? How's she doing?"

"She's fine." His second glass was already empty but he tipped it up anyway. "How about Genny?"

"She's good. She's making brownies with Chloe tonight."

"Good." He leaned forward. "Niceties aside—"

"Do you have a hollow leg or what? Let's get you another." I looked for the waitress. A table of frat boys was talking her up.

"Where are you on your project? How's it going?"

I looked him in the eye. "I'm doing research right now."

"Seriously."

I waved but failed to catch the waitress's attention. Meanwhile, I could feel Farley's gaze on me.

"The truth, bub. What are you doing, really?"

"A great thinker once said that Truth does not exist in the objective sense."

"Don't try that on me. How's it going?"

The waitress was oblivious. No joy there. He had me cornered. I turned to meet his eye again. "Not good."

He waited.

"Ideas," I said, slumping now. "There are none."

He considered this and nodded. "That's happens. It's not unusual. A writer's just someone who finds writing harder than others do. Thomas Mann said that."

"You've got a quote for each and every occasion. I bet they're all made up. Does anyone ever challenge you?"

"Are you writing at all?"

I shrugged.

"You've got to," he said, leaning in again. "You've got to fight it and work your way out."

"You think I haven't tried?"

"Look. Think of it this way: you're mired deep in the doo doo."

"What a frank and honest assessment. Thank you for it. Very helpful. And sensitive. Thank you kindly indeed."

"Hear me out. You're blocked. *That's* the story. Your struggle is the story. *You* are the story. Make it yours. Make a silk purse from a sow's ear. Lemonade from lemons."

"Night soil from—"

"A poioumenon."

"I'd go with the Anglo-Saxon. More punch."

"No no. 'Poioumenon'. It's a type of metafiction. A story about the creation of a story. Look, bud: you're here, whether you like it or not. Write about it. About *this*. Your creative process, your development as a writer. It's the journey not the destination, that makes it art."

Art. My art. I wondered if he was mocking me. "'Poioumenon'," I said spitefully. "Is that one of yours?"

"No," he winced, suddenly deflated. "It's somebody else's."

CHAPTER TWO

There are three rules for writing a novel. Unfortunately, no one knows what they are.

Somerset Maugham

If I had to give young writers advice, I would say don't listen to writers talking about writing or themselves.

Lillian Hellman

The next morning I decided to try Farley's idea. Anything to break the logjam. Things just weren't flowing, not like they had before. But I'll get to that. Right now, I'll start at the beginning.

*

My parents were prairie people, child survivors of the Dust Bowl and Great Depression, the dual cataclysm that levelled a generation. Yet neither of their families was ever reduced to relief, not a single voucher or charity shipment from the East. They were farmers, self-reliant despite the times; they subsisted on what they grew, pulled out of a lake, or shot; they sold what little surplus remained to buy essentials.

They were raised to be hard working and stubbornly independent. They believed the Good Lord helped those who helped themselves, that beggars can't be choosers, that children should be seen and not heard. Charity began at home, pride went before the fall, never blow your own horn. They passed these sturdy values on to my brothers and me. We were taught to finish what we started, to never give up, to suffer in silence and eat our vegetables. Look a person in the eye, give a good handshake, always wear clean underwear. Nobody, we were told firmly and often, is better than anyone else—with the possible exception of Anglicans.

I concluded from these parental adages, from careful observation of my father, and from the old movies shown on our one TV channel in Poplar Lake, Saskatchewan, that a man should be like John Wayne or Gary Cooper—quiet, diligent, and dependable. Men minded their own business, until a thug like Hitler came along, then they got the job done. Women, by contrast—well; women were a mystery, an object of fascination for me. The only female in our house was my mom and she, being a mom, wasn't really a woman. Frankly, outside of a tattered back-issue of *National Geographic* in our local library (the volume with pictures of bare-breasted pygmies), I was lacking in sources on the topic. I could hardly ask my mother about females, and my three older brothers, being worldly and sophisticated—they'd all played in the school marching band—would ridicule me mercilessly if I asked them about dames.

I was left to draw impressions from those old movies on TV. It seemed women were either callous and cold, or cheeky and rude—until you saved their lives. Then they got real clingy. That sounded good. Mushy stuff aside, those cone-shaped fifties breasts looked mighty interesting to me. Alluring, I might have said, if I'd known what alluring meant.

While my brothers were hardy, rough-and-tumble and athletic, I was clumsy and uncoordinated, easily distracted, a knee-bobbing fidgeter to boot. "He'll grow out of it!" my mother insisted. She forced my brothers to take me along with them to ensure I did, and if they objected she whapped them on the head with a spatula. Thus I was included in neighbourhood games and outgrew my extreme spasticity to appear, at first, only possibly handicapped, and then passably middling—that is, competent enough to avoid embarrassing my brothers. But truthfully, when it came to physical challenges, I had to work at it; I was a late-bloomer, bordering on never. In the water I never got beyond the dead man's float; at the plate, I could not connect eye, brain, and body to deliver even a glancing blow to a baseball. I struggled for years to ride a bike, although this might have been because my parents eschewed the tyke-sized options for a model I could ride into adulthood. "He'll grow into it!" Mom maintained. "He doesn't need training wheels. A fall or two won't put him off. Will it, Junior?"

I had few friends and didn't make new ones easily. Frankly, I didn't connect well with others. My interests were solitary, and my distraction amongst people, my challenges in the physical world, turned into laser focus when I was on my own. I was happy to read or do math, make up stories, or pour over my collections (of which there were many: stamps, hockey cards, match books, ticket stubs, cash register receipts, and coins, to name a few).

Early on, I showed an affinity for numbers and words—I saw patterns in both. In Grade Two, I could add a column of figures in my head and recite Dr Seuss from memory. Then I discovered history, which had discernible patterns as well. I memorized all the prime ministers since 1867, the presidents since 1789, the Big Power monarchs since 1492 (an arbitrary figure, I admit), along with the dates of their ascension. My father was an army veteran with a bookshelf full of history, much of it about his war; I consumed it all. By Grade Five, I was doing algebra and writing stories in iambic pentameter. To me it seemed right, to write it that way. Not everyone understood. "There's nothing odd about that," I overheard my mother say sharply during a parent-teacher interview. "It's just a phase, not some syndrome. That boy's quick as a whip." Or a spatula. "They want to give you some kind of test, honey," she told me later, "but we already know you're smart. *That's* what you are. Smart. We don't need specialists to tell us that."

There's nothing odd about that. I heard her say that many times. But I knew there *was* something odd, something different about me.

My parents gave me lots of positive reinforcement, but they were not evenly disposed to my two scholastic affinities. Numbers, they approved of—there would be jobs for a whiz at numbers. Words, not so much. They worried I might become a politician or a poet, or something even worse.

But words were my true passion. I wanted to write.

*

What if I'd committed myself to writing, way back then?

At university in the eighties I majored in math and economics while Farley, intent on becoming a Serious Writer, majored in English. We met in a compulsory first year English course. Half the students were engineers grumbling about having to take an artsy-fartsy class when there were more important subjects, like experimental fluid dynamics and petroleum geo-mechanics; the rest were artsy-fartsy majors embarrassed by their scorn. And then there was Farley, the flame-headed fellow with the Fu Manchu and black beret who sat next to me on the very first day. He plunked down a ratty copy of *Iron in the Soul* and said "Fuck you" to a sniggering engineer.

The course was taught by an elderly Yorkshireman named Yeares. That first day he stood at the lectern and looked out balefully, perhaps wondering how he had gone from brilliant Young Turk at Cambridge to sessional lecturer on the frozen prairie. And then he spoke. From Chaucer, through Shakespeare and the Romantics, to Dylan Thomas and Walt Whitman, he had an encyclopaedic ability to quote verse from memory; drama, prose, his range was prodigious. He talked about the methods and goals of literature, the influence of society and philosophy on all things literary, and vice versa, all without notes. He threw out examples and citations like a bird lover feeds pigeons. "Pearls before swine," Farley called it, referring to the engineers—half of whom dropped out before Christmas.

As we filed out of class on the first Friday of term, Farley pulled me aside and suggested a barley sandwich.

The words were barely out when a door crashed open at the end of the hall, and a crowd spilled into the already-jammed corridor. For a moment the newcomers shoved and jostled among themselves. Some flailed and shouted, others stumbled and fell and shouted back. It was like a Roughrider rally, only more orderly. Then a whistle blew, a blaze of crimson unfurled from a pole, and they shuffled forward beneath a banner proclaiming them the *Saskatchewan Student Movement (Marxist-Leninist) (Anti Socio-Imperialist Vanguard)*.

"I had one of those this morning."

I glanced at Farley, uncertain what he meant.

"A movement, bud."

We were witnessing the SSM (ML) (AS-IV)'s weekly spontaneous demonstration of proletarian anger. Two standard-bearers held the banner taut and advanced with chins jutted, vanguard of the vanguard. But behind them came no revolutionary legion, just a few scruffy men in work boots and four or five spotty poli sci majors. In their midst marched a Stone Age mother goddess in a plaid shirt who punched the air with her fist and bellowed, "Down with capitalism! Death to the running dog lackeys of imperialism!" into a dented megaphone. She was (we later learned) Cathy the Commie, mainstay of the SSM (ML) (AS-IV) and its de facto leader since 1973. Her cadre dutifully repeated her chants while the Masses, the students they intended to mobilize to The Revolution, grinned and gawked and scratched their mullets, oblivious to The Struggle. Cathy's obscure slogans didn't help. "Death to the Fourth International!" she shrilled into the bullhorn, echoed by her followers.

"The fourth international *what?*" whispered Farley, affronted by the absence of a noun. A moment later he edged out of their path and pulled out a notebook.

"What are you doing?"

"Lit-rah-chah, old boy," he said in good approximation of old Professor Yeares. "The characters, the strange oddities of life . . . I've got to get this down."

Week One, and he was already committed, already working on his first novel.

"Down with the military-agricultural complex!" Cathy shrieked, her voice a tinny bleat.

That one lit us both up. She was really trying to connect.

"Go home to Russia!" taunted a Don Johnson look-alike from the crowd of onlookers.

"War mongers! Sell-outs!" returned Cathy, meaning the Russians, not *Miami Vice* wannabes.

Cathy the Commie became a mainstay of our Friday schedule, memorable beyond her sloganeering for what Farley called her "anarcho-feminine charms." He had a theory about the SSM (ML) (AS-IV): that its members, male and female alike, were not attracted by the incisive clarity of Lenin's thought, or by the spellbinding prose of Karl Marx, but by Cathy the Commie's capacious, unrestrained breasts and oversized booty. He was only half-joking when he proposed joining the rally some Friday to see if her revolutionary tenets included free love. "The socialist paradise isn't Albania," he averred. "It's between the sheets at Cathy's."

Farley had set himself a life goal of introducing a hundred words into the English language. He was inspired by the Germans, with their knack for stringing things together, and he tested his prototypes on me by slipping them into our conversations and watching my reaction. "Cathy's got *bosomheft*," he told me once, observing my face.

I envied him his devotion to language, his freedom for invention. While he focused on writing and literature, I was immersed in the mechanics of the Capital Asset Pricing Model and Keynesian theory, both of which marked me as Cathy's class enemy.

After observing the weekly People's rally from the

sidelines, we retired to Gabe's, the student union bar, to drink and talk about literature, art, politics, and the world in general. One of our mutual passions was the environment, and we spent hours debating and comparing the effectiveness of activists like Greenpeace and Sea Shepherd to that of more radical political groups like the Red Brigades and the Baader-Meinhof Group. We were both convinced that for the right cause (and the environment was the right cause) direct action was justified—necessary even.

We never chose to do anything about it, mind you, but the principle was fascinating.

Over the course of an afternoon others joined us, and there was a distinct shift in the dynamic. We started with impassioned debates about principles and causes, but alcohol uncorked Farley's inner blarney; inevitably he lost interest in the original topic and took fresh note of his surroundings, and as he hit his boozy stride he morphed from serious young intellectual into bold raconteur. He became boisterous and loud, and others, mostly female, were drawn to the flame of his personality. The girls, pretty young things from towns like Meadow Lake and Watrous, new to the Paris of the Prairies, were infatuated. A man in a beret! A charmer, a sophisticate—he'd been to Winnipeg! And Farley, north of .08, inherently knew what to do. He had a natural touch, a matchless technique. While regaling the group his eyes scanned over the laughing eager faces until he found his mark. I always knew who she was, for from the moment he spotted her he behaved as though she did not exist. He ignored her so thoroughly, charmed others so obviously to her exclusion, was so blatantly oblivious to her presence that it was downright hurtful—until, late in the going, she took the lure and came to *him*. "Reeling in the b-ass," he called it privately, miming the motion. From that point it was as good as over; a half hour of his attentive patter made panties drop like walnuts in September. Farley was a closer, a red-haired Casanova.

I had none of his booze-fuelled talent. Whatever my

blood-alcohol level, I was hopelessly inept at conversation with girls. Whenever I was nervous (and pretty girls made me nervous) I blabbed inanely on subjects I'd previously discussed with lucidity. Farley coached me on what to say and do. "Make eye contact," he said. "Try not to fidget. It makes you look shifty. And don't talk about World War Two. I know you know all the details. Girls don't care. Stick with unthreatening subjects. Remember, they like to talk about themselves." It didn't help. I'd start with an icebreaker, something inoffensive like "What's your major?" A proven opener, but when she returned the question I'd tell her about mathematical finance, and how it differed from mathematical economics. Rational pricing, probabilistic risk assessment, and value-at-risk were concepts that needed explaining. "Consider the Black-Scholes option pricing model," I'd say. As I prattled on, careful not to break eye contact, her gaze inexorably drifted towards Farley. Or the door.

I lacked the gene for small talk, and if a girl didn't flee at the first opportunity, but stayed—inexplicably interested, or shy and inept like me—I invariably still blew it. If she bantered back, I blathered in return; if she challenged me on something, I changed the subject. (Drop back and punt—that always worked for me.) My problem was that I could make no sense of verbal hints or visual clues. Nuance was entirely lost on me. On occasions when I seemed to be connecting, when a girl did not escape to the bathroom or wave a friend over for help—as she, arms raised, splayed her long hair across her feminine shoulders, her exquisite breasts straining against the fabric of her blouse; or as she studied me with eyes narrowed and head tilted, a knowing Mona Lisa smile on sly ruby lips—I would ask if she lifted weights or had done something to her neck.

I learned to disguise my haplessness and the anguish it caused me by affecting a cerebral impatience for the Game. From a certain point in the evening, talk of direct action, punk rock and Sartre forgotten for the night, I sat back and observed the bacchanal that surrounded Farley. While he stumbled into bed with many a nubile lass, I tumbled into bed with many a good book.

The day after a night of letting loose Farley was the soul of discretion. He never bragged, never embellished; and our friendship never wavered. Somewhere along the way I realized I was a touchstone for him—although I never understood exactly why.

Our academic paths diverged after first year. Having committed himself to writing, he continued in English; old Professor Yeares became his mentor. As much as I wanted to do the same, I continued instead down a rabbit hole of arcane specialization from which I would emerge years later, battered and wheezing, back where I should have started.

*

When we graduated we were both awarded full scholarships at the same English university, he on the basis of editing the campus paper and authoring a slim volume of sex-obsessed poetry, me on the basis of my acumen with numbers. In the first glorious weeks of Michaelmas term we attended sessions with our respective tutors until we realized they were optional, at which point we both adopted a program of "self-study," which allowed us more time to explore the city's many interesting pubs.

After the Christmas break I realized I would wash out if I didn't reform. Besides, I was feeling the combined effects of the lack of sunshine and a diet of fried fish and mushy peas. Farley, though, was made of sturdier stuff; he was able to sustain, even thrive on, an unstructured lifestyle. His tutors, when he met with them, had similar work habits, so his seminars rotated between various public free houses. This fluid regime brought out his innate talent, which blossomed in Blighty. British girls, Americans, Europeans, they all succumbed to his charm, and as his experience deepened his repertoire and understanding of women grew. He became more than a one trick pony—he became a master in the field of seduction. Over the winter term and into the spring, as I buckled down to work, he seduced and bedded most of the pretty young undergrads enrolled in English and literature at his college, then branched into the social sciences and out to other colleges.

He also found time for activism. He became involved in what he viewed as *the* most important political cause of our day: not Greenham Common, the campaign to ban deployment of nuclear-tipped cruise missiles in Britain, but CAMRA—the Campaign for Real Ale. By our second year he was on the executive of the university's CAMRA chapter; he became secretary, then treasurer, and finally vice-president. Only a schism in the movement (precipitated by a heated debate over the Bavarian Purity Law of 1516) prevented him from assuming the presidency. It would have been a first, a colonial as chief executive, but he took a stand on a matter of principle by championing the Bavarian brewing standard, a position which made him suspect among CAMRA's Little Englander faction.

At the height of the rift the Little Englanders papered the campus with posters proclaiming. "Say NO to Europiss!" and (more cutting to Farley) "Foreigners don't know ale from lager." No one slights like an Englishman. The vitriol directed at Farley caused him to become disillusioned with both the cause and his fellow travellers. "They're acting like beercompoops over the bloody *Reinheitsgebot*," he told me, closely observing my face. I was careful not to react. He was still working on his hundred words, and I had resolved to be a hard judge.

By our third year he'd put it behind him, although it was clear the beer wars had left a bitter aftertaste. "I'm over it," he told me. "I'm no ideolager." (Again, that hopeful, inquiring look, but I refused to blink.) I didn't believe him, for he was a man who needed a cause. Luckily, his interests were evolving, and he soon found another movement into which he could pour his passion. He became founding president of the local chapter of the Campaign for the Purity of Single Malt Whisky.

He loved the horses and I sometimes joined him at the

track, or for a night at the pub, but those occasions grew rare. I was a slave to routine, in fact I thrived on it; and I'd found a girlfriend. Farley called me slave to something else, but sex was better than a hangover. He could handle both, the former with herculean enthusiasm, the latter with epic stoicism. I never acquired his taste for whisky, and when we met up he'd drink two or three shots for my every pint. Appropriately, his dissertation was on Dylan Thomas.

CHAPTER THREE

The parody is the last refuge of the frustrated writer. Parodies are what you write when you are associate editor of the Harvard Lampoon. The greater the work of literature, the easier the parody. The step up from writing parodies is writing on the wall above the urinal.

Ernest Hemingway

It's not a good idea to put your wife into a novel; not your latest wife anyway.

Norman Mailer

Morning on the home front. Chloe has already left for school. Genny has a meeting at the faculty club, for she is deep into the machinations of the faculty association. Before she goes she is all business—this for supper, take it out of the freezer at noon, Chloe has piano after school—then she is out the door, moving at a brisk pace to catch the College streetcar. She is methodical and purposeful in the morning, anticipating every eventuality, a choreographer arranging a can-can through life's cow pasture. But today, five minutes after her departure, I'm standing in the kitchen, avoiding writing by wondering what to cook tonight for supper, when I find her lunch on the counter. This is one of her belt-tightening measures, adopted since I gave up my job as a financial Frankenstein.

I sling on an old coat, slip on my muddy garden shoes, and clomp towards the streetcar stop. She's still there in a crowd of commuters that spills onto the road as the streetcar arrives. I call to her and she turns, sees me, and for a moment worry clouds her brow. She steps out of the queue and I sprint the last twenty yards to meet her.

"Are you okay?" she asks.

I hold up her lunch. "Delivery."

She smiles. There is relief in her eyes. "Thanks, you." My gallantry earns me a kiss on the lips and a hug, a nice close one. I know she hears me wheezing from the run. She wears no scent, avoiding chemicals for me.

I watch the streetcar rumble across Roncesvalles. I don't mind her forgetfulness today. It's gotten me out of my funk for a few minutes. I like the mornings, being out and about, but it's also my most creative time. I return home, savouring the dank smell of slick leaves on wet asphalt, the rare brightness of a clear October sky. When I enter the house I kick off my shoes, see that there's compost to take out, and slip them back on. I'll do some raking while I'm out.

*

Genny is an Irish Catholic from Nova Scotia, the product of six hard-drinking generations of grinding rural poverty and priestly oppression. As a consequence of her ancestors' deprivations and humiliations, she is ardently anti-cleric and anti-capitalist. Yet her own upbringing was decidedly middle-class. She was the brainy middle child of a teacher and a librarian, both the first of their line to survive childhood *and* the rigours of Grade Eleven.

Genny the bluenoser and I the stubble-jumper would never have met in Canada; it was our fate to meet in England, where it was her exotic looks that first drew my attention. She claims to be part Mi'kmaq but that is based on circumstantial evidence and wishful solidarity. I first noticed her at a reception in the quad at Farley's college, where she had arrived to reside at the beginning of my second year. Maybe she did have a smidge of Mi'kmaq, or maybe she was a pure black Celt as her granny stubbornly maintained, but she stood out in the pallid throng, with her strong features and lustrous black hair. She also had big blue eyes and an ooh la la bod shown to stunning effect in a little black dress.

She was being chatted up simultaneously by Chuck from Denver, a pasty string-bean I assumed to be English, and an Aussie we called Fair Dinkum Bruce, a second year law student and celebrated cocksman. Even Farley had come to respect him for his shameless effrontery with women. ("It's his technique," he told me once. "It works for him, but it's really in-your-face. Risky. Myself, I don't get it.") I jostled through the crowd to say hello to Bruce and Chuck, but really to see Genny up close. When I arrived she turned her eyes on me for the first time and I went blank. Bruce introduced me and she said, "Genny Paterson," and shook my hand.

"So where are Saint Fwancis the Saviour and Dollhousie?" the pasty Brit put in quickly, resenting my interruption and seizing the conversational initiative—but he was defending against the wrong guy.

"Nigel, old bean, they're in the bloody *colonies*," said Fair Dinkum Bruce. "In snowy Canada, land of winter. Genny here is a real live Eskimo. I'll wager there were no Eskimos back at Eton College, were there?"

"Wugby," said Nigel.

"Inuit," Genny said, frowning at Bruce.

"Oh me too," Bruce said. "You bet I am."

Chuck from Denver, who had hair like Robert Redford, asked if she was a skier.

"No," she said.

Chuck opened his mouth but Bruce beat him to it. "Too cold, I'll bet, in Dal-Howzy. I skied one year in the Rockies. Jasper. Worked mornings, skied afternoons. Had a fantastic bloody time. It's a party place, but cold as a witch's tit. Some days you could freeze your nuts off. How do you stay warm there, Genny, in freezing cold Dal-Howzy? I'll bet you've got a snug little parka, haven't you?"

Our small circle seemed to freeze, as though someone had just tinkered with the space-time continuum over in Professor Hawking's lab. Genny and Bruce held eyes, while waiters with platters of fancy British hors d'oeuvres wandered through the crowd. I plucked an orange lump on a toothpick off a passing tray and, thinking I should say something in the sudden silence, rather than appear mute and stupid, held it out for all to see.

"Oh boy oh boy!" I said. "It doesn't get any better than this. Plenty of *cheese* around here, eh Bruce?" I sniffed the cube, popped it in my mouth and took a swig of Sainsbury wine.

Genny laughed, which made me feel good. After all—a pretty girl laughing, and a tasty piece of cheddar: life was swell.

Chuck grinned and grabbed some meat on a stick before moving off into the crowd. Nigel begged off, too ("Excuse me, fwiends fwom Wugby," he explained); then Bruce, who was still hovering near Genny, got tugged into another conversation, something about diving. All this party flux left Genny alone with me, so we chatted, me inanely, as I do when I can't believe my luck, she with sober intensity. I wasn't sure if that sobriety was begrudging, as in, "Oh god, what a bore," or just the way she was, but I learned in those few moments that she'd arrived the week before to start her doctorate in social anthropology, and she was a bit lost in the scale and traditions of the place. She gestured around at the clock tower, the spires, the quad and crowd. "Don't you think this is all a bit snotty?" she asked, one perfect brow raised in inquiry. "So witty, so pretentious. After just a couple of days here I had to get away. I went down to London for the weekend." We both marvelled at how good the British trains were, she mentioned a few of the galleries she had visited, and I was telling her about the World War Two exhibit at the Imperial War Museum when Farley arrived and I introduced them.

"Hello," he said, distracted, then looked to me. "We've got to go or we'll be late. Time's a wasting." Time was drinking time. We were only going down the road to his local.

"Why don't you come with us?" I asked Genny, riding a wave of reckless courage. "This thing will peter out in a half hour. All the welcome receptions do, then everyone heads for the pub anyway. Might as well get there early with some friendly unpretentious types."

She smiled. "I'd better stay. Meet people in my college, mingle, that sort of thing."

Once we were out of earshot, past the porter's lodge and out in the street, me picking cheese from my teeth with a toothpick, I said to Farley, "Wow. She's a fox."

"She's a bitch," he said. "Sometimes you can just tell."

*

It was a few weeks before we met again, around the end of November. I was crossing St Giles and ran into her coming from the direction of her college. Literally, ran into her, for her head was down and she barged straight into me. As we picked ourselves up off the pavement she recognized me. "Oh I'm so sorry!" she burbled.

"My fault entirely. I should have looked where you were going."

It was a drizzly grey day and I could see immediately that she was blue. I don't mean her eyes, which were still intensely blue. I mean down; those beautiful peepers were if anything a bit teary.

"Are you all right?"

"Yes. Yes, I'm— I'm fine." She wiped one cheek with a hand scraped from her fall. "Sodding weather. Hello, by the way."

"Hi. You get used to it. I hated my first winter here."

Her eyes dropped to the ground and she knelt to pick up her bag and a few scattered books. I knelt to help and kept talking. "I eventually took up running, which helped, when I couldn't make the hockey team. That was some kind of first.

No Canadian ever *didn't* make the hockey team before. Seems I can only turn left. Why do people always skate counter-clockwise in Canada? Don't you think that warrants a Royal Commission, or some kind of public inquest?" Here I was, babbling, improvising, even telling a small fib about trying out for hockey. I just wanted to engage her, get her talking, cheer her up and see her smile.

We both stood and she smiled tentatively—success! I forged recklessly ahead.

"You know, if you don't mind me saying, you look like you could use a cup of coffee."

For a moment she stood looking uncertain. She used her palm to wipe her cheek again, then a pinkie to wipe beneath both eyes. An icy drizzle doused us both.

"Come on. Let's go somewhere warm and have a nice cuppa."

She nodded.

We went to a Greek take-out and sat in for a watery cup of Nescafe. We talked about the prairies and the Maritimes and laughed at our provincialisms. She told me why she was interested in social anthropology (a fascination with social class, stratification and the role of gender); I told her something about my work on financial risk and changed the subject as quickly as I could.

Within fifteen minutes she had disarmed me so effectively that I confessed what I really wanted to do.

"I can tell you're thoughtful," she said. "That's what it takes to be a writer. You'll do it, someday."

I affected a shrug and for the first time avoided her gaze. Beneath the table, my knee began to jump.

"Really, I think you have the right personality. Still waters run deep and all that."

I dared not correct her; instead I changed the subject. "Do you think there's an ideal temperament for it? Many of the greatest writers were outrageously extroverted. It's amazing they ever found time to write, or that they were ever sober enough. Maybe they wrote drunk. Look at Hemingway or

Faulkner, or Eugene O'Neill. Do you remember my friend Farley? You met him at that start-of-term reception. He's doing his dissertation on Dylan Thomas. Now there's a guy with the artistic temperament. Talk about living life to the full."

She flinched as I said this.

"It's not full, it's not real, if you live it drunk," she said, a spark in those lovely eyes. "On the contrary. And it's not fair to anyone. I've seen it over and over. I keep seeing it. The outcome is predictable. People get hurt. There's no honesty in a drunk."

Her fervor surprised me, and in the silence that followed I looked for something to say. An earworm presented itself. "Honesty," I said, "is such a lonely word."

Suddenly her eyes were sapphires in a welling spring. Could she object to a shameless paraphrase? Maybe Billy Joel made her sick.

"Are you okay?"

A tear slid down her perfect cheek. She rubbed it away

"You're different," she said after a moment.

Now it was my turn to flinch. I had always felt I was *different*, and I didn't like hearing it confirmed by anyone, especially a pretty girl whose company I'd been enjoying immensely, and whose eyes made me giddy.

She read my reaction, for she reached over and touched my hand. "Don't. Please. I mean, you're not like others. There's something about you . . . I remember how you put that pig Bruce in his place, the day we met."

I had never thought of Fair Dinkum Bruce as a pig; nor for the life of me could I remember ever putting him in his place. But I nodded silently and held her eye.

*

After that day we spent all our free time together. We talked, we walked, we laughed and listened to music and went to movies and plays and had dinner together and argued with friends and talked some more, just the two of us, long into the night. I had never known anything like this before, this sensation of being complete.

We even worked together, researching and writing academic papers, she in her field, I in mine. She filtered her studies—indeed, everything she encountered—through an intellectual prism reflecting her world view and beliefs. And she was a woman who believed. Her many positions forced me to think about things I hadn't thought about before, even if, after reflection, I discarded them as Not For Me.

She never relented on her initial opinion that the traditions of our ancient university were pompous and pretentious; she saw despicable class distinctions behind them all. She was an unremitting champion of the downtrodden, the abused and disenfranchised, of immigrants, refugees, the displaced and the poor. Life's little people, the unassuming and unaffected, the humble hard-working sorts who kept the world running. And there was something about her presence, her sincerity and earnestness, her intensity (not to mention her beauty) that converted such people to her cause. She conveyed empathy, understanding and total acceptance. In her presence they felt—knew—that they mattered to her, that she cared.

I first recognized the effect she had on others in her interactions with the staff at her college. Although it was against the rules, I stayed over in her room, especially on weekends. "This is my male physical lover," she told Basil the porter and Tilda the housekeeper, eschewing boyfriend/girlfriend terminology as manifestations of patriarchy. "He's going to stay over now and then. We'll have sex in my room." "Have a nice stay," they said to me, the designated MPL. Tilda beamed adoringly at Genny. "Would you like some tea, luv, in the morning?" Without artifice, never striking a false note, Genny had bonded with them on a class level, commiserating over the depredations of wealth and privilege, and gently proselytizing on the need for proletarian solidarity. They responded with slavish devotion. "Don't you *dare* break that dear girl's heart!" Tilda once hissed at me as she rooted through the trash, checking for signs of my decadence, while Genny was in the lavatory.

"Now then, Young Mister Numbers," said Basil, an ex-Guards non-com. "I've got my eye on you." He went on to explain, in meticulous detail, how to string a man up with piano wire. "If you have to," he said ominously, eyes narrowed. "The privates," he concluded (not referring to the Other Ranks) "swell up enormously. Fat lot of good it does anyone. Hah!"

"Yes, I'll try to remember that," I replied carefully. This must be what "nuance" is, I thought; then, to change the subject: "Do you have any tattoos, from the service?"

On Sunday mornings we would lie in her narrow single bed, she pouring over the weekend *Guardian* and the *New Statesman*, me over *The Independent*, which was new and refreshing and struggling for readership. I made my case about the ossified perspectives of the established papers to deaf ears. For Genny, class solidarity was key; also, the *New Statesman* made her horny.

*

I will not say, in hindsight, that the volume and intensity of her beliefs struck me then as odd. Rather, I admired her for them, for she was remarkably consistent, and my own world view was anything but. She approved of my agrarian Saskatchewan roots, and assumed I was a fellow-traveller in the proletarian cause. My parents, though, had been big fans of Dief the Chief who, like the CCF, was also home-grown. That didn't make them Tories, but frankly it was hard to tell what their political views were, they were so close with them—the exception being the rare occasion when my father could be goaded on the subject of draft-dodgers, separatists, or Pierre Trudeau. From them, I had learned to be close with my own views. The acorn, it is said, does not fall far from the tree.

"It must be wonderful being from Saskatchewan," Genny cooed.

I was raised to return compliments. "Down East, though, you can get *real* oysters. And pogey lasts forever!"

"Some day," she said dreamily, "Nova Scotia will elect the

NDP, and that will be the start of the revolution we need."

"Never going to happen," I said, "not east of Manitoba."

She sighed. "You're right. Everything's stacked against people power in this country." She meant Canada, although we were lounging naked abed in England.

That's not it at all, I thought. Too many wing-nuts, like that guy Bob Rae in Ontario.

Her beliefs were not just firm and resolute, they could be scary-intense, like those of a Bolshevik learning of the latest Menshevik deviation. You just knew if *she* were in charge, there'd be a little shake-up at the politburo.

"Things won't really change until women take power," she asserted.

"What about Margaret Thatcher? She's a woman."

This earned me a disdainful scowl and some worrisomely closed body language. "What we need is a vaginocracy, not another woman with a penis."

Rather than debate her, I thought selfishly about my own penis, and that worrisomely closed body language. "Yes, I see that now," I said.

Privately, I filed "vaginocracy" away for Farley.

*

It wasn't always politics. We had fun. We could be giddy-silly with each other as well as deeply serious. I loved to watch her just being Genny, engaged with the world and interacting with others, committing her many acts of kindness. We entrusted each other with thoughts we'd never shared with anyone. We revelled in the joy of finding a kindred spirit, a soul to complement our individual existence. And for me, her confident femininity (wrapped as it was in an assertive brand of feminism) was complementarity incarnate for I—youngest of four boys, sisterless, shy, and ungifted in blarney—had had little prior experience with Females. Sure, I was fascinated by their breasts and curves and whatnot, but I'd had precious little congress with them (women, not their whatnots—although that was true as well). To me, they were a strange and exotic species, one I could not quite comprehend.

Often I could not quite comprehend Genny either. "It's not working," she said one night, a few weeks into our relationship. "We just can't get beyond 'man' and 'woman'. That's the root of our problem." I nodded, terrified at her earnest tone and thinking this talk of a problem was her way of breaking up. It turned out "we" was inclusive of the human race and not a specific reference to us. "I'm a woman," she said, "but first and foremost I'm a person. We all need to see the person beneath the skin."

I agreed solemnly, although I liked the skin just fine. Still, it didn't take her long to realize what she was dealing with. "You're a blank slate," she marvelled when the full extent of my ignorance dawned on her. And bless her heart, she made it her mission to rectify it by educating me on what being a woman was like.

When she proposed this I thought-chortled dirtily, tingling at the wonderfully kinky possibilities. Beautiful her on top, getting a bit rough, me in her silken undies . . .

But practical Genny had something else in mind. First, in instalments over several days, I received a lengthy clinical description of the menstrual cycle, complete with compelling demonstrations on my body to simulate cramping, bloating, and breast tenderness. She provided me with mind-numbing details about flow, vaginal discharge, and the pros and cons of pad versus tampon, as well as the symptoms of toxic shock. "You're very quiet," she said at one point, giving me a hug.

"Hhgm," I mumbled faintly, worried about lunch.

In the next module of lessons, I learned what a pap smear and mammogram felt like. She had had exactly one of each, but still believed them both essential to my education as a rounded person. Owing to my inconvenient anatomy, my pap smear was an improvised procedure involving a dry Q-tip and much writhing. When it came time for my mammogram, she allowed that I lacked sufficient breast tissue for a realistic simulation. I thought this would put me in the clear, but she opted to abandon realism for analogy. I'd always been fuzzy on the concept of analogy, so I followed her preparations with interest. First she splayed a particular appendage of mine, and its two best friends, across a cold glass plate. Hmm, I wondered; but in a short time I'd come a long way in my confidence, and rather than ask, I said something flippant like, "Hey, baby, you want some of *this*?" I did not truly fathom her intentions until she, concentrating on the task and humming quietly to herself—the very picture of the detached clinician—pressed a second plate over the first. With my privates sandwiched between glass, I was understandably less sanguine than she. Imagine pressing fragile botanical specimens—say, a couple of kiwis—between the covers of the Gutenberg Bible. Still, I kept my cool.

"Can we stop now?" I whispered, careful not to move. "I get the picture."

"Hold still," she said, "there'll be a brief burst of radiation."

But she was just joking about that, ha hah.

Next I was instructed, with demonstrations, on the many degrading abuses women endure at the hands of men: unwanted attentions, physical bondage, sexual slavery and violation. This was the only element of her program that she did not anticipate and plan for effectively, because she naively opted to play the role of smut-talking tough guy, with me her bitch. But she didn't have it in her to be truly tough, and for a short while I lived the fantasy I'd imagined. When she realized I wouldn't call, "No, no, please, not again! Don't touch me there!" she halted the lesson and changed tack entirely to read me stomach-churning accounts of botched deliveries, female genital mutilation, HIV infection and the like. We finished up examining ghastly pictures in a medical textbook, of people suffering the various manifestations of advanced syphilis. I realized only later that all of them were men.

CHAPTER FOUR

> I find in most novels no imagination at all. They seem to think the highest form of the novel is to write about marriage, because that's the most important thing there is for middle-class people.
>
> Gore Vidal
>
> Oh FUCK the longings and agonies of youth.
>
> John Irving

My education at the University of Genny had crushing effects on my libido. For several weeks after I "graduated" (I'll relate that adventure separately), whenever she came on to me I couldn't help think how selfish she was being, and did she not understand the *consequences*? There were other . . . complications. When we went all the way, I had to hum a Sheena Easton ditty in my mind, and concentrate on Sheena, taking the morning train—innocent, wholesome and not in the least clinical. Or the Bananarama girls—poppy, pert, and not in the least clinical. This was a travesty, because Genny was far more desirable than Sheena and all the Bananarama girls combined.

All her earnest lessons had robbed the act of its magic; and now the genie was out of the bottle, for she continued along a clinical vein, analyzing everything within a leftist-feminist framework, every perceived ill another building block in the development of her General Theory of Human Oppression with capitalists, men, or capitalist men at its centre.

Her general disapprobation of males was exacerbating my specific male issue. I realized I had to confront the matter head on. "We need to talk," I said, sitting her down.

She gave me a look that was both quizzical and concerned.

"It's about me being a boy and you being a girl."

"You mean man and woman," she said. "Equal persons."

"Whatever. I mean hetero-humans. I'm not—"

"Of course you're not."

"Let me finish. I . . ." I lost my train of thought and needed a moment to regroup. "I need some of the mystery back."

She looked at me with total incomprehension.

"I can't be as clinical as you. I can't dissect everything on a feminist-socialist theoretical level. I can't explain in words why I'm attracted to you in particular or women in general. Why I think about Sheena Easton or Bananarama—"

"What?"

"Never mind. The point is, I don't have to talk about every feeling I have or every thought that flits through my head, let alone form a thesis on it. I know you're a woman. That's enough for me. I lose your essence if I try to analyze it. I love you, not the idea of you."

"You love me?"

"Don't change the subject."

"You love me?" Eyes boring into me like cobalt drill bits. I had nowhere to hide. No changing the subject this time. How had I, the master dissembler, stumbled into this conversation?

I swallowed hard, and nodded. I may dissemble shamelessly, but I am no liar.

*

The time I spent with Genny further cut into the time I spent with Farley. At first she was disapproving and cool to him, very cool. There were occasional touch-points of tension between them, like the time he and I came into some money at the turf accountant. He had helped me operationalize a betting system I'd thought up, a fun little applied detour from my theoretical studies on probability and risk. It was based on the posted odds, the trend in those odds, and a few statistics on the horses themselves. Problem was, the odds moved quickly towards post time, leaving little time to play the system. We had to huddle inside our Ladbrokes outlet, Farley watching the Tote and reading me stats from the racing form as I worked the calculator (it was the eighties, remember), then one of us had to run to the window before it closed. The day we tested the system it worked, modestly not splendidly, just enough to attract the attention of a couple of cranky punters without a system of their own.

That night we met up with Genny after some celebratory G&Ts and split a gut telling her how we'd dodged the yobs and about the glorious potential of my wagering scheme. It was the Gordon's talking, and the adrenalin, and when we finally calmed down I noticed Genny wasn't laughing along with us.

"Jack, you could have been hurt," was all she said.

Farley and I exchanged glances. A few minutes later he remembered a place he had to be.

"I don't like you hanging around unsavoury characters," she said when he was gone.

"It was just a bit of fun. And Farley was with me."

She gave me a look. Later she asked me, "Did *he* put you up to it?"

"He likes to play the horses, that's all."

Eventually they reached a sort of accommodation, and she seemed to become fond of him, tolerant even of his transgressions with women. It wasn't his many seductions she objected to, it was what she saw as his callousness, the falsities he used to manipulate women into the sack. These she considered irresponsible, unethical even; but she took the criticism no farther than that, out of deference, I felt, to me and my friendship with him. I admired her for this; it was a generous gesture for an unremitting champion of the downtrodden, the abused, and women everywhere.

For his part, he was reserved when she was around, perhaps even a bit intimidated. And he was curious about our relationship.

"How is she in the sack?"

I fixed a deadpan look on him.

"And why's she call you 'Jack'? What's that about?"

"It's just a pet name. Sometimes she calls me 'Jack Hammer'."

"You dog!"

"It's because I bounce my leg. I'm kind of fidgety. You never noticed?"

He grinned evilly. "So you say, Hammer. So you say."

Over time they became understanding, even affectionate friends, like a cat and a dog sharing common territory.

*

Over the years Genny and I learned to live with each others' quirks. I am not without my own, although they are minor in comparison to hers. She is smart and beautiful and oh-so stubborn, and a little bit crazy, excuse me for calling a spade a spade. While I breathe I'll deny saying that, but if you're reading this I must be dead and it's safe to disclose the fact— alongside its corollary: that I loved her profoundly.

To her credit she came to exempt me (more or less) from her General Theory of Human Oppression; she even acknowledged my counterarguments and grew more flexible and forgiving in its application. Yet on a personal level, she pursued ideological purity and political correctness with dogged intensity. Her world was fair trade and organic, union-made, free-range, non-sexist, non-racist and non-nuclear. She wanted to prohibit animal testing, boycott South Africa, and save the whales, the forest, the ozone layer—in fact the planet in general. This gave us plenty of common ground, although my few hard principles were focused narrowly on the environment while hers were all-encompassing, so much so that they limited what she could eat, drink, read, think, and wear. Once, I sat chuckling over a book by one of my favourite writers, looked up and found her eyes on me. "Have you read him?" I asked. "No," she replied, horrified at the thought. "He's a misogynist. His women are caricatures. They're all either whores or saints." She'd heard that, somewhere.

The strength of her convictions amazed and sometimes frightened me. Indeed, there were certain discussions which brooked no debate, and I shrewdly learned to be careful with my opinions to avoid a diatribe or a hurt, pitying look and a withholding of certain affections until I saw the light. Thus she came to assume that I endorsed employment equity, approved of blanket indictments of white men, disapproved of beauty contests, pornography, and boxing. Whenever she asserted that women were inherently peacemakers, that union leaders spoke for the common person, or that Eddie Murphy was not in the least bit funny, I stroked my chin thoughtfully and went, "hmm." And whatever my true opinion I answered "No!" forcefully when asked if paisley made her hips look big.

Even I knew what "all politics is local" meant.

She considered my agnosticism on many matters a lack of rigour, yet she excused it. Thus I could eat meat, wear commodity cotton, read Mordecai Richler, that sort of thing, with only a frown as consequence. Live and let live, when it came to me; and full credit to her, for she was a true believer on her own account. In the cause of political correctness she was forever embracing causes and embarking on lifestyle experiments. The latter she tried to extend to me. Case in point: the time we gave up soap and deodorant, I can't remember why. "Why do we fear our bodies?" she asked at the outset. I lasted a couple of days, she a couple more.

Thankfully, she could change her mind, but she was disturbingly contrarian on some things. She favoured holistic-alternative therapies over evidence-based medicine, which she decried as a tool of the "phallocentric medical-pharmaceutical complex." Her chief informant on the subject was her friend Cindy, a straight-laced prude from Utah doing a PhD in pharmacology. I could tell that Cindy disliked me, and I wondered if it was because she had a thing for Genny. If so, Genny seemed oblivious to it and the tension between us. "They're afraid of us," she informed us both one day, referring to those phallocentric pharma baddies. "That's why they burnt us as witches. And it's why they still reject our traditional cures." She huffed this while ingesting some herbal hell-broth concocted by the witch Cindy, her trusted source on pond scum remedies. I responded with a spirited defence of the scientific method, fact-based analysis of risks and benefits, and clinical trials, to which Genny rolled her eyes and countered, "There you go again," that old Reagan brush off. Cindy tittered at my expense and I clammed up, even though I knew a lot about the analysis of risk, it being the focus of my degree.

From our earliest time together, what perplexed me most was her intellectual struggle with her own good looks. Genny had always turned heads; she was confident, and carried herself proudly. She was aware of her animal qualities and enjoyed the effect she had on others. When I first met her she dressed like a raven-haired Madonna (the singer, not the mother of Jesus), with plenty of trinkets and skin. Yet she denied, even railed against the notion of being prisoner to her outward appearance. "What's the first thing that attracted you to me?" she asked once, her head resting on my chest. "Your mind, of course," I lied wisely. But truthfully, I could not understand what was wrong with being a stunningly gorgeous woman. Beauty is a gift to the world, one that should never be squandered. We are but briefly alive, and only fleetingly paragons of our kind.

Whenever I meandered conversationally towards this, my true opinion, she rolled her eyes and rumbled "Arrgh!" and railed against the oppression of gender roles. According to her, *I* was as much a captive as she. " 'One is not born, but rather becomes, a woman'," she told me once, quoting some

French guy, Simon somebody.

"That sounds exactly like something a French guy would say."

"*Simone*, not Simon. *Simone* de Beauvoir."

"Oh. Right. Sartre's girlfriend."

"Arrgh!"

While we were still in England she stopped wearing makeup. She'd never used much, but when I incautiously inquired if she'd forgotten, she said, "Fine. You like makeup—you wear it." But a couple of weeks later, she was wearing lip gloss—to prevent chapping, she said; I could tell she'd also applied some blush, and something to her lashes that made her eyes smoulder like blue coals in a simmering brazier.

Next it was clothing. She began to buy shapeless garments of rough but easily washable sackcloth at Olga's of Volgograd, a Marxist-feminist collective on the edge of Camden Market. The collective failed, thank God, but I think she would have abandoned it anyway, for she was turning heads now for unaccustomed reasons. I was relieved to see her back in more form-fitting garments, because by God she had the body—all womanly curves, and a butt you could crack an egg on.

One morning I took a double take as she was getting dressed. "Are those jockeys?" I asked.

"Yes. Much looser. And cool! Look how much room there is in front. Why should women suffer yeast infections to fulfill some male fantasy? You wear a thong for a while." That was how she challenged me: if you like it so much, you wear it—makeup, panties, perfume. Then she abandoned her bra. This gave her a delightful jiggle in the chest area; but when I asked innocently if the girls, unsupported, would, you know, succumb, maybe, over time, just a little—not enough to notice!—to Newton's law of universal gravitation, she looked at me intently and played her trump card.

"Would you still love me if my breasts sagged?"

The answer to this question can have no "but." Even I

knew that.

"Of course," I replied, and dropped the subject. But for an horrific moment I imagined us in the shower, twenty years on, the distended nipples of her drooping jugs tickling my lower abdomen and pointing accusingly at my own gravity-ravaged bits. Little did I realize then that old people, people in their forties, didn't shower with their lovers every few hours after a wild session of sex. Who knew? Gravity and life both settle on a person. You get busy. Responsibilities and all.

Within a couple of weeks of that conversation, she was wearing a sports bra. I dared not comment. Shortly thereafter, she retrieved all the bras she'd put, pragmatically, in a pile for the Sally Ann.

For a while, when we first moved to Toronto, she stopped shaving her legs and armpits. She said nothing to me in advance, but I noticed soon enough. Her story about being part Mi'kmaq was just that—she was definitely black Irish. It took me a couple of weeks to figure out a way to bring the subject up. "Hey, Genny!" I called, just in the door from Shoppers. "I bought some Foamy. Do you want to shave your legs?"

She looked up from a treatise on gender roles among the San peoples of southern Africa. "No." But I made the mistake of meeting her eye, and she rightly concluded I had missed the meaning of her glare. "Why should I? Why should women pretend they're pre-pubescent children, just to fulfill some sick male fantasy?"

Well, that wasn't one of *my* sick male fantasies. I just liked those silky smooth legs, those clean smooth naked pits. "Come on, be reasonable," I said. "You're all stubbly. It's like . . . it's like cuddling with Farley," then quickly added, because I had never cuddled with Farley, "I mean, how it must be."

"You pig!" she said, with a vehemence that surprised me. "That's . . . that's . . . just not called for. You-have-no-right! How dare you!"

"I just meant—"

"Why is it with you people, anyway? This is *my* body. This

is how *my* body is."

"You people," I assumed, referred to all men, and I felt compelled to differentiate myself from that slavering pack.

"Genny, listen to me: I love your body."

"Ahrgh!"

She flew into orbital dudgeon about sexual objectification and the infantalization of women; and the fact is I couldn't disagree. I respected her viewpoints and learned from them. She forced me to question what I might have taken for granted, to recognize my many contradictions.

And hers, too. Come the hot weather she began to shave and pluck again. By then she'd returned to mostly-conventional female garments and looked mighty fine in a little black dress.

*

But before that: we were still in Britain. Still in the early days.

For the first anniversary of our collision on St Giles she arranged a romantic yet frugal getaway. We took a succession of buses to spend four days walking the windswept hills and frigid beaches of Wales, dining in pubs at night. On the last day of our stay we hiked up a low mountain, and as we crested a rise the drizzle finally stopped, the sun appeared, and we stripped off our wet jackets to eat our box lunches in unexpected warmth. And felt like lingering, for the rolling green hills, the valleys dotted with sheep, were no longer dreary in grey half night but brilliant with light. We sheltered in the lee of a ridge, snuggled with backs against a boulder, sun full on our faces, and talked about the future. I was nearing the end of my time in England and she still had a year to go. She wanted to pursue a university career and still had field work to do to complete her degree.

"You'll make a wonderful academic," I said.

She glanced sideways at me. "I'll take that as a compliment."

"It's true. You've got the passion and smarts. And you look hot in a mortarboard. I can't think of anyone better suited. Maybe Farley but—"

"What about you?"

I looked away. "I couldn't. You know that."

"I meant, what'll you do?"

I reached for her. "If I practice and truly commit myself, I could become a gigolo. But I'd need your help."

"Be serious! Stop . . ."

She pushed me away a couple of minutes later. "You always think you can change the subject."

"Pardon?"

"Why don't you try writing?"

The sea to the south glimmered before us. The sun at its zenith seemed barely at our level. I squinted into it, feeling Genny's gaze on my face.

"You can do it," she said.

"I'm not so sure."

"You can! Come on, why don't you write? Take some time off."

"I don't want to take time off."

"When will you ever take time off again?"

"I don't know." Unlike Farley, I'd been disciplined. All of my attention had been focused on Genny and my degree. I'd had no time for writing. More correctly, I'd made no time for writing. And now I was close to graduation, to adulthood and the rest of my life. "I won't take time off. I'll get a job."

"You can write, too."

"Maybe."

We fell into silence.

"What about us?"

Oh god. Farley always said no good could come from the Relationship Talk. This called for some serious dissembling. "I know I can get a job in the City. With Big Bang, there's going to be plenty of opportunities for my—"

"Yes! We can be together on weekends. I can come down to London."

"And I can come up."

She snuggled closer and I realized I had not evaded her question, but answered it.

"You can write when I'm not around."

"When you're not around I'll work. People in the City work sixty, seventy hour weeks."

Genny clicked her tongue at capitalist exploitation. "A year from now, I'll be in Africa for my research. You could come with me."

"That would be good."

We gazed out on Cardigan Bay and the Irish Sea beyond, as the future nestled on us like a mantle of down, comforting, warm, and only a little suffocating, where it drifted up and over our heads.

I closed my eyes.

When I awoke the sky was overcast and Genny was sitting a few feet away, propped against her day pack, reading a tattered copy of *Pride and Prejudice*. She sensed me stirring, looked at me and smiled, her eyes dazzling in the now-pallid light; then she returned to her book.

I reached into my pack and pulled out my new Moleskine notebook, her anniversary gift to me. I opened it, ready to begin. Below me, the splendours of north Wales: rugged hills, verdant valleys, flocks of woolly sheep, and nary a sign of humanity. On the horizon, a glittering sea stretching to the ends of the earth; a few feet away, a beautiful, quirky, contradictory woman, engrossed in Jane Austen, her guilty pleasure.

I was ready to begin.

A half hour later I capped my pen and closed the book. I hadn't written a word.

CHAPTER FIVE

A novel is balanced between a few true impressions and the multitude of false ones that make up most of what we call life.

> Saul Bellow

In the writing process, the more a story cooks, the better.

> Doris Lessing

In the morning Genny hovers around me before she leaves for work. "What are you doing today?"

"Writing. New project."

She looks pleased and hugs me. "What is it?"

"It's . . . well, I'm still working it out. It's historical, though."

"You and history! I should have known. I'm so glad to see you working again. I know how hard it's been." She lingers in my arms, suggests something for supper, reminds me when Chloe will be home; then she is gone.

As I read over what I've already written I have a flash of déjà vu, remembering how I used to record things as a kid. It helped me make sense of the world, for I was lost, hopeless with the rules of social interplay. Straight talk I understood but subtlety escaped me. Polite evasions, hints, sarcasm, irony—all missed. So too was body language. Where others found fluency in looks and gestures, I saw looks and gestures, nothing more. I could not grasp why people spoke with shoulders and eyes when they had voices and tongues. "They just do," my mother told me. "So you watch them. You watch them close. You be a detective and work things out."

I became an observational gumshoe. I took notes and organized them and studied them methodically, looking for meaning hidden in words, trying to recognize when silent conversations were underway around me. I posited interpretations and theories, and sometimes I had a sudden moment of clarity, a revelation: I understood.

Those moments were rare. Mostly I was wrong. I could not crack the code. My world was peopled by cuneiform characters, human squiggles. Perhaps this explains my fascination with words, my ambition to use them, to write and, just maybe, to reach others. Yet in the end I chose numbers. And numbers were what led me to the World Trade Centre.

*

London's financial sector exploded after Big Bang, the deregulation of Britain's financial markets. For a while, the City was the most dynamic place on earth, and there was a lot of money to be made, both in the UK and on the continent. My arcane specialty—or as Farley now called it, my idiosavancy with numbers—came into its own. Prices, values, volatility, risk, the probability of every eventuality—all these could be modelled. The very world could be modelled. All possible hazards could be mitigated, all conceivable assets monetized, packaged, securitized, and sold. Liabilities could be collateralized, synthesized, and swapped, risk diversified away, obligations engineered into default-free assets. Firm after firm, market after market, country after country was seduced by financial wizardry, and people like me made it work. ("People like me" were what Farley called "financial Frankensteins." He soon abridged it to "Finanstein." Neither term ever caught on.)

I quit that world to be with Genny in Africa. Our six months there became a year, her field research on migratory labour patterns transitioned into work with South African refugees; and my numeracy won me contract work with a multilateral agency. We didn't make much money but we lived life, inhaled new experiences, saw how the other half lived, and did some growing up. In the process, Genny finished her PhD. After that, she did a post-doc in New York, and I found a job in the heart of Wall Street, in one of its tallest towers, where there was always demand for people who understood risk and knew how to mitigate it. I was a capitalist, Genny a socialist, and we lived happily in Morningside Heights under the terms of an ideological armistice. Our life together, our relationship, was very New York.

All that changed in 1993 when the World Trade Center was bombed. It felt like a very close call, my building and our city under attack. It made us think. We had been rootless for a long time; I had been away from Canada for seven years, Genny for six. Suddenly it was time to go home, but where was home for us?

We decided on Toronto, a place neither of us knew, reasoning we could both make a living in a city its size. She applied for positions at universities in the area, while I canvassed the financial players and found that experience like mine was in demand. I knew I'd be able to land on my feet when Genny found a position. That took almost two years, and when she finally accepted an offer she decided to shuck a lingering vestige of the patriarchy, one that had bothered her for ages: her surname. Thus on our arrival in Toronto the woman formerly known as Genny Paterson became Genny Patersdotter, Associate Professor of Womyn's Studies at the self-styled Harvard of the North.

I always admired her decisiveness. Once she made up her mind, it was full steam ahead; she asked no questions and brooked no objections.

"But Genny—" I began, when she first told me of her intention.

"Stop right there." (I felt my testicles shrivel and retract at her tone.) "I will *not* change my name to yours. Full stop."

That was not what I was going to suggest, but when I tried to make my point again (my voice an octave higher) she cut me off abruptly and got angry, convinced I was an agent of The Man if not The Man himself.

From then on I adopted a demeanour of studious neutrality, knowing she would not be amused if pater knew best.

*

I found a position with the investment banking arm of a Canadian financial services company. The Firm had been founded by a prominent brewing family; for decades it sold insurance and annuity products to farmers and homeowners. By the 1980s, though, the members of the family's fifth generation, needing cash to sustain their lifestyle, and so lacking in acumen they could not recognize a cash cow when it mooed, sold their venerable namesake to an American holding bank. The employees, who held a minority stake, supported the deal, thinking it would vault the Firm out of its dull niche into the big leagues of global finance. And this seemed to be the case. Within months the American parent merged with an even larger Japanese company, an insurer flush with overvalued yen. Three years later, the resulting multinational, headquartered in Luxembourg for tax purposes, was brought to the brink of collapse by the American savings and loan fiasco and the bursting of the Japanese asset bubble. It was rescued by a German financial conglomerate which, two years after I began in Toronto, got into a patch of trouble itself over Asian debt. The Germans were bailed out by a Russian oil oligarch who, only a year later, was caught short by the rouble crisis. Finding himself no longer an oligarch, and facing hard time in a Siberian prison, he was forced to sell his holdings to the Russian government. Soon, facing a liquidity crisis of its own,

Moscow put the international affiliates acquired from the oligarch (who'd been jailed anyway) back on the block.

Uncertainty again swirled at the Firm, until a white knight appeared, an American company specializing in sub-prime home lending. Mortgages had always been seen as stodgy but safe, and after years of ownership flux, revolving door executives, and flavour-of-the-month strategies, my colleagues were ecstatic when the Americans closed the deal. They welcomed the new focus, relieved that there'd finally be some stability at the Firm.

Through all the turmoil I worked in an area called Structured Products, building financial models to operationalize my theories of risk mitigation and diffusion by creating new securities, assets themselves built from other assets. The Firm sold this expertise to others, but our new American parent saw the potential and put it into practice on its own portfolio. It pressed me to move back to New York where the real action was, but I said no. Family reasons. This marked me as odd, but we worked out an arrangement. I had to travel a lot but the Firm and our parent gave me free reign, and it was interesting work at the cutting edge of financial innovation. Others like me in other firms were working on similar advances, similar products. We were pioneers, racing to innovate, pushing the bounds of knowledge. Some days I felt like Orville Wright.

*

In Toronto Genny and I grew comfortable. We had long hours, regular salaries, nice holidays: we had careers. But we were in our thirties, not getting any younger, and sometimes we wondered (when we paused to wonder) what we were doing with our lives, and was this *it*? We'd never seen ourselves as ladder climbers. Tenure track and partner track seemed eight-track to us.

Still . . . we had a great lifestyle. We made good money.

We'd shake things up later. In the meantime there was something we could do, something we'd always intended, and what were we waiting for? Ten months after Genny went off the Pill, Chloe arrived, and we bought a big old house on a leafy street, not in Rosedale or Forest Hill or Oakville, the usual Bay Street enclaves, but off Roncesvalles, the city's Polish heart. It was considered ethnic and bohemian, a bit dodgy for its proximity to poor people, but acceptable for academics and their spouses. At the Firm I was already viewed as eccentric, someone who might vote Liberal or Green or read poetry.

Chloe was a marvel, and Genny and I had each other; but now we also had a mortgage, and responsibility, and where did all our money suddenly go? You forget about your dreams, about changing the world, or writing, when you are sleep-deprived, on the treadmill of life, working on the next article, another lecture, a new course (her); the next transaction, another new product, another financial close (me). A grad student struggles, a new analyst screws up, and Chloe gets a tooth. A road show in New York to explain an offering, a panel at the Learneds in Montreal, quarrels over picking up Chloe followed by makeup sex, more lectures and refereed articles, more lawyers and securities filings, now another merger and more days in New York. Clinton is impeached and the dean pushes teaching loads, management gooses the revenue target, and the roof needs doing, the drains are crumbling, the basement floor and driveway, the rads the boiler the car the knob and tube. Chloe on her first day at Montessori, Chloe dressed up at Halloween, Chloe hanging tinsel on the tree; and after she's asleep just us alone, a quiet laugh together and sex comfortable like a Perry Como sweater. Meetings and presentations in Chicago and New York, Brooks Brothers suits talking dotcom and Y2K, pressure unrelenting to think outside the box, everyone's creating new products processes mechanisms, SPEs and SPVs, synthetic obligations and credit-linked securities, default swaps and asset-backeds. Look at Goldman Lehman Bear, look at Morgan, eating our lunch, mowing our lawn, just put lipstick on it, crate it rate it and get it out the door, it's the quarterly target, it's the profit forecast, it's the annual meeting, it's *bonus time*, so book it quick and get it off-book, we need results and we need them—

Now what?

Hanging chads—

What happens next?

And so we entered a new century, Y2K technically being the end of the twentieth, and the Firm was a key member of a syndicate behind an innovative offering, a multi-sector CDO which everyone wanted to close by October. That spring and summer I flew to New York almost every week. By late summer we'd nailed it, and the first full week after Labour Day we scheduled a round of meetings in Manhattan with lawyers and investors, midtown all day Monday and at the World Trade Centre on Tuesday, which dawned as clear and beautiful as any day ever will.

BOOM

"Jeezuz, what was that?"

"Get to the stairs. Just get to the stairs—"

"Hey, don't—"

CHAPTER SIX

A man writes to throw off the poison which he has accumulated because of his false way of life. He is trying to recapture his innocence, yet all he succeeds in doing (by writing) is to inoculate the world with a virus of his disillusionment. No man would set a word down on paper if he had the courage to live out what he believed in.

Henry Miller

If I don't write to empty my mind, I go mad.

George Gordon, Lord Byron

There's nothing like a brush with death to clear your mind of clutter, to force you to reassess your life and prioritize what you want to get accomplished. For me, it wasn't another securitized, collateralized, hybridized, credit-enhanced, ring-fenced, tranched or otherwise-structured product of financial engineering and creative accounting.

"I want to write," I told Genny when I finally figured it out.

"I know, baby," she said.

But what would I write?

I had been lost in the suffocating smoke and chaos of a doomed monolith. I had emerged from the ruins coughing, sputtering, wounded. I had wandered among the dying and the maimed, cheated death, and survived to bear witness to a calamity that changed the world. And I could not bring myself to think of it.

I chose instead to write a nautical-themed historical thriller. I'd always had a thing for history, and once I studied the convolutions of eighteenth century diplomacy, the logistics of a round-the-world voyage, the mathematics of the era's navigational techniques, I was hooked. I may not understand body language or metaphor but I see needles in haystacks, patterns buried in detail that others easily miss. Perhaps that's why I thrived at slicing and dicing and bundling financial assets into higher, purer, risk-free securities—though all that bores me now.

My central character was an explorer, and his story became an outlet for me, an escape from the numbers that had always controlled, even defined my existence. Thus I set off on my own voyage of discovery, my eyes gleaming with pious intent. I was going to write a Novel.

*

You quickly realize that wanting to write is not enough; that deciding to write will not fill a page. Contrary to the expectations of people who have never tried writing, words don't flow by divine inspiration. Writing is hard work. It's heavy lifting with your brain. The brilliant ideas you start out with are almost certainly wrong. What you thought about your plot, your characters, the chronology of your story, the scenes you envisioned, the way you peek over a shoulder or look through a character's eyes—most of it, upon reflection, you must reject. It's not worth snuff. You have to be prepared to discard what you write, every word, until you develop some craft. And even then, you must accept that what you've written is not worth reading and start again.

The sooner you realize this the sooner you can go beyond empty ambition and actually write.

That's just my experience, of course, and I've never published a word.

As I set out to write, I wondered about the choices I'd made so many years ago. For all my youthful blather, I hadn't believed in myself. I'd taken the safe option and defaulted to numbers. I simply hadn't believed I had the words to say anything of substance. Now I had a second chance, and knowing life was finite, every day a gift, I was determined not to falter. This time I'd have the strength of my convictions.

In those early days I often thought enviously of Farley, who had dedicated himself to literature years before and paid his dues. After his PhD he taught at six universities in ten years, adapted his dissertation on Dylan Thomas into book form, and pumped out paper after paper on the same basic theme. (Each was nuanced, of course, but that was lost on me.) He knew that bibulous Welshman like the bottom of a shot glass, and his interest in Thomas's evolution from poet into icon stoked his curiosity on the phenomenon of literary fame. He published widely in that arcane field too.

Our paths had diverged, but to my delight we were reunited just after the millennium, when he arrived in Toronto to assume a tenured position at the U of T. He was the same old Farley, albeit older and wiser; the Fu Manchu was long gone, along with much of his fiery red hair. He had two kids, one of whom lived with his ex in Philadelphia, and a current marriage he was working on.

We picked up as if the years that had passed were but days of the week. Like old times, we'd go to the track—he still liked a good wager and respected my take on the odds; or we'd meet for a drink and a cheap nosh and, inevitably, more drinks. Our conversations were as wide ranging as ever, but whenever I asked about his writing, he turned vague. "I keep a hand in," he'd say unassumingly. "A few stories, when there's time, in and around academic papers and bumph like that. You know what they say about the ivory tower. Publish or perish. And then there's teaching. Bloody students. I'd love the job if it weren't for them." At this, he'd grin and drain his glass and signal for a round.

At least he'd spent his life studying what he loved. And as

he put it, out of modesty I felt sure, he kept a hand in. He'd never given up.

Given up? I'd never even started.

When I first told him I was writing I expected his enthusiastic, uncritical encouragement, the kind we always gave each other as students. Instead he grunted, "Huh," and signalled for a drink. It was as though I'd just announced my intention to strip naked on Yonge Street to fornicate with a tree.

*

I was back at the Firm but I no longer poured my creativity into the mechanics of asset-backed securities and credit default swaps. Default scenarios, risk profiles, the tiered structure of securitized debt obligations and their waterfall payments no longer consumed me. I worked in a drone-like trance, modelling and pooling and packaging assets that our sales department sold to investors to get off-book. Everything was as before but I was changed. I had cheated death. The quarterly revenue target seemed trivial now.

Writing was an escape. I wrote late at night and early in the morning, but that wasn't enough. I needed bigger blocks of time. I took random vacation days off. Full days were what I needed to sustain the creative process, to let me imagine another era.

Like a junkie, I craved my fix.

I began to take mental health days. Officially, I'd be "working from home," but the work was all on my Novel. On weekends, I'd block off a day and more if I could. On long weekends I stayed behind when Genny and Chloe went away to visit relatives or friends. I spent these days in splendid isolation with my books, notes and laptop, the nights devoted to research.

In my sleep, I worked out plot points, just as I'd solved differential equations as a student, or processed risk parameters and distribution functions during my years at the Firm. I awoke in the dark and jotted ideas by flashlight as Genny slept unaware next to me. In the peaceful moments of clarity at dawn, I'd find the solution to an issue of perspective or voice and scrawl it down before it was lost.

I was finally doing what I wanted to do and felt a profound sense of fulfillment. And promise, for I saw writing as a means of deliverance, an opportunity to end my lifelong isolation. I knew how awkward and maladroit I was in person. Beyond a conceptual level, I seemed unable to connect with people. I'd rail at poverty and social injustice, citing statistics to support my case, but barely notice a beggar when I stepped over one on the street. In writing, though, I felt the possibility of transcending my limitations, of finally linking with the outside world and touching the lives of others.

To be certain I wasn't naive or crazy, I took an objective look at myself. In my favour, I was prepared to work hard and learn from my mistakes. Ego wasn't a problem; in fact, introversion might finally be an advantage. And I had a prodigious vocabulary. I loved words. While Farley invented them, I collected them, the more obscure the better. I'd always known they'd be proficuous some day.

On the other hand, there were certain mechanics that gave me trouble. Literary devices, for example—irony, sarcasm, hyperbole, analogy, metaphor, simile and the like—these I couldn't capture without painstaking study. These, I had to work at. Along with hanging prepositions. And sentence stubs.

*

To get feedback I took creative writing courses. They were offered at night on a downtown campus. There were usually about a dozen students, mostly women. Yummy mummies, Farley called them, familiar with their ilk. There were one or two men in every class. From the looks of them and what they wrote, they lived in their parents' basements.

There were no formal lessons. Instead everyone shared something they'd written with the group, and everyone else provided comments. It was an all-accepting, nurturing collective, the writing class, conducted within safe, semi-academic confines. Every voice was valid, every submission treated respectfully. The instructors acted as moderators. Their own advice on storytelling revolved around three things: don't use adverbs; show, don't tell; and write what you know.

Anguish, despair, psychological darkness—that's what everyone seemed to know. My classes were full of people writing about how they were cracking up, how their marriage was falling apart, how their spouse or child hated them, ran away, or died. Or all of the above. It seemed the way to get respect in a creative writing class was to write about your breakdown. Under 35, you could write about youthful angst, your character a lovelorn ingénue or a slacker man-child who drank too much and avoided gainful employment. Such an existence was considered rich, for it foreshadowed mid-life crisis. Over 40, you had some heady material to work with: life experience, psychic wounds, plenty of break-ups, some even with other people.

My story was considered unusual. "A talking sea otter?" one instructor said in a rare one-on-one session. Do you have the *craft* to do that?" He'd written a national award winner, a thinly disguised novel about his own nervous breakdown, not a big seller but an artistic accomplishment, at least in Canada. "My advice," another counselled, "is to write what you know." He had mutton-chops and a goatee, which gave him the air of an artiste. The protagonist in his novel was a writing instructor who dreaded reading his students' work. "So," he said, struggling with my storyline, "what century is it again? And what are they? Pirates? Where's the conflict? Find some inner pain, man, and write about that."

I nodded respectfully, wondering what he knew about inner pain.

CHAPTER SEVEN

Writing has laws of perspective, of light and shade just as painting does, or music. If you are born knowing them, fine. If not, learn them. Then rearrange the rules to suit yourself.

Truman Capote

Beware of advice—even this.

Carl Sandburg

Morning again, and when Genny walks in to say goodbye I hotkey off Word and find myself on Bloomberg. She bends, kisses me, glances at the screen. "Any change?" she asks.

"None for the better."

She rubs my back, says nothing. A short while later she is out the door. I switch back to Word to read and collect the thread from where I left off yesterday.

*

No one at the Firm really understood what I did. Few outsiders did either. This gave me a great deal of freedom, and I took measures to preserve it. I avoided peers and industry events; I rebuffed outside calls with a cranky demeanour. When asked to appear at Management Committee I gave detailed presentations calculated to intimidate and bore. I replied to queries with lengthy technical explanations, my expression composed to suggest mild astonishment at the questioner's inability to grasp a fundamental principle like the concept of a Markov chain.

I was eventually exempted from Management Committee. As long as I met my numbers, I was left alone. Trevor Larkin, one of the Firm's senior managing directors, was delegated to keep tabs on me, and to avoid my excruciating PowerPoint presentations he insisted we meet informally over lunch. "We'll get out of the office," he said, all chummy. "Have a chat. Get to know each other." We'd both been at the Firm for years and that had never been a priority for either of us. Anyway, as we were wrapping up one of these lunches, he was regaling me with details of his latest golf-and-hookers getaway in Florida when, as an afterthought, he asked what I did for hobbies.

I was still absorbing his and replied without thinking. "I'm writing a novel."

He chuckled appreciatively. "Good one. That's bizarre. Really, what do you do for fun?"

"Look at the time!" I signalled for the cheque. "I've got a two-thirty with Lehman about their next synthetic credit-linked mini-bond issue. They set up an SPE in Hong Kong to—"

"Oh my God. You're serious." He looked worried, not about Lehman Brothers' offshore mini-bonds but about my novel. He asked what it was about and I dissembled. No one does that better than me.

"But it's a *novel*," he said. "That, that, that's fiction, right?" He looked relieved when I said yes. Still, from that day on he pondered me with apprehension, like I was a convicted pervert discussing plans for his son's Cub jamboree. There was no more small talk at lunch about any of his hobbies. In my hearing, he never again asked if there was anything *creative* we could do to beat the quarterly target.

A few months later we were out for another session, waiting in line at Jump in Commerce Court, when a voice bellowed from across the way. "Trev! Trevor! Trevor Larkin!"

I turned to see a beaming giant, broad across well-tailored shoulders, wading towards us through the crowd. "You shrimpy little S-O-B!" he exclaimed when he reached us, clapping Trevor across the back. "How's it hangin', boy?"

The force of the blow propelled Trevor into the group ahead of us. He apologized and turned to face the man who'd struck the blow. "Murray. What a surprise." He offered his hand, reluctantly it seemed, and Murray scooped it up and shook it like a piggy bank.

"Have you met my colleague?" Trevor gasped.

Murray let him go and took my hand, his head cocked to hear Trevor's introduction. "Glad to meet you," he said, still all jovial, but his handshake was nothing more than firm. He turned back to Trevor, who was wiggling his fingers, testing for fractures. "How's things at the candy store, Trev?"

"The Firm's having a good year."

"Too modest!" Murray's voice echoed through the lobby. "I hear you're big swinging dicks these days. Overcompensating, heh? Eh, Trev? Hah! In the old days we weren't much but we could take a dump without calling Compliance. Remember that? You were just a young whippersnapper then, a bum boy in the bullpen. Oy, that takes me back." He shook his head in fond remembrance and clapped Trevor another good one, sending him lurching again into the suits ahead of us. They were starting to get annoyed with Trevor Larkin.

Murray, Trevor explained for my benefit, had been a managing director at the Firm. He'd retired a year or two before I arrived from New York.

"Speaking of retired, Trev," Murray said, suddenly all confidential, "I'm having lunch with a senator. I simply must scoot. I need to catch him before he's too far into the brandy, know what I mean?" He laughed and raised a fleshy paw to slap Trevor on the back but this time Trevor intercepted him mid-air and made an awkward fist bump, probably the first ever delivered in the line at Jump. I heard his knuckles crack in Murray's palm. The big man held his gaze, beaming affectionately, before releasing his hand and inclining his head to me. "A pleasure," he bellowed, like Pavarotti at the Met. He lumbered to the head of the line where a harried hostess was trying to seat a party without a reservation, two lawyers I recognized and a group of Japanese. She frowned at her book and bit her lip but when she looked up and saw Murray her expression softened, her face transformed. "Murray!" she exclaimed, smiling brightly. They exchanged hugs and kisses, a few whispered words, and then she took him by the arm to the senator's table. They shared a quiet laugh along the way.

The Japanese businessmen exchanged glances, clearly reconsidering their choice of counsel. Ten places to their rear, Trevor's face was an unhealthy shade of purple. "Murray *Fucking* Rothstein," he muttered to himself.

Over lunch, he forgot all about the original purpose of our meeting (work I'd been doing on the cross-market correlation of default risk on securitized subprime loans—there were some interesting and counterintuitive trends in the data) and ranted about Murray Fucking Rothstein.

Murray had joined the Firm in the 1980s, an up and coming M&A whizz who quickly became its rainmaker. He was a shark in an eat-what-you-kill world, and he produced a lot of revenue, but he was unconventional, a bull in the china shop, an alpha wolf among alpha dogs. He flaunted rules, upset apple carts, mowed others' lawns, sailed close to the wind. Time and again the regulators rapped his knuckles, but they could never cuff his wrists.

Trevor's facility with metaphor, I realized, far exceeded my own.

The publicity was embarrassing so the Firm pressed Murray to stop cutting corners. He agreed but nothing changed. He kept doing what he did best. As the Firm climbed in the M&A league tables, as fees poured in and the senior partners bought Bahamian islets and private jets, the controversy and scrutiny Murray generated became intense. The Firm felt it necessary to act. It created an oversight committee to manage its top performer, and that committee implemented approvals processes, vetting procedures, risk management protocols, compliance checklists. The times were changing, Trevor said, but Murray couldn't adapt. A year into the new regime, still in his prime, he quit.

"We all thought, good riddance," Trevor said. "The scrutiny we were under . . . But then he wrote that fucking book."

It was a titillating insider account of filthy lucre and dirty tricks, none of which directly incriminated its author. It shone an unwelcome light on certain Bay Street practices, and the government tightened oversight as a result. A lot of people were still angry with Murray for breaking *omertà*, the code of silence. Trevor, it appeared, was among them.

Back at the office that afternoon, I wondered why Murray had burnt his bridges. Was it revenge? He must have bridled at all those procedures the Firm had put in place. Imagine harnessing Northern Dancer to a chuck wagon. But maybe there was more to it than that. Maybe he'd ignored his muse and later—relaxing on the deck of his fifty-two foot Dufour yacht, in his castle in Tuscany, or on his private Georgian Bay island—he'd regretted doing so. Maybe the book was his way of making amends.

I nosed around and learned that his former secretary still worked at the Firm. I knew Gizelle vaguely as a smart, competent woman, a striking blonde in her mid-forties, the chairman's executive assistant. When I approached her about Murray her eyes narrowed and she appraised me coolly. I felt myself blush under her gaze. She smiled faintly, glanced over her shoulder, and slipped me his number.

A week later I called him and arranged to meet at a place called Bistro des Artistes.

*

"So you worked with Trevor?" I said to make conversation.

"No, he carried my briefcase. Trevor wouldn't know a deal

at a poker table. He's a lick-spittle, kiss-ass toad. Gizelle says you're different."

"This looks like a nice place," I said, casting around.

"I like it. The waiters are all performers and actors. The owner likes to support the arts." He caught the eye of our server, a pretty blonde. "Darlene, could we have the '97 Brunello, please?" He admired her backside as she left. "Like two cats in a gunny sack," he said. "She's an actress. Graduated from Guildhall. Going to be a star."

We drank the wine and swapped histories. He was a Jew from Winnipeg and he'd always felt like an outsider on Bay Street. "My mother's side were all socialists, communists even. The old man was an anarchist. His bubby was Emma Goldman's cousin. Now that's a pedigree for an anarchist. And me, I show interest in writing. 'Wasn't Emma a writer? Look at Hannah Arendt!' I played football for the Bisons—'Shouldn't a Jew know how to handle himself in a crowd?' Oh, they had high expectations. 'He's going to be a shop steward someday! Maybe a lawyer!' I was their golden boy but I was just a kid and had to rebel. Believe it or not, business was my rebellion. I became a huge disappointment—an embarrassment, even. I have cousins who stopped talking to me."

Now, a decade removed from his Gekko-Milken days, he'd reconciled with everybody. His book had helped. "They think of me now as a sleeper agent. Maybe I was." He drained his wineglass and looked around. "Oh, Darlene? Darlene?" After a few glasses, her name came out sounding like "darling." "Could we get some of that nice Calvados, please? The Napoléon? There's a batch just in." He watched her bustle away then turned back to me. "Tell me about your book. You don't mind me saying, it sounds like a stretch from what you do at the Firm. But I guess you need a good imagination for that, too."

Murray listened closely while I talked.

"Sounds interesting," he said when I finished, toasting me with Calvados and ordering another. "I wish you every success."

His manner was so courteous and dignified (and I'd had so much to drink) that I was finally emboldened to get down to the question I'd really wanted to ask: how he got published and what I should know.

"Funny story," he said.

He'd met a well known literary agent at a charity fundraiser, a woman named Barbara Edgeley. They'd hit it off (here, his eyes shifted discretely down to his glass) and she'd liked the concept of his book. When his manuscript was ready she read it and agreed to represent him. "We signed a contract and Barb started shopping it around. But I got impatient." Behind her back he approached the president of a publishing house, a former client he'd helped with a management buy-out. There'd been some issues at the company that weren't disclosed to the MBO's financiers, nor discovered during their due diligence (Murray coughed discretely as he skirted over the details), and when the president learned that Murray had retained certain working files, he expressed a sudden interest in reading his manuscript. "He signed me to a deal, and Barb still got her percentage on sales. I didn't mind. I'm a man of honour and a contract's a contract."

Darlene brought us cappuccinos, and Murray waited for her to leave before he continued. "Barb and I are still friends," he murmured, barely audible, "socially, so to speak. Although these days we don't see much of each other."

I asked him about football, something he'd mentioned earlier in passing.

He'd been a linebacker at university but injured a knee in second year. That ended his playing career, but he still loved football, especially the game with three downs. "When I was a kid in the 'Peg it was the only game in town."

Being from the scattered town of Saskatchewan I knew what that was like. We spent the next half hour talking about the CFL, something that never happens in Toronto, where a foreign league rules every sports bar every Sunday.

For a man known for ruthlessness, his ego didn't overshadow the table. When we parted he gave me a firm handshake and gripped my elbow hard, and for a moment I saw the titan he'd been, saw the eat-what-you-kill look in his eyes, the hard-nosed stare he was known for on Bay Street. But it was just gas. He let my elbow go and belched into his fist. "I enjoyed this," he said. "Let's stay in touch. I'm going to Italy on Sunday for truffle season but I'll be back in three weeks. Let's get together next month."

I was heading back to the office, he for his Bentley. "Say hello to Giselle," he called after me. "I should have never let her go."

We got into the habit of meeting once a month at Bistro des Artistes. It turned out he had a thing for Darlene. It remained undeclared, though it was obvious even to me; he pined for her like a grizzly-sized teenager. "She's just my type," he'd lament after a few glasses. "Smart. Beautiful. Way too young." For a man with a take-no-prisoners reputation, he was an unaccountable romantic. Genny liked him immensely, even though they had a drawn out argument the first time they met. It was over the Arab-Israeli conflict. Genny was on the side of the Palestinians, Murray an unrepentant supporter of Israel. I watched them go at it, knowing she liked the sound of his lefty family in Winnipeg, and that she, black haired and intense, reminded him of the Emma Goldmans of his childhood. That first debate set the tone for the way they'd interact ever after.

CHAPTER EIGHT

When one burns one's bridges, what a very nice fire it makes.

Dylan Thomas

Writing was therapy, an escape, an affirmation that I was alive, that I wasn't just another empty suit. But after five years, I was worried about *Blown to Hell*. I still didn't have a complete manuscript. I knew I needed more time to work on it or it might never be finished. I couldn't tolerate that thought, for I couldn't shake the notion that I had cheated Death, and that it (sore loser that it was) would return for me whenever it liked. I knew with certainty that I had to do *this*, what I wanted to be remembered for, while I had time and all my faculties.

I decided to quit my job.

I thought Genny would be enthusiastic about me making something of my second chance. After all, years before, she'd encouraged me to write. And I thought she'd welcome the notion of shucking another irritant of traditional marriage, the Man as Breadwinner. But she did not at first embrace the notion wholeheartedly.

"How will we pay the bills? The mortgage?"

"We'll have to watch our spending."

"But . . . but . . ."

"Not to worry. I've been well paid at the Firm. I put money away and built a portfolio. It'll generate dividends. And you've got your job."

"But you always made more money."

"I won't any more. But there'll be dividends, and capital gains. Look at this spreadsheet. Look at the five-year return we had to the end of Twenty-Oh-Six. If we can get the same return . . ."

I'd done my homework, but she didn't care what the spreadsheet said. She'd always left that kind of thing to me. She took no interest in our finances beyond periodic questions around ethics.

("Any tobacco? Anything in Chile?" "Chile's okay now." "Mexico, then. The *maquiladoras*? What about fair wages? Child labour? Dolphins?")

As we talked it through I reassured her that I had a plan.

"I won't manage the portfolio myself. It'll be managed by professionals. They're big on diversification—that's how they deal with risk. It's the same thing I do with collateralized debt obligations, except with equities. They invest our money in a range of stocks and sectors. If one goes down its effect gets offset by the others. They change the allocation now and then, depending on what's happening in the economy. Right now they're heavy on high tech, commodities, and US real estate. Dotcom's come back from when the bubble burst, and the housing market will always be secure. The bottom line is, we're totally diversified. Our nest egg is safe. Don't worry about it. I know what I'm talking about." I was tempted to make a self-deprecating joke about idiot savants—Farley's favourite gibe.

Over many months we went around and around, not on the numbers but the idea. "Are you sure you won't get bored?' she asked.

"I am bored."

"But won't you miss going to work? Contact with

people?"

I was beginning to wonder if she'd miss contact with the exotic vacation spots we'd enjoyed at spring break.

"Can't you do it part time, like you were doing? Do you really want to write full time? I remember when I wrote my book on the Basarwa—"

"You always told me I should write. To do what I wanted."

"But can we afford to lose one salary?"

"It'll be all right," I said.

"Chloe . . ."

"She'll be all right." I said, now stubbornly.

Genny eventually saw I had to make a break of it, that I needed to grasp this particular nettle. We tightened our belts, and the stress level in our household went up; but I give her full credit: once she agreed she never looked back. And anyway, I wouldn't exactly be a kept man. I had means. I wasn't an idiot savant for nothing.

CHAPTER NINE

> A good novel tells us the truth about its hero; but a bad novel tells us the truth about its author.
>
> G.K. Chesterton

> Being myself of colonial extraction, I have a keen nose for colonial anxieties, and the notion of a "Great (Your Country Here) Novel" seems whiffy to me.
>
> Peter Carey

After Genny leaves for work I check the market.

It's a bloodbath again this morning. The crisis is far from over; exchanges everywhere are in turmoil.

There's always a price for risk; but people get lazy. That's what happened here. They should have paid attention. They were too trusting and, admittedly, there were abuses. Disclosures were not transparent. Snake oil passed as extra virgin. Someone should be held accountable.

Until things bounce back we'll tighten our belts. Make economies. It's like living on the prairies.

The good news is that *Blown to Hell* is finished. Long finished, in fact, although it remains, lamentably, unpublished.

I should describe it for you. I need to get better at

summarizing it anyway. Sometimes I go off on tangents or into too many details. Get to the point, Genny says, while Farley likens me to Tristram Shandy.

Blown to Hell is set in 1792, during the forgotten voyage of William Broughton, the re-discoverer of the San Juan Islands, the second man to explore the Columbia River, and sidekick to the redoubtable Captain George Vancouver. The book has everything required of The Great Canadian Novel. A multinational cast of Britons, Spaniards, and Americans, all cavorting with Indians. ("First Nation Peoples," Genny always interjects.) Imperial powers manoeuvring for advantage, the Royal Navy engaged in some old-fashioned gun-boat diplomacy. Revelry, sword fights, and reflections on age, maturity, duty, honour, love. There's sex, skulduggery, and a murder. It's a mystery, set on the eve of the French Revolutionary Wars.

Uh-oh. You see it too: the *French* Revolutionary Wars. The French in Quebec, they were on our side by then, weren't they? (Aren't they still? I can never tell.)

Could the Wars, which ended badly for France, be construed in Quebec as another historical humiliation?

Okay. *Blown to Hell* has all the makings for The Great *English*-Canadian Novel.

What it does not have is a publisher.

Perhaps it would have been easier if I'd centred *Blown* on Broughton's boss, the testy, mercurial and driven George Vancouver, but for me Broughton is a more compelling character. He was Vancouver's deputy for two years, on the voyage out from England and during a year of exploration in the Pacific north-west. He commanded *Chatham*, the rinky-dink brig that accompanied Vancouver's more dignified flagship *Discovery*. *Chatham* was pug-ugly, an historical also-ran that leaked like a sieve and wallowed embarrassingly in even the calmest conditions. Her own crew referred to her as a dung-barge. The term was not meant with affection.

Broughton himself was a decent sort, a dutiful if stolid Number 2; something of a plodder, sometimes inept, always cautious—he must have recognized his own limitations. The exasperated Vancouver, in the midst of a tense standoff with the Spanish over possession of the region, decided to send him home to England, ostensibly to report on the situation. It was a smooth ruse by Vancouver, an obvious contrivance to be rid of an annoying subordinate. The made-up mission spared Broughton's honour, an important consideration back then. Nowadays he'd receive a patronage appointment on top of three years severance. Forget honour, these days. Go for the pork.

Bearing his commander's secret dispatches, Broughton sailed with the Spaniards to Mexico, travelled overland to the Caribbean coast, then on to Cuba and Spain on a Spanish man-of-war. Quite a trip, for an Englishman of the day. Were the Spaniards tempted to bump him off en route, or at least get him drunk and peek at his dispatches? Probably, but Broughton made it home unscathed. The Admiralty considered Vancouver's report, heard Broughton out, and ordered him to rejoin Vancouver somewhere in the Pacific. (Why did everyone want to see the back of Broughton?) The ship they gave him was the *Providence*, a vast improvement over the rinky-dink *Chatham*; Captain Bligh of *Bounty* fame had recently sailed her to Tahiti and back to complete the mission so rudely interrupted by Fletcher Christian.

Now Broughton had orders for sea and a prestigious command; yet he seemed in no hurry. After a lengthy home leave, an extended refit, and a leisurely outbound cruise, he finally arrived in Nootka Sound on Vancouver Island in the spring of 1796. It was almost four years since he'd departed the place as Vancouver's emissary. In the meantime, the Spanish had abandoned their local bases, and Vancouver had returned to England, his mission accomplished.

Broughton must have been concerned that his dilatory voyage now had no purpose and might reflect badly on him. He decided to sail for Asia. There was still mapping to do there. He'd finally lead his own expedition, no longer subordinate to a demanding tyrant like George Vancouver.

Over the next year, he languidly charted the coasts of Korea, Japan, and China, until he ran the *Providence* onto a reef off the tiny isle of Miyako-jima. He and his crew were briefly marooned until, improbably, he acquired another vessel and continued his voyage. He returned to England at last in 1799 to complete his seminal work, *A Voyage of Discovery to the North Pacific Ocean: in which the coast of Asia, from the lat. of 35 north to the lat. of 52 north, the island of Insu (commonly known under the name of the land of Jesso), the north, south and east coasts of Japan, the Lieuchieux and the adjacent isles, as well as the coast of Corea, have been examined and surveyed: performed in His Majesty's sloop Providence and her tender, in the Years 1795, 1796, 1797, 1798.* History does not record whether book buyers confused his tome with Vancouver's more catchily-titled best-seller, *A Voyage of Discovery to the North Pacific Ocean and Round the World.*

Broughton had a colourful run in Asia, and there is plenty of dramatic fodder in his shipwreck on Miyako-jima; but I chose to set *Blown to Hell* in Nootka Sound during Vancouver's tense stand-off with the Spanish. It was not the most swash-buckling period of Broughton's career, and I think he gets overshadowed by the domineering Vancouver; but it had a Canadian angle, which interested me, and it seemed the place to begin with Broughton. I'd had a trilogy in mind for him but now I don't know. I just want to get Volume 1 published.

*

"How am I ever going to get published?" I asked the one person I knew with an eye to literary matters.

"Just do as I do, old boy." Farley looked at me over the rim of a shot glass before chugging it and pouring Żywiec down his throat to douse the flames.

I was confused for only a second. "No, not rubbished. Published."

"Eh?"

We were in Gzbrnznkwyc's on Roncesvalles for one of our regular sessions. It was payday, late afternoon, and the place was packed with Poles. The air was redolent of comfort food, full of noise and consonants.

"I asked about how to get published."

He observed me thoughtfully for a moment, raised a finger to emphasize a point but burped before he could make it. "Same way you get to Carnegie Hall," he said, his eyes watery. He waved to get our waitress's attention.

"Carnegie Hall?" I asked, confused again.

His head swung my way. "It's just a saying, bud. Look, the thing about publishing is, it's a tough, bloodthirsty, unforgiving industry run by piranhas. Don't forget that. It's a business. It has nothing to do with the creative process, or literary merit, or art. It's about selling books, and the bottom line when it comes to your book, every book, is that sometimes the sizzle sells the steak but the proof is in the pudding and the pudding—"

"No. Is not. No pudding."

We both looked up at Ludwika, the pretty Polish waitress who always seemed to be working at Gzbrnznkwyc's.

"I'm sorry?" I said.

She signalled another table she was coming and looked down at us. "Just *naleśniki*. You want? With two forks, like woman?" She smiled coyly and looked from me to Farley but the smile faded as she registered our confusion. "We no pudding. *Naleśniki* instead. Polish pancake. Is better."

"But we don't want pudding or—"

"You wave me like you want order, then you pudding this, pudding that—"

"Oh. I get it now." Farley circled his finger over our table. "We just wanted another round."

"Ah. Okay." She raised a hand to the other table and looked at Farley. "Just Żywiec? Or shot too?"

Farley looked at me. "Shots too."

"Why you no try shot of Polish Scotch?"

"Polish Scotch?"

"*Torfowisko*. Is good."

Farley looked doubtful. He was a stickler when it came to Scotch. "We'll stick with vodka."

Ludwika shrugged. She was always trying to get us to try things Polish. One night she'd guided us through Gzbrnznkwyc's extensive list of Polish beers. For the last hour before closing we were her only customers so she sat down and Farley got her talking about herself, an old trick of his. She was twenty-three, a trained engineer, but her credentials weren't recognized in Canada. She worked nights and studied days to qualify.

"Why didn't you stay in Poland?" I asked.

She turned her green eyes on me, and she was so beautiful I felt myself blush. "Everyone with baby or gone to England. Men drunk and violent. Canada is better. My uncle," (she nodded towards the kitchen) "came during communism, years ago. He likes here. I like."

"What about Canadian men?" Farley asked.

She sat back in her chair and lit a Dunhill (although we were in No Smoking Toronto). For a moment she stared at the ceiling, holding the cigarette out from her side like a thirties film star. Finally she exhaled and brought her eyes down to us. "They think Polish girls easy to fuck. They think Polish girls are like French, only cheaper."

"We'll find you a nice Canadian," I said. "You'll like."

"Not *too* nice," Farley said. "You'll like even better."

"Is too bad you both married," she said. "You very handsome, for old peoples." Then she smiled to show she was joking and went to help her uncle close up.

But this night, she had no time to dawdle. She hurried off to take the other table's order then headed for the bar. Farley watched her go. "Where were we?"

"Publishing. My book."

"Oh yeah." He drained the last suds from his beer glass and looked back to see how Ludwika was doing with our order. I craved his advice but I knew then he wasn't going to answer. He grew distant whenever I brought up my writing, and never talked about his own. I recognized this as aesthetic detachment, and I respected him for it. He must reserve a place, I reasoned, one exclusively his; one he cannot share with anyone; a place where he *creates*. This thought, this glimpse of his artist's soul, moved me deeply. I envied him. He'd paid his dues. He'd pursued his passion. He'd never sold out.

And then he surprised me by speaking.

"It's the work, bud, the work that counts. Just the work."

CHAPTER TEN

When a true genius appears in the world, you may know him by this sign, that the dunces are all in confederacy against him.

Jonathan Swift

This novel is not to be tossed lightly aside, but to be hurled with great force.

Dorothy Parker

"Of course, it's the work that counts," I told Murray. We were in our usual place. I'd just brought him up to speed.

"Sure, but you need an In of some kind," Murray said. "I wish I still had some pull with my publisher but we had a gentleman's agreement. I destroyed my files. I've got bupkis on him these days."

"No worries. I'll figure something out." Murray didn't know it, but I already had. "How about those Leafs, eh? Oh, by the way. Totally different subject. What was your agent's name again? Beverley?"

"Barbara?" Murray looked startled, then glanced towards Darlene, who was taking an order across the room. "Barb Edgeley. I haven't seen her in a while."

"Right. Right. That was the name."

Murray's eyes couldn't seem to settle on anything.

"Yes, Barbara Edgeley. I just couldn't remember her name."

We both fell silent.

"I suppose I could introduce you to Barb."

"Murray! No. I couldn't ask . . . Would you? Really? That would be great. Gee! Thanks."

I was rather pleased with myself. Recently I'd been studying subtlety, trying to work it into my writing; and they do say life imitates art.

When Murray phoned a couple of days later he sounded miserable. Barbara had agreed to meet, but she'd suggested Bistro des Artistes. He hadn't been able to persuade her otherwise.

"Any advice?" I asked.

"Just tell her what you tell me all the time," he said, preoccupied.

We were scheduled to meet on a Monday. I spent the weekend making edits. Little Chloe was bursting with excitement that I was finally meeting an Asian about my book.

"*Agent*, Chloe," Genny clarified, without explaining the distinction. She kept Chloe busy and out of my way all weekend while I worked. They went shopping in Chinatown and watched *Mulan* on video. "It's for good luck, Daddy," Chloe whispered, "with the Asian-ttt."

The day of the meeting I spent the morning formatting, reformatting and editing; then, when I was satisfied, I ran over to the print shop to make a clean copy. *Blown to Hell* came in at 780 pages, and I wanted Barbara to have a professional-looking manuscript, to show I was savvy to the business.

At Bistro des Artistes, Darlene was unaccustomedly cool to Murray and almost rude to Barbara, who seemed like a nice woman. She was about Murray's age, a striking woman with strawberry blonde hair.

"So you've got a novel," she said after the preliminaries.

"Yes. I've been working on it for years. I began it in my spare time—"

"Well, don't give up your day job, that's what I always tell people starting out."

We all laughed, me clicking my tongue at the very idea.

They hadn't seen each other in a while and their discussion seemed a bit stilted. As they chatted about acquaintances and social events, I sipped my merlot, swallowing around my beating heart, which was lodged in my throat. At my side, my briefcase, stuffed with the magnum opus that was *Blown to Hell*. The last thing I'd done before printing was tweak the dialogue in Chapter 12—did it foreshadow what I wanted? Had I used the right font? Were the margins industry-standard?

Darlene delivered our entrees (steak frites for Murray and me, salad for Barbara). A few moments later she circled the table to grind pepper onto our steaks and, unbidden, onto Barbara's salad. She was quick, and just as Barbara realized what she was doing and opened her mouth to speak, she nodded a curt Your Welcome, wished us *bon appétit*, and sashayed away towards the kitchen.

Barbara stared after her. Murray's eyes followed her also before returning to focus on his steak. I tasted mine. Barbara looked at Murray. A silence settled over the table. I tasted another piece of steak just as Barbara turned to me and said, "Tell me about your novel."

This was my moment, the dawn of my future, the instant in which my destiny would change. And I had a mouth full of steak and a throat full of heart.

Speaking around a chunk of juicy meat, I began with some background. How Broughton had been dispatched with George Vancouver to explore the Pacific coast from California to Alaska. I explained that Francis Drake first coasted the area in 1579, fully two centuries before Cook, but that Britain hadn't followed up on his territorial claim. The Spanish hadn't pushed their own exploration in the area until—

"Your book . . .?" Barbara probed.

"Is set in 1792." By then the Spanish were worried about the Russians coming down the coast, and the British and Americans coming across the Pacific or around Tierra del Fuego. Cook had—

"What's it about?" she asked. Murray was looking at me oddly.

"It's about diplomacy and exploration on an unknown coast. An unknown chapter of history."

"But the story . . . There's a *story*, in the novel. How would you summarize it?"

"It's very difficult to summarize."

Silence again fell over our table. Barbara frowned at her salad. She'd asked for a lemon vinaigrette but seemed to be finding it sour. Perhaps it was the pepper she was finding disagreeable. Around us, the murmur of lunch conversation, the clink of cutlery and glass.

"Well, it's a mystery, isn't it?" Murray put in.

For a moment I thought he was referring to Barbara's choice of dressing, but he was speaking about my book. "Well, there's a mystery to it, but it's not a mystery novel per se," I said.

I was beginning to regret my morning of fine tuning on the manuscript. My brain was swimming in details, and I seemed unable to get the story across. "It has a nautical theme," I said with growing desperation. "There's seamen."

"Well," Barbara said, starting afresh. "What's it called?"

"*Blown to Hell.*"

She giggled.

"Barb," Murray said. "It's not that kind of blown. Clean it up. Besides, it's a working title."

I hadn't thought of that. Who would? This was not going well. "There's a love story," I offered. "And a death. But I wouldn't describe it as a romance or a murder-mystery. There are Indians. And lots of alcohol. They get really drunk. That's when things get ugly. I've used the voice of a sea otter to emphasize the spiritual aspect."

"A sea otter?"

"It's based on a legend. He speaks in these dream-like sequences. But that's only one of the points of view I've used."

As Barbara appraised me silently, Murray pinched his fingers together and slowly pulled his hands apart, like God stretching a mote of dough into a universe of bread.

Big picture. I had to go big picture. "It's . . . uhm . . . historical fiction?"

That wasn't supposed to come out like a question, so I cleared my throat and repeated, this time with emphasis, "Historical fiction!"

I won't relate the rest of the conversation, but it ended as ingloriously as it had begun when the normally efficient Darlene, bustling around to refill our water glasses, splashed ice into Barbara's lap. When that kerfuffle was tidied up none of us had the juice to discuss my novel. Barbara declined Darlene's offer of "a free no-fat, easy-on-the-hips latte" with a scowl and a wave. I picked up the tab, which I think compelled her to accept my proffered manuscript when we parted. Still, she hesitated before taking it. "Are you sure it's ready?" she asked.

"Absolutely," I replied. "I haven't explained it very well, but I know you're going to like it."

"I'm very busy over the next month."

"No problem."

"One thing you should work on," she said, "is your elevator pitch. You have about ten seconds to say what it's about."

Ten seconds. I wondered about those 780 pages, every one of which was filled with words. Which ones to emphasize in my ten second pitch? Back at the Firm, the sales guys were always talking about what to say and not to say in sales presentations. But how could they explain the nuances of an asset-backed security, the complexity of the tranche structure of a collateralized debt obligation, without knowing the specifics? "Let the sales guys take the lead," Trevor always told me. "You come in if there's any technical questions." There were hardly ever any of those.

On the way home I couldn't get *One Froggy Evening* out of my mind. Released by Warner Brothers in 1955, it's considered one of the finest short films ever made. Stephen Spielberg calls it "the *Citizen Kane* of animated film." Accolades aside, mention it to anyone who grew up in the sixties or seventies and they know it: it's the one with the singing frog. Discovered by a greedy everyman, the frog's range is prodigious—ragtime to opera, sung in a rich and reedy baritone and performed with a showman's zest. The man envisions riches—a Singing, Dancing Frog! But the frog performs only for him. In the presence of others, it behaves like an ordinary, leaden, garden-variety amphibian.

I'd had my chance to sing, and I'd produced a creaky *ribbit*.
I felt sufficiently insecure to email Barbara that night.

> **Dear Barbara,**
> **The 10 Second Pitch: It's a tragedy, set amid a high-stakes game of diplomacy at the edge of the known world.**

Ten seconds means you have to be economical. I'd left out all the details. I sent Murray a message too.

> **I blew it, didn't I?**

Murray's reply was waiting for me in the morning.

> **Probably, but work her. See what she says. She knows the business. BTW she's pissed with me—nothing to do with you. Let me know how it goes. Glad to help any way I can. Remember, publishing is way more cut-throat than finance. Illegitimi non carborundum, as we say in yiddish.**

Barbara's reply came in later that morning:

> High-stakes diplomacy doesn't cut it. Calling diplomacy high stakes doesn't make it more dramatic. Tragedy, edge of the known world? Conveys nothing. Try to get specific on who, where, and what happens. You have no verbs like Prince Kills King, Kills Himself. You are missing the most saleable elements.

"Saleable elements" was a good sign. Best of all, she'd replied. I set to work.

> Blown to Hell is a murder mystery, a love story, a tale of diplomacy, intrigue and compromise, an epic adventure set in the Pacific north-west at the start of the Napoleonic Wars.

Exactly ten seconds. I felt I was getting it. She replied an hour later.

> I'm not going to read it right now. I looked at it and don't think it's ready. It's complicated and confusing. A mishmash. I don't see the bones that give the story tension or movement. My advice is to start over from scratch. You know your characters and the story. Pick your hero, pick your point of view and stick with it. Make it a straight-ahead narrative and cut everything—the history, the back story, everything that doesn't further the action. I'm not sure about the otter. This is only my view. Others will feel differently. If you do decide to stick with it, by all means let me know when you have the next draft.

Ouch. "Others will feel differently." Maybe my granny.

That night, I said nothing to Genny or Chloe about my first rejection. Instead I drank a few glasses of wine and entertained them with comic repartee. Next morning I cheerily saw them off, checked they were well and truly gone, and collapsed into bed.

I hadn't presented well, and Barbara hadn't understood what I was trying to do. Still, she'd given me feedback. There *were* too many voices, too many perspectives; there *was* too much history. I could deal with all of that. I could drop some scenes, delete some of the back-story, rewrite sections from a different point of view, even reconsider the role of the sea otter.

After a few days I got back to work.

CHAPTER ELEVEN

All writers are vain, selfish and lazy, and at the very bottom of their motives lies a mystery. Writing a book is a long, exhausting struggle, like a long bout of some painful illness. One would never undertake such a thing if one were not driven by some demon whom one can neither resist nor understand.

George Orwell

If it sounds like writing, I rewrite it.

Elmore Leonard

This past weekend Genny was incensed over an article in the newspaper. It was about those metallic water bottles that are all the rage because they contain no bisphenol-A, a synthetic compound used in everything from plastic pipes and DVDs to the lining of cans and bottles. BPA was long billed as inert yet ninety-five percent of us have measurable levels of it in our bodies, and clinical tests have linked it to cancer, decreased sperm count, early puberty, and other reproductive and neurological problems.

Just last year, when Genny learned about BPA, she threw away all our expensive polycarbonate containers and vowed not to eat canned food.

"But it's cheap," I said, tartan even before the market turned.

"You of all people," she chided, "should know what ingesting chemicals can do."

She banned canned food from the house (I hid a supply in the basement for when I cook; you can't beat the convenience) and replaced all our plastic bottles with thirty dollar metal ones made by a European enviro-company, Heil AG, because *its* bottles were safe. No BPA. Totally inert. Nothing leached from them. Except, as Genny discovered in the weekend paper, they *do* have BPA.

After she read that she scoured through our cupboards once again, this time to collect all our trendy, expensive Heil bottles.

"And they're *European!*" she said angrily. "Who can you believe anymore? Where's the obligation for ethical behaviour? One day it's safe, the next it's not."

"*Mais, zut alors*, eet's only a leetle leachate," I said in my best French accent. "It won't hairtt yew."

At least Chloe laughed. Genny scowled. "They feed us such pap. They just keep repeating it. 'BPA is no risk to your health.' 'There is no such thing as global warming.' No wonder people are so apathetic these days."

I felt a pang of guilt. The comment hit close to home. I remembered the impassioned arguments Farley and I had had back in undergrad. I was all about environmental causes and direct action in those days.

I picked up the paper and read the article Genny had read.

Heil is covering its tracks. Apologies galore, sorry for the inconvenience, and for anyone concerned about their bottles (". . . but they really are safe," a spokesperson assured reporters) the company is offering a voluntary exchange. If you send your old bottles to Heil, at your own expense, they will send you a BPA-free replacement, free of charge. They are careful not to call this a recall—perish the thought of admitting liability. This from a company that made such comforting claims and rode a wave of greenwash to handsome profit.

Now, Monday morning, and me with the house to myself, I can't get the environment out of my head. We *are* apathetic. We just go with the flow. We need to act on many fronts, but that takes political will. It takes courage and foresight, research and innovation, money for new technology, *lots* of money, and the *cojones* to stand up to the naysayers and yeah-buts. Most of all, it takes leadership.

We face big challenges—forget BPA, think climate change; but we've overcome big challenges before. Years ago we phased out the chemicals that cause ozone depletion, reduced emissions that cause acid rain, cleaned up the Great Lakes, banned DDT. Recently, there have been many examples of concerted global action—just not on the environment. Look how the disparate countries of the world acted quickly and decisively to prevent economic collapse during the financial crisis. Now, as I write in 2009, there is a new threat, and another heartening international response. The world is mobilizing to deal with swine flu, a particularly virulent and deadly strain of influenza that's killed hundreds and has the potential for much worse. Millions of doses of vaccine have been ordered; mass immunizations are planned, and billions of dollars have been allocated to the campaign. Admittedly, there's some petty waffling over terminology, as the name "swine flu" has raised needless concerns about the safety of pork. To ameliorate the impact on pig farmers the CDC is calling it a "novel form of the H1N1 virus"; the European Commission has gone one better and called it simply "the novel flu." That's politics for you. It doesn't matter what it's called. It matters that it's nipped in the bud.

(Genny is also concerned about the impact on swine producers—not the factory farmers in Iowa or Italy for whom the authorities invented these innocuous labels, but the women who tend pigs in traditional societies. Now, in their interest, she is quick to correct anyone who mistakenly calls the swine flu the swine flu. It's strictly H1N1 or the novel strain to Genny; this, from a woman who hasn't eaten bacon in years.

She has also started Chloe and me on an herbal preventative recommended by her pharma-friend from our England days, Cindy, who found religion on naturopathy years ago. Cindy now heads a booming herbal supplements business based in Salt Lake City, and Genny consults her regularly for holistic remedies. Incidentally, my long-ago speculation about Cindy proved unfounded; she has been married to a man these sixteen years and is mother to six young Republicans. Genny ingests her supplements, but not her politics, which by unspoken agreement they never discuss.

Genny's faith in traditional cures has never faltered. Over the years, whenever I've had a cold, a sniffle, any ailment at all, she's been quick to prescribe a herbal remedy; and to please her I've taken it, reasoning it could do no harm. In a relationship, you choose the hill you want to die on.)

*

I spent the better part of a year on the rewrite. I revised, cut, rethought, rewrote, and cut again. I went through successive drafts (retaining them all, thinking the parts I'd deleted might be useful some day). I joined a writer's group to get feedback. I listened to what its members said as well as what they didn't say. And I asked Farley for help.

Despite the reticence I'd sensed in him, he agreed.

We met for drinks after he'd read the manuscript. "It's . . . original," he said. "And complicated. Lots of detail. I can see you in it." He peered at me for a moment over his bifocals. "Look, bud, before we get into this. It's your book. Don't ever forget that. Everyone will tell you what it should be about and how you should write it, but in the end, the decisions are yours. You with me?"

I nodded.

"Okay. Having said that, there are certain conventions a writer can breach on his fourth or fifth book. Not his first." He handed me a sheaf of paper, his handwritten notes on

Blown to Hell. Next he handed me the manuscript itself, tagged with stickies and heavily marked up.

An hour later he leaned back in his chair. "I hope this is helpful."

"You know it is."

"Just remember, it's your call. The burden of decision is always on the writer." To emphasize his own burden, he observed me through a glass of Dewar's. We were in a bar near the university, a faux-British pub that stocked no single malt. "T'were best done quickly," he said, jiggling the glass andpouring its contents down his throat. Inspired, even giddy with his insight, already thinking about what I'd do first, I tossed mine back too.

"If you don't mind me saying," he said when we both had our wind back, "you're an odd duck. Married for years, faithful even." His eyebrows rose, he seemed to be waiting for me to speak. "You were respectable. You wore a suit and built derivatives for a living. Now you turn to writing. Writers are scrofulous by nature, but you don't have a disreputable bone in your body."

"I've got a lot of catching up to do." I signalled our waitress.

"Hmm." We fell into silence. His eyes wandered onto a table of undergrad women.

" 'Scrofulous'?" I asked.

He grunted. His gaze stayed on the undergrads.

"That's good. Is it one of yours?"

He still didn't look at me, and I realized it wasn't just the presence of those pretty girls; his mood had shifted, a veil had descended, a gulf now lay between us. "No. It's not one of mine. It's not original in the least. That was Dylan I just shamelessly, unoriginally, unimaginatively paraphrased."

"Bob?"

He knew I knew he meant his Welsh blowhard, but he didn't smile or even glance my way.

*

Months later, I was ready to approach Barbara with my

revised manuscript.

"I wouldn't do that," Murray said under his breath.

We were at Bistro des Artistes, and Darlene was serving our table. He looked around, spotted her across the room, and relaxed. "Well, do what you think," he said. "Just don't mention my name."

Why Barbara, after she'd blown me off? Because she'd taken the time (albeit a New York minute) to comment. She'd given hard advice that I'd found useful. And she was an In to publishing and I had no other.

I called her office and left a message.

No response.

A week later I sent her an email.

> Dear Barbara,
> I took your advice to heart and completely rethought Blown to Hell. I knocked out a prologue, eliminated two first person voices and all the second person narrative, cut the Latin section, and got rid of the interior monologue by the sea otter. I simplified the structure, streamlined the narrative, tightened and refined the plot. I've written new sections to aid continuity. I've edited, cut and crisped up my prose. Blown to Hell is down to 600 pages, and it is now a very different book from the one you saw. I have complete confidence in it and in myself as a writer. I wasn't ready at our first meeting. I am now. If you're willing to take another look, I'll deliver the manuscript to you. Say the word and it will be there.

I appended a half-page synopsis, with this for a clincher:

> Blown to Hell is a story of coming of age but it is also a tale of diplomacy, intrigue and compromise;

> it is a love story and an epic adventure set in the Pacific north-west on the brink of the Napoleonic Wars.

I'd covered all the bases with that, but it didn't satisfy Barbara.

> Your pitch isn't there yet, and I fear this still reflects a problem with the novel. I still don't know what your book is about. "Coming of age" of whom? Whose story is it? What happens? You've given background but nothing of the dramatic action. And I just don't see any point in a talking sea lion. I hate to sound negative or undermine your confidence, but from what you've said, you may want to consult with a professional editor or get feedback at a creative writing class. Also, is it for young adults (i.e. "coming of age")? I don't do young adults.

I wasn't sensing any benefit of the doubt. I responded:

> Although I seem unable to summarize it effectively for you, I fear you judge this book by its cover. I've restructured and rewritten it completely. I've received plenty of feedback. The sea <u>otter</u> (in first person) is gone. The book stands on its merits. It isn't young adult/juvenile; its themes are universal. I'm attaching a detailed outline of the book that describes its flow and summarizes its plot. If you feel it's not for you, I'll understand and we'll both move on; but please review my outline before you make that call.

She replied:

I read the outline. I may just be the wrong reader for this. I don't see the bones of a rip-roaring yarn that will sell in the commercial marketplace. Yes, you do have to learn how to pitch your book. But perhaps you have presented it accurately and what I need is different from the book you want to write. I wish you great success with this—the topic is enormously appealing. I am certain someone will pick it up, or that you will succeed in publishing it yourself. Best wishes, Barbara

Kid gloves and an iron spine, that was Barbara. She'd brushed me off, but I was grateful. The dialogue had been worthwhile. I'd listened; I'd responded. I'd operated on my love child to save its life; and now I knew that the story wasn't everything—*I* was also part of the equation. I'd fallen flat in our first meeting and no revisions, however radical, would ever convince Barbara Edgeley that I had the stuff.

"I'm sorry, baby," Genny said when I told her. "You'll find someone else. Cream always rises."

I grunted.

"Why don't you have a cup of that nice tisane Cindy sent? It's soothing and it'll give you energy."

I let her make me a pot of herbal tea. I hate the taste but it makes her happy to fuss.

"What'll you do now?"

"Go back to the drawing board. I'll go online and start looking for an agent."

"You'll find one."

I didn't say anything, but I was embarrassed. Here she was, commiserating with me, when we should have been celebrating her success. A paper she'd co-authored with her colleague Andrea had just been published in *The Annals of Womyn's Social Commentary*. It was called "The Stunting of Male Capacity for Emotive Expression: Enculturation or

Biology?" and in it they'd covered a number of scholarly issues such as why men can't talk about their feelings or say "I love you." It must have been Andrea's idea; she was chronically unsuccessful with men.

CHAPTER TWELVE

Writing a book is a very lonely business. You are totally cut off from the rest of the world, submerged in your obsessions and memories.

Maria Vargas Llosa

Writing is pretty crummy on the nerves.

Paul Theroux

Last night I had a dream in which I stood before the UN General Assembly to defend my literary pretensions. Speaker after speaker hurled abuse, and I looked down and realized I was naked, and aroused by all their literary criticism. "That looks like a penis," shouted the French ambassador spitefully, "only smaller." Hilary Clinton looked disgusted; she rose to rebuke us both. "I would remind all members that this is no place for petty displays." She was clearly annoyed with the French over some other matter, but I felt bad. I was always a fan of hers, and once she dumped those honking big horn-rims—well, she was really hot.

This thought did not help my predicament.

Meanwhile the Israeli and Palestinian delegations, staring daggers at each other, seemed relieved that something had

come up to divert her from their own little boy games.
What can it mean, this dream? I lay awake trying to make sense of it. Even now, in the cold light of day, I wonder. Today I'll continue documenting my writing journey. At least it's got me writing.
My mind drifts back to Hilary.

*

I was down for a few days then I got back to work. I googled "literary agent" and made a list of the ones who emphasized words like "literary," "upmarket," and "quality." They'd be the ones interested in *Blown*. They all had similar submission processes: send us a query letter, some information about yourself, a sample of your work. No phone solicitations, please. Just follow our submission guidelines.

(My search also turned up countless websites brimming with testimonials from happy writers I'd never heard of. Flashing banners proclaimed "Your career as a published author starts here!" These weren't agents at all but vanity presses that would rush my novel into print with none of the bother that came from dealing with a traditional publisher. Their only prerequisite was the possession of a credit card.

There is no respect for a self-published novel. None of these so-called "agents" made it onto my list.)

For the record I designated Barbara Edgeley Agent #1 and chose Agent #2 on the basis of her promise to reply in six weeks. I spent a few days crafting a query letter, several more redrafting the fifty pages I'd submit. I delivered the package myself, pretending I was a bike courier so I could get an impression of the place. It was quiet, three or four offices off an un-staffed reception area. A young man with spiky hair came out of an office to accept the package. He stood waiting for me to go, a wary look on his face, holding my submission like a soiled adult diaper.

"Well, I'll wait to hear from you, then," I said, blowing my cover.

"Yes," he said.

Eight weeks later I called to follow up. Whoever it was

that answered—it might have been the spiky-haired young man, I couldn't tell—was cold to inquiries. Frankfurt Fair, he explained. Everything's backed up. We're doing our very best.

Finally, after twelve weeks, I received a rejection letter. I showed it to Genny and laughed it off.

"Are you okay?" she asked. There was a crease of concern on her brow.

"Never better. Why?"

"I know it's a disappointment."

"Plenty of fish in the sea." I pulled the letter from her fingers, convinced it would have historical value. Her eyes followed me as I crossed our bedroom to slip it into a drawer.

"I think you should get out more."

"Genny, my next novel's not going to write itself."

"How's that going? You haven't mentioned it in a while."

"Still doing research. Have you seen my car keys? I thought I left them by the stairs."

I selected Agent #3 because she was acknowledged by a writer whose book I'd admired. Her guidelines called for a query letter and the first five pages of the novel. I dropped this slim submission off myself, once again disguised as a courier. Mid-afternoon, the office, located in a house on a quiet street in the Annex, was locked. I stuffed the envelope through a slot in the door and called the next day to confirm receipt. Of course I knew she had it; I just wanted to appear keen and establish human contact.

My call went into voicemail. I left a message but received no return call, no confirmation by email. I called again after six weeks. Emailed after eight. At the end of week nine, I hung around down the street, tinkering with my bike, ignoring the cold stares of neighbours and watching the house. People came and went, packages were delivered. I gave up at the end of the following week. I never heard a word from Agent #3. Someone lives at the house, the lights are on at night and the ground-floor blinds get drawn. The blue bin gets put out (lots of chardonnay and Canadian champagne, surprisingly little red); and her web page is still running. She must still be in business.

Agent #4 was efficient. I had a rejection in four weeks. Agent #5 took six.

Agents #6 and #7 were concurrent. Here, I was breaching convention, for I'd been told that simultaneous submissions really pissed agents off. They don't want to be bothered with you, they won't deign to reply to an email, but they want an exclusive look-see on your manuscript. Fortunately, #6 and #7 never discovered my duplicity. They both rejected me within a week of each other. It took three months but at least I heard from them.

By then I'd burned through the better part of a year. I should have been writing but I wasn't; I was completely bereft of inspiration. There seemed no words left to me. Perhaps I had nothing left to say. I couldn't rule that out. Philosophers thought, writers wrote; but I stewed on vapours and wasted time, consumed with angst or captivated by trivia, the more arcane the better.[1] I told myself I was doing

---

[1] Did you know, for example, that David Foster Wallace's 1996 bestseller *Infinite Jest* (one of the lesser-read best-sellers of all time, owing to its hefty 1,079 pages) became a phenomenon again in 2009, when *The Morning News* sponsored an on-line book club called "Infinite Summer." The challenge was to read the entire book at a rate of 75 pages a week over the 13 weeks of summer. Organizers created a web-site to provide literary guidance and a forum for discussion; readers also wrote and exchanged commentary on Facebook, Twitter and other social networking services. The initiative became a viral phenomenon, generating unexpected sales and new interest in Wallace and his works.

David Foster Wallace was a gifted, respected, even beloved writer, who struggled for years with depression. He was able to write with the help of antidepressants, which he stopped taking because of side effects. He committed suicide in 2008. He was a brilliant ironist, an innovative stylist who made extensive use of endnotes to disrupt

research.

I craved a return to the Zone, that place I'd found while working on *Blown*, for when I'm writing and when it flows (oh, sweet dysentery of words!), I am content.

*

Genny commiserated at every rejection, fussed and reminded me to take my vitamins and supplements; her faith in them and me helped cheer me. Murray was sympathetic. Farley clucked and shook his head in sympathy and reminded me of the indignities suffered by writers. Faulkner sorted mail, JD Salinger apprenticed in meat packing. *Watership Down* was rejected twenty-six times, *Gone With The Wind*, thirty-eight—

When he got going like that I'd distract him by signalling a waiter or staring at a passing woman.

One night he and I were in Gzbrnznkwyc's for one of our regular sessions ("That's *not* what I meant by 'getting out more,' " Genny grumped as I left the house to meet him) and we were talking about one of his academic interests, the study of literary fame. I had always thought it would lend itself to quantitative analysis. "I'd start with Zipf's Law and test a hypothesis," I told him. "After all, Lotka's and Bradford's are just variants on Zipf." He looked confused so I explained about Zipfian frequency distributions, which are based on the power law curve, so basic a concept that I had recently shown it to Chloe."So if you use citations, or the number of studies devoted to a writer's work, as the parameter—"

"Hold it, bud. Whoa." He must've had a long day in the classroom because he stifled a yawn. "You're barking up the wrong tree. Mathematical models can't measure the qualitative factors that contribute to literary fame. Besides, literary reputations aren't static. They evolve over time."

"That could be captured with a temporal analysis."

Infinite Jest's linearity. Reality is fractured, he said; he wanted to fracture his narrative to reflect that fact, and endnotes did the trick. I see his point but stylistically, for my digressions, I prefer footnotes.

His eyes narrowed. I was sure he'd seen my logic. But then he spoke. "It's a writer's work that counts. It's what makes his reputation in the first place." He fiddled with his glass, gathering his thoughts like the professor he was. "And then, sometimes, something about a writer builds into myth. Some writers' reputations just cross into legend. Maybe it's their love affairs or epic benders. Or the anonymity they worked in—Herman Melville as a customs inspector, T.S. Eliot in a bank." He looked at me for a moment, as if suddenly struck by an idea. "Or their exotic pasts. Ian Fleming and John le Carré were both spies. People love that kind of thing. They remember it."

I nodded along, disappointed that Farley didn't see the potential I saw. What he was talking about would be captured in Lotka's general formula, although it might be hard to disaggregate.

"Joseph Conrad was a sea captain . . ."

I realized I was hungry. It was two-for-one wing night at Gzbrnznkwyc's. The table next to us was already chowing down. It was the aroma from there that was making me peckish.

"It's the body of work that counts, of course."

"Of course," I agreed. "The work."

For a moment I contemplated suicide.

"Now, *you* have an exotic past, designing derivatives . . ."

No, not suicide—honey-garlic. My mouth began to water.

". . . people don't understand derivatives. They'd find your background intriguing. Did you ever think about letting it be known, just as a biographical fact, what you used to do for a living?"

I took a drink and pretended to consider the idea. Farley liked his wings hot. Maybe we'd get half-and-half. I caught Ludwika's eye and signalled her over.

"Or, maybe, that you were there in New York on—"

"No!" I slammed my glass down and recoiled from the table. "Uh uh. NO."

Ludwika, half way to us, stopped in her tracks, shrugged,

and turned away.

"That kind of detail would help create a persona. It would differentiate you and—"

"No way."

I glared at him but he held my eye. Finally he looked down at his drink. "It was just a thought. Hey, you hungry? I'm feeling a bit peckish."

*

Everyone had a suggestion on how I could grab an agent's attention. Build your resume with some short stories. Enter the CBC's annual literary contest. Set up a web page, go on Facebook and Twitter, write a blog. Have you considered self-publishing?

"Hmm . . . I'll think about it," I said to every well-intentioned idea, then smoothly changed the subject.

An opinion piece, Genny said.

There was the germ of a good idea in that suggestion. Writers had hard opinions; they spoke truth to power. They spoke out against what they knew was wrong. Noble or curmudgeonly, everyone respected truth-tellers. Take Solzhenitsyn, Havel, Zola; or Mordecai Richler, facing off against separatist lies. Then there was me, eternally uncomfortable in my own skin—I'd learned to dissemble instead of confront. No more: I resolved to crystallize my thinking around the causes I held dear. I would formulate opinions. I'd take a stand. The environment came to mind. I'd been catching up on the issues since Genny's diatribe against Heil.

"Dirt," Murray suggested. "You need some dirt on these guys, pictures with an underage boy or a goat. I'll ask around."

Trust Murray to think outside the box. That's how he had wooed Darlene, calculating that slow and steady, rather than a linebacker blitz, would win her heart. It had. Over time, she'd fallen for the courtly giant whose table she always seemed to serve, the perfect gentleman with the old world manners and those doleful dark eyes; there was something sensitive, even tragic about him. "I grew on her like athlete's foot," he said after the fact. He'd left nothing to chance in the wooing process. It turned out that *he* was the mysterious owner of Bistro des Artistes, the anonymous benefactor of struggling artists and actors. He'd arranged all of Darlene's shifts with the maitre d'; his supposedly random seating was never random at all. "She must never know," he told me severely, scaring me a bit.

She was just a decade younger than Genny and they became good friends. The four of us sometimes got together for dinner, and one night Darlene, trying to be helpful, suggested I attend a PEN Canada benefit, a play about an imprisoned writer. "There'll be a lot of publishing people there," she said. "It's a great chance to network."

"Hmm . . . I'll think about it."

Darlene had a plum role in the play, that of a sadistic prison guard. Murray had seen her in rehearsal. "Her character's like an Iranian Ilsa of the SS," he told me (a bit breathlessly) when Genny and she were out of earshot. "Whips, indignities, degradation . . . I'm telling you, she's marvellous."

"You should go," Genny said later when we were alone. "It's a chance to make connections."

"I hate 'making connections'," I whined.

"Why don't you go with Murray?"

"He can't make it. It's truffle season in Italy."

"Well, you should go anyway. Give it a try."

Genny was nothing if not persistent, so on the night of the benefit I was there to support imprisoned writers everywhere, and to troll shamelessly for contacts like everyone else; but I was inept at the fake bonhomie of schmoozing, and quickly found myself on the margins of the crowd glancing at my watch as if waiting for someone, or edging in behind a potted plant. I finally realized what I had to do and worked my way towards the bar.

Soon, wondering why I'd been so uptight, I set off to mingle. I joined a succession of strangers in their cocktail clumps, smiling, nodding, laughing when they laughed, and nudging the person next to me good naturedly before wandering away as the group dispersed; but as I joined one couple they fell silent and glared at me. The woman, gaunt and sour, held her wineglass in front of her nose, her other arm tight across her chest, hand snug in armpit. Even I could sniff a spat.

Party protocol demanded that we engage briefly, but she took my arrival as her opportunity to leave. I was left alone with the man, a plump, exotic fellow whose black eyes followed her across the room. He would have gone after her but I was standing in his way.

"I'm looking forward to this play," I ventured after a silence, taking a swig of my drink to confirm its level. My glass was full, his was too. Neither of us could politely break off for a refill. "The dominatrix is a friend of mine."

"Hmm."

I'd prepared for the night with a list of small talk openers. "Do you come to many of these events?"

"Sometimes." He scanned faces in the crowd over my shoulder.

"It's a good cause. PEN."

This time, silence.

"Are you in the business?" That sounded stupid. "I mean, the creative sector?" That sounded stupider.

He glanced at me. "Yeah." His eyes wandered away. He waved to someone.

"What do you do?"

He mouthed something, nodded, smiled, and replied without looking at me. "I deal in IP."

"Intellectual property."

Now he fixed me with a look, the kind a cool kid gives a geek. "That's right."

"What kind?"

"Entertainment." His eyes again scanned the room.

"What's that entail?"

He sighed and looked at me. "I work with rights-holders

who want to expand their narrative brands and franchises. I license IP rights internationally for film, television, video games, graphic novels and books. I work directly with producers, studios, game developers, publishers, and other rights-buyers."

Blah blah. Narrative brands, franchises, licensing. It sounded like hot air. Then it registered. Books. Publishers.

"Are you a lawyer?"

"I'm an agent."

"Hah!" I cried. A woman nearby jumped and looked around, startled over something. Jittery. She was drinking coffee (at that hour!). "I'm *looking* for an agent!"

"Really," he said, unmoved by the coincidence. He looked to either side for a gap and found none. After a long pause he asked why I was looking for an agent and I began to ramble. His eyes roved the crowd.

". . . It's a story of coming of age, but it's also a tale of diplomacy, intrigue and—"

"Who have you shown it to?" He lifted his glass to acknowledge someone across the room.

I had a choice: I could be candid, or I could obfuscate. The latter came easy for me, which is why I opted for candour—nothing about writing had been easy. "I've made some submissions but haven't found any interest. I met with Barbara Edgeley a while ago. She saw a draft and gave me feedback."

Now he looked at me. "What did Barb say?"

"Well, simplify the structure, focus on the story, cut, cut, cut. I took it to heart. It's a much better book for her input."

"Did you show her the re-write?"

I felt myself blush. This was what came from candour. "She took a pass." The house lights flashed, signalling us to our seats. "Listen, would you take a look at my manuscript?"

"David!" he called across the room. "Hang on a sec." A tall gangly guy with owly glasses waved at him. The agent drained his glass and made to go in his direction. "Nice to meet you," he told me.

"Wait! I didn't actually meet you." I blocked his way and introduced myself, offering my hand. He looked at it for a moment.

"I don't shake hands." He started to edge around me.

"Would you take a look at my manuscript?"

His eyes narrowed. His face was very close to mine. "Send it to my office." He slipped past me but I followed and tapped him on the back. He flinched and turned.

"Do you have a card?"

He handed one over his shoulder and disappeared into the crowd.

This was how I met Phil Regency, Agent #8, face to face, sort of.

CHAPTER THIRTEEN

> Go on writing plays, my boy, One of these days one of these London producers will go into his office and say to his secretary, "Is there a play from Shaw this morning?" and when she says, "No," he will say, "Well, then we'll have to start on the rubbish." And that's your chance, my boy.
>
> George Bernard Shaw

> Shall we forever make new books, as apothecaries make new mixtures, by pouring only out of one vessel into another? Are we forever to be twisting and untwisting the same rope?
>
> Laurence Sterne

The day is hot and steamy, the kind Torontonians pay good money for during the winter but complain about all summer long. Heat advisories and health warnings have been issued. The smog is so bad that anyone with a respiratory condition is advised to refrain from strenuous exercise or going out of doors.

"Jack Hammer, don't run outside today," Genny tells me at breakfast.

"Perish the thought! Outside? In the summer?" I'm rather pleased with myself—I've been working on irony and think that's pretty good.

Genny gazes at me over her copy of the *Guardian Weekly*. "You know what I mean."

"It's preposterous. We pay taxes why? So they can give us helpful advice like 'don't go outside'. Disgraceful. Did you hear the beaches are closed again? We live next to the largest fresh water mass in the world and they tell us not to swim for fear of poop."

"Daddy said poop!" Chloe says, then repeats "poop" a couple of times, sure she's gotten away with something.

"He meant water-borne fecal contamination, Chloe," Genny says. Then, to me: "Don't go swimming either." There is a smile at the corners of her mouth then she grows serious. "Take your ma huang and some lobelia too. It's good for your breathing. And try the snakeroot brownies at lunch. You'll like them."

"Okay."

I am not a swimmer but I run, which I find therapeutic for my creative ills; but I have some lingering respiratory issues from inhaling toxic dust. Yes, I'm one of those vulnerable souls advised to avoid heavy breathing and to stay inside. I bridle at this but I'm just one of millions affected by air pollution.

Some mornings I stand on the pedestrian overpass at Sunnyside Beach to watch the slow commuter cortege roll into the downtown core. An acrid pong rises from the clogged lanes below. I feel my lungs constrict and scuttle on hurriedly.

I've been thinking a lot about the environment lately. So many missed opportunities. So much damage.

*

In between submissions to agents I tried to write. I did. My problem was—what would I write about? Conventional wisdom has it that an up-and-coming writer must build his résumé by getting published in a literary magazine. A short story in *The Kamsack (Sask.) Literary Review*, a thoughtful poem in *The Blasphemer's Journal*, a personal reflection in *Onan*

Today—it doesn't matter how obscure the organ. It all helps establish a catalogue of credible work.

I had no catalogue. I had one unpublished novel. No back list, no short stories or poems, no book reviews or think pieces. No quirky demi-essays on the *Globe's* Facts and Arguments page. Not even a misspelled shocked-and-appalled diatribe in *The Toronto Star*, which will print anything.

I knew I should polish my credentials but I had no interest in doing so. I wanted to forge ahead and focus on writing that appealed to me; and only long-form fiction appealed to me. Yet the tank was dry as a Saudi wedding. Instead of writing I worried and obsessed, or pursued dead ends and trivia, unable to concentrate. At night I tossed and turned, sleepless; yet I must have slept, for I had vivid dreams, like visions, fevered. Afterwards I fretted over my mental state, wondering if this was the price of the writer's life. Of creativity.

Creativity? In truth I was creating nothing.

I told anyone who inquired that I was doing research, which worked commendably until Farley called me on it, kicked me in the ass, and told me to snap out of it. "Write about your journey," he said, and I tried. I plugged away at it (I still do); but in truth I needed a destination, something I could work towards. I needed to find a topic that lit a fire in my belly, the kind I'd had with Broughton.

And so, waiting for inspiration, I continued my so-called research. The cursor winked, devilish and teasing; and I avoided its gaze.

*

I heard nothing after delivering my manuscript to Phil Regency, Agent #8. After four weeks I called his office. I finally reached him a week later by calling his cell phone.

"Just wondering how it's going," I said after repeating my name, "on my manuscript."

It took another moment for him to place me. "PEN. The guy with the dominatrix?"

"She's not my dominatrix. She goes out with a friend of mine. It was just a role, anyway. I thought she played it—"

"Right, right. Now I've got it."

"So, how it's going," I said, switching gears from social banter, "on my manuscript?"

"How'd you get this number?" he asked.

"It's on your card."

"Sorry, you're breaking up."

"I'm on a land line."

There was a pause. "This'll just take a minute," he said, muffled, to somebody. Then he was back. "You're the one who knows Barb Edgeley."

"Well, kind of. I met her. Briefly."

"I saw her last week at the Trillium Awards. I asked her about you."

My stomach performed an uncomfortable manoeuvre.

"She said you're not ready and neither's your book."

"But . . . she hasn't read it. Have you?"

There was no answer.

"Have you read my book?"

A pause. "Someone in my office looked at it. We have to work quickly. I got a verbal report. Barb said there was too much history, not enough story. And those fairy tales. Barb said—"

"What fairy tales?"

"The animal stories. About the sea lion and the crow."

"They're not animal stories, they're Indian legends. The crow's a raven, and I took out the talking sea otter. I told Barbara that . . ."

In the end, this spoke volumes about Phil Regency. Where was the independence, the objectivity, in asking Barbara about me? It was lazy to go with the flow. How could a new voice ever emerge that way? Convention, it must be said, is the enemy of invention.

CHAPTER FOURTEEN

All good writing is swimming under water and holding your breath.

F. Scott Fitzgerald

Some who have read the book, or at any rate have reviewed it, have found it boring, absurd, or contemptible; and I have no cause to complain, since I have similar opinions of their works, or of the kinds of writing that they evidently prefer.

J.R.R. Tolkien

I ran for the phone. Agent, book deal, it might have been important. But it was just a man from Porlock Polling, asking me to participate in a survey on voting intentions.

"What's it pay?" I asked, irritated at the interruption but knowing that focus groups paid upwards of fifty bucks for an hour's work.

There was a delay at the other end. "This is a just telephone poll, sir, not a focus group. It doesn't pay anything, but I'll only take a few minutes of your—"

I hung up and returned to my research, shaking my head at the calls I field every day: pollsters, charities, offers for fireplace maintenance or a free insurance quote, banks pushing credit cards, cruise operators announcing "Congratulations! You've just won . . ." I'm bombarded by pitches for stuff I don't need. The Ask is relentless.

I used to wonder who responded to telemarketers. Now I know: they are the lonely. They buy unneeded doors and windows, another tier of cable, even subscribe to the *Toronto Star*, just to connect fleetingly with a voice in a call centre, an installation man, a chimneysweep. They take vacations they can't afford, fill their homes with bric-à-brac and exercise machines, and pay for everything with a credit card offered and accepted over the phone. And nothing they acquire quite fills the void.

I could have really used that honorarium.

The doorbell now.

*

It was two men in suits; youngish, fit, short hair. Images flashed through my mind: loved ones, tax filings, the contents of the medicine cabinet. I felt a sudden deathly chill. But they weren't detectives with bad news or awkward questions. They stood stiffly on my porch proffering a copy of *The Watchtower*.

I am never rude to JWs but I refuse to be drawn into conversation. I closed the door as quickly as I could. It took about a half hour. It turned out they had to rush off somewhere. We'd had a little chinwag about creation. The seemed like nice guys but they could not convince me, and I would never convince them.

*

"You need to get out more," Genny told me. "You can't just write all the time."

"I'm doing research right now."

"Research then. You need to get out."

"But with Anthony? Thanks a lot."

"It'll do you good."

"That's what they said about bloodletting."

She gave me the look that said, "Don't make me make you."

Anthony, our next door neighbour, made his living giving

seminars on spiritual awareness and self-fulfillment. He taught people how to move to a higher, purer plane of existence by embracing Selfishness. "To achieve True Self you have to transcend both Ish and Ness," was how he explained it.

This higher, liberated embodiment of Self cost upwards of five hundred dollars for a day-long seminar (or "Selfinar," as Anthony preferred). There were longer programs as well, even retreats for the truly stubborn cases. Corporations paid a premium for his workshops and consulting services. They wanted to harness the power of Self once it was liberated from the yoke of Ish and Ness, the plodding oxen of inefficiency.

Anthony often collared me when I was out puttering in the yard. We'd stand surveying our respective gardens over our shared fence while he quizzed me about my palpable failure as a writer. "How long do you think you'll stay with it? Does it ever get you down?" He wanted to know the details of every rejection. "I've followed your journey," he told me once. "You've embraced your Self. I've seen your Ish and Ness recede."

"Get a load of my rhubarb," I said, to get away from his. I'd never been comfortable with deep philosophical conversation.

"We have to get out one of these times," he said, his long face blank as a wall. "Paint the town red-Ish."

I had carefully avoided that until Genny, behind my back, set us up on a man-date.

Thus I found myself nursing a Polish beer in Gzbrnznkwyc's one evening, with Anthony opposite me sipping Doctor Pepper through a straw. He liked to talk about himself and was in high spirits—he'd just landed a contract to run a series of Self fulfillment seminars for a big financial services firm. "They're going to put all their high-flyers through my program," he said. "It'll keep me pretty busy over the next eighteen months."

I pictured him leading a band of dancing, chanting

accountants through the streets, the men in business casual with finger cymbals ringing while the women, in flowery dresses, sold pencils to passersby. I must have smiled at the thought because Anthony, sitting straight as a flagpole, smiled back, raised his glass and held the pose, waiting.

"Congratulations," I said, finally getting his point. I lifted my stein and he clinked it.

"Thank you, thank you, very kind. It's all worked out extremely well. I'm now recognized as *the* national thought leader in this field, and one of the top three in North America."

Recently I'd heard people pontificating about the strangest things. Now there was thought leadership on selfishness. Curious, I asked, "How does that happen? Is it word of mouth? Satisfied customers talking you up?"

"That's part of it, me helping people find themSelves. Not many people do what I do and touch so many lives. It's a spiritual thing . . ."

Well, here I was, sipping a beer with the Mother Teresa of Selfishness.

". . . but probably the biggest factor is the internet. I pop up high on key-word searches."

"What kind of key-words?"

"Well, 'selfishness', 'selfishness counselling', 'embrace selfishness', 'all about me', 'I self'. A few others."

"Why does that happen?"

"I pay for it."

"*That's* how you become an expert these days? You pay for it?"

Anthony's smile disappeared. "How's your book going?"

"Good. Fine." I wiped the condensation from my stein and examined my palm.

Above our heads the Polish news blared on a TV no one was watching. At the table next to us, two middle-aged men in leather caps were pounding it back.

Anthony sipped through his straw, his expression again blank. "You know, I cite you as an example in my seminars.

You set off on a journey to change your life, embarked without hesitation and risked everything in the pursuit of Self. Against the odds and with no real preparation, you wrote a book. It's an inspiring story. I salute you."

I took a swig of Żywiec. "They have polka here sometimes. Late at night."

"My own books have been hugely helpful in spreading my reputation. I get a lot of media inquiries and calls to speak—"

"What books?"

"I thought you knew. I've written four over the last six years. They've done quite well. Excellent reviews."

I stared at him. "You're a writer? A published writer?"

He inclined his head modestly. "I suppose that's encouraging for a fellow just breaking in. Well, it's possible. Everything's possible." He raised his glass and waited—and waited—for a clink. Then we both drank to him, or to everything being possible. A silence followed.

"My latest one's my best seller: *Hug the Self*."

"Your bestseller? You mean, nationally?"

"No . . . I mean, my best seller."

Questions tumbled in my mind like boots in a dryer.

"My self-massage book also does quite well," he added after a moment.

My mind reeled at the images this produced. "Do you have an agent?"

"Hah ha. I didn't need an agent." His gaze shifted to the window at the front of Gzbrnznkwyc's. He waved to someone and grinned. When I looked there was no one there.

"Friend of mine. Must be going home. She lives over on Pearson. They bought a fixer-upper and renovated. It took them more than—"

I knew this ploy. "You got published directly?"

"Yes. As an author you always—"

"Who's your publisher?"

"You probably haven't heard of them."

"What's the name?"

"It's a small press in Indiana—"

"*Indiana?* How did you find them?"

Anthony looked up at the Polish news. A farmer was dumping a load of potatoes in front of the Polish parliament. Others were burning the European flag. "Well, I wanted to get my first book out into the market, and I didn't want to fiddle-fart around with edits and submissions and stuff like that. So I wrote a business plan and project-managed the roll out on a single media self-directed push market platform."

It took me a moment to decipher what that meant.

"You self-published."

"I call it seamless integration of the intellectual and production processes. The costs are reasonable, the returns are good. It got me out there quickly and raised my profile. The business model is dollar- and time efficient. It would work for your nov—"

"How do you sell?"

"Every seminar participant gets a free copy. I get hits on my website and I go to book fairs and festivals and sell there. I get some orders through Amazon and the big retailers. They get requests—word gets around. Quality sells itself."

Normally I found Polish beer smooth, but that night it was giving me heartburn.

"I manage everything. I keep my inventory in the basement and expense the space. But I won't even need inventory soon. Everything's going print-on-demand."

There was a sudden loud crack close by. One of the men at the next table had fallen forward—his head had hit the tabletop. His companion quickly grabbed both their teetering glasses before either spilled a drop.

The beer was saved, but the first man lay slouched face-down, unmoving.

"Good lord," Anthony said.

The other man smiled at us and said something in Polish. It sounded slurred, but how could you tell? Anthony made to stand just as Ludwika arrived and pushed him back into his chair. "Sit, sit," she said and switched into Polish to confer with the Flash. Customers at nearby tables eavesdropped and chipped in. A hubbub arose and the cook, Ludwika's uncle, came out from the kitchen to see what was happening. His arrival was the signal for everyone to repeat what they'd just said; and when by chance the Żywiec sales rep walked in the front door a few moments later, the crowd beckoned him forward and began again.

It was proof of the vigour of Polish democracy, and it might have gone on indefinitely, like a Polish parliamentary debate, had not Ludwika lost patience and silenced everyone with a curt comment and an appeal to the ceiling. She grabbed the unconscious man's wrist, held a finger to a vein, and closed her eyes.

Above us the TV cut from the news to a commercial, blaring even louder in the sudden stillness. All eyes remained on Ludwika until she opened her own and nodded. A murmur of relief rose from the room. It became a cheer when the Żywiec rep announced, first in Polish then English, a round for the house.

Ludwika rolled her eyes at me as she headed for the bar. Next to us, the man with the quick hands took a thirsty pull from his friend's glass and smiled contentedly to himself.

Anthony blinked, bewildered.

"You mentioned reviews," I said.

It took him a moment to pick up the thread. "Uh, yes. Yes. Very positive reviews."

"Who?"

"People with an interest in the field."

"In the *Globe*?"

"No."

"The *Post*?"

"No."

"Oh, my God, not the *Star*."

"No. The dust jacket. Look, it doesn't matter. The point is, I practice what I preach. Do you want to get published? Do it yourself. Why deal with middlemen when you can be recognized as a published author instantly. On your own terms."

He mistook my open mouth for admiration.

"My books build profile for my speaking engagements, which build profile for my True Self seminars."

I had to think about that for a moment. His real business was seminars. His books tied into them. My book was a stand-alone. I had no tie-ins to sell—

I had a sudden image of a blue-coated William Broughton action figure, free with a Happy Meal, or as a limited edition adult collectible. Ridiculous. I dismissed it immediately. He began telling me about a reading he'd given at a recent self-love convention in Las Vegas. I drained my beer. I was ready to leave. I'd had enough of Anthony and his True Self mumbo-jumbo; but he was nursing his soda slowly, as though taunting me with it: the Pope jiggling the world's last Viagra tablet in Hugh Hefner's face. I slapped a twenty on the table just as Ludwika plunked down two fresh beer glasses.

"Żywiec. Is complementation."

"Oh no. Not for me!" Anthony said.

Ludwika frowned and slid his glass to me.

I handed her the twenty. "Thanks but we're done."

"Nonsense," Anthony said. "We're having fun." He looked from me to Ludkwika's chest. "I don't drink liquor but I'll have another Dr Pepper please. With a bendy straw."

Ludwika's eyes narrowed. She smiled faintly at me and departed.

"I like this place. We should do this more often, you and me. So. What's your plan, if you're not going to self-publish? How are you going to get your novel into the hands of readers?"

"I'll get an agent and go through a traditional publisher so I can focus on writing."

He gave me a published author smile. "And how's that working?"

"Slowly," I said between gulps of beer.

"An agent won't do anything for you that you can't do yourself. And doing it yourself gives you all the control."

"Hmm," I went thoughtfully and downed the first Żywiec. "I'll think about it."

CHAPTER FIFTEEN

Send it to someone who can publish it. And if they won't publish it, send it to someone else who can publish it! And keep sending it! Of course, if no one will publish it, at that point you might want to think about doing something other than writing.

Robert B. Parker

The profession of book writing makes horse racing seem like a solid, stable business.

John Steinbeck

In the end I caught a break. It came through Farley. We were in the Faculty Club one night for one of our sessions, and I'd just brought him up to date on my agent quest (I was on #11), when he slammed his glass down on the table and declared, po-faced, "I know a guy."

The ice in his glass tinkled with the impact. A couple of tweedy emeritus types looked up at the noise then went back to reminiscing about the sixties. *I know a guy* . . . I thought he meant, "I have to see a man about a horse," and waited for him to push himself upright and plod over-slowly towards the bog. But he remained seated, watching me.

"So, what are you saying?" I said at last. "You got a date?"

"Fuck off. I know an agent."

I took a pull of Tankhouse Ale and considered how to respond. "I appreciate it, bud, but an academic agent isn't—"

"He handles fiction. He handles my stuff." His eyes roamed the room then came back to me. He flinched as he met my eye. "Look. I'm a better critic than I am a writer, but I always wanted to write. I kept at it over the years. I've written, uhhm . . ." He tipped up his glass to drain whatever residue remained in the melt-water of his ice. "Some novels."

"Really?"

"Really."

"Published?"

He nodded.

"How many?"

"Seventeen."

"Jesus Christ! *Seventeen?*"

"Since I left the U.K. Two over there."

"Why didn't you say anything? Why didn't I know?"

"Pen names. I'm Basil Letherman, Cynthia Powell Ducat, R. Lucius Benny. And Pussy Hindmost. She's my favourite."

I stared at him.

He glanced away to signal for another round, and I drained my pint in a single go.

"I like to write but I'll never be F. Scott Fitzgerald. What I produce wouldn't have helped me get tenure, and it wouldn't have helped my reputation as a 'serious literary scholar'." He made quotes in the air to punctuate the phrase. "So I kept it to myself. I wrote sci-fi, crime, some gothic horror. And ladies romances that were somewhat beyond the Harlequin category, ratings wise, if you know what I mean. Now *those* were fun. As Pussy Hindmost I could get literary without fear of discovery. No one will ever compare *Möbius's Dick* or *Captain Ahab's Glad Hand* to Melville, but they sold amazingly well."

I could think of nothing to say.

"Look. I've got a wife, an ex, and a kid with each," Farley said. "Baby needs new shoes, and I could never rely on winning at the track. So to the point, *paesano*, as it pertains you: I have an agent, a guy named Peter Wannacutt. Are you interested, or are you just going to idiot-stare me to death?"

*

I met Peter in the bar on Danforth Avenue that doubled as his office. Despite the casual venue, he was dressed for business in a blue blazer and open necked button-down. He was stick thin, his head big and out of proportion to the rest of his body. He had a close-cropped fringe of grey, a ruddy face, a nose like Farley's. Late afternoon, and he was slightly hung over from lunch. "Had a meeting with a client," he explained in a comforting baritone drone, the voice of a smoker. "Lovely gal. Needs reassurance now and then. Took a few snoots of wine today."

He'd worked at Sporran & McGonigle for twenty years with Jock McGonigle himself. "Started in the mail room. Summer job. Jock liked me, taught me the ropes. Had fun, those days. Used to fly by the seat of our pants. Followed our gut. Pissed most of the time, got laid seven ways to Sunday. Before I was married. Happily, too. Widowed now. Cancer. Ten years ago. Kids grown up. Anyway. Brought along a stable of home-grown talent. They don't do that now, these big foreign houses. It's all changed." He shook his head sadly at the thought. When Jock retired the company was taken over by one of those multinationals. "Didn't want to be a cog inside a big corporation. Decided to leave and do some writing myself. And some agenting. Still know the head honcho at every serious house in the country. That's who I meet, not the kids with the fancy titles. *Commissioning* editor. *Acquisitions* director. Those kids make coffee for my guys."

As he sipped his G&T, I realized he spoke like a telegram, dropping the superfluous for economy.

"Farley says you're a friend. Your book. Got a title?"

"*Blown to Hell*."

"Nice! Action. Story?"

I told him.

"Good, good. Big market for nautical thrillers. Anything

with Indians, too, these days. Sounds like a swashbuckler. Could swing a nice advance. Any romance?"

"Yes, there's—"

"Forbidden love, eh?"

"Actually—"

"Thought so! From the title. Had to be! Sailors, heh? Long voyages. Pity the cabin boy! Clever."

I explained it wasn't *that* kind of romance but a conventional boy-girl one, albeit across races.

He shrugged. "Hmm. Not quite so forbidden. Big market for gay, you know, these days. Oh well. Your book, your call. Still, like what I'm hearing. Like it a lot. Big houses will too. Chance Manor, Mulroney de Valera. Spheniscus. I'd start with them. Also, the guys in New York and London."

"New York and London?" I squeaked. Cash advances, big publishers, international exposure. It was all happening so quickly.

"Know all the top people there. Met them all through S&M, over the years. Shared history. Girlfriend's high up in Chance Manor in London. Works with the parent company, too. Bertelsberg. I go over there two-three times a year."

"You really think there'll be interest that broadly?"

"Depends on your book. Have to read it."

He would read it! I felt like Sally Field at the Oscars. For a moment I grinned stupidly, then thought I should say something to appear professional and not too desperate. "How many people do you represent?"

"Not that many. Handful. Don't want to get over-extended. Lot of agents take on too many and don't do a good job for any of 'em."

"Anyone I might know?"

He rattled off a few names I didn't recognize. "And Farley, of course. Got the manuscript with you?"

I handed it to him, the whole manuscript, not five, or ten, or fifty pages. This version was a slimmed-down six hundred pages. He weighed it appreciatively in his hands. "Bit of time now. Should get into it over the next day or so. One more thing to mention. Need to sign a contract. If, that is, you want me to represent you. Just a one pager. Simple thing."

"Of course."

"Way I work, bit different. No fancy proposals or submissions. Meet the top boss, buy a few drinks, push my authors and their books. New York, London. Means I've got expenses. Usually ask for $7500 up front. Credit against future earnings. Fair and square. Means there's no commission on the first $50,000 in sales."

He must have read my expression. "Know what you're thinking. 'Don't put anything up front to an agent.' Hogwash. Lots of bafflegab around. Business is changing fast. Anyway, that's the way I work. Works well for everybody. No complaints yet for the five grand."

"I thought it was seventy-five hundred."

"Oh. Should've said. Reduce it for referrals. Friends' friends. Known that piss-tank Farley for years. Done pretty well for him, too."

When I got home it struck me that he'd been pitching me, rather than the other way around. I wondered if Farley had pulled in a favour.

*

A couple of days later I received an email from Peter.

> I have not yet completed my reading of Blown to Hell, but I shall over the next couple of days. I can tell you, however, that the pace is good, you write with a natural style that is easy to read and have the wonderful traits of a good storyteller. I have no doubt that whomever you choose to represent you will have little trouble finding a home for this intelligent and highly readable book.

By the end of that week he was done, and he sent me another epistle.

Among my favourite aspects of your remarkable story of adventure in the north-west waters of our continent has to be your uncanny interweaving of the compulsive jottings of your protagonist into and around the historical fabric of the larger work. As a literary device, I found it helpful, skilful in fact, in cementing events and chronology in the reader's mind with lively reportage, all from the perspective of a very believable and engaging observer. I liked the sea otter's perspective as well. It was, all in all, a very rich and satisfying read. I found myself struggling but once—and that I may ascribe to the hour and, perhaps, to one-too-many martinis—where Broughton relates in flashback his altercation with the headhunting Tahitian midgets.

I am not, I must confess, a big reader of historical fiction which, I hasten to add, does not interfere with my knowledge of, or access to the houses that publish it. I would be pleased to act as your representative in finding this epic a worthy home. Until I hear from you, I will hold the manuscript here; and should you wish to proceed, and I sincerely hope you do, I must advise you to print a new page 46 and a new page 105, as I managed to decorate both, one with a ring stain, the other with lunch.

I met Peter the next morning at a coffee shop in his area, his office not yet being open.

"Awful headache," he said. "Client session last night. Here's the contract. Sign here. Got the cheque?"

I didn't answer but read the contract. It was a single page. Percentage, exclusive, etc. etc. I took my pen out. "Where are you going to start?"

"Meeting S&M next week, Spheniscus in a couple. Pretty sure I'll get it in for readings there."

"I thought you had to go one at a time. Give them an exclusive look."

"Hah. They say that. Wouldn't you? If they want it they'll understand."

I grinned happily at his insider perspective.

"N'other thing. Idea I had. Something Farley said about you in New York."

I felt my grin freeze on my face.

"Lot of interest in a novel by a 9/11 survivor."

"It isn't about 9/11."

"Still, everyone loves a hero—"

"No, that's not me. I just happened to be there."

"Seems what they call everyone, these days—a hero. Survivor, then? Victim? It might—"

"No."

He peered at me for a moment before giving a nod. "Okay. Thinking out loud, is all. Focus on *Blown to Hell* then. Not 9/11."

"Good."

"Interesting coincidence, though, the name."

I said nothing.

"Maybe you'll write about it sometime. Next book, eh?"

"Hmm. I'll think about it."

"Atta boy! Going to New York end of month. Meeting Antilles Press. Slip it in for a read there."

"Please, Peter, nothing about 9/11 to them, or anyone. All right?"

"Okay. S'aright. Your call. Also in New York, meeting with Mulroney de Valera—my girlfriend there. Give it to her, too."

"I thought your girlfriend was in London."

"Sally. Yep. Vice-chairman, now, at Bertelsberg. Got a promotion. Real darling. This is th'other one, Sue. Plan is to get it into at least five, maybe six houses. Give it lots of exposure."

I signed the contract and opened my cheque book. Things seemed to be happening at last. Now I truly could focus on writing.

CHAPTER SIXTEEN

Writing is finally about one thing: going into a room alone and doing it. Putting words on paper that have never been there in quite that way before. And although you are physically by yourself, the haunting Demon never leaves you, that Demon being the knowledge of your own terrible limitations, your hopeless inadequacy, the impossibility of ever getting it right. No matter how diamond-bright your ideas are dancing in your brain, on paper they are earthbound.

William Goldman

Research is usually a policeman stopping a novel from progressing.

Brian Moore

"Now I truly can focus on writing," I told Genny as she left next morning.

"Break a leg, Jack." She smiled and kissed me on the lips. Then she headed for the door. "Oh! Don't forget to take your ginseng and B complex. And a few drops of St John's wort."

I grinned. Genny had my back. "Okay. Have a good day."

An hour later I still hadn't been able to get down to work

and decided to try a writing exercise I'd thought up after reading one of Farley's Pussy Hindmost novels. I went to a coffee shop on Roncesvalles and spent time watching women and scribbling in my Moleskine notebook. "It's a shopping list," I protested when the manager approached, but she still asked me to leave. After that I made my observations in a Tim Hortons on Bloor Street, and when I got home I read over my notes, closed my eyes, and began to type.

It was coming along, I had ideas, they were flowing— when the phone rang. I stopped what I was doing (which was WRITING, dammit) because I thought it might be Peter with news of a publisher. But it was Porlock Polling, with an automated poll on political preferences.

I hung up and returned to my screen and read what I'd typed. Collision of random glances, musk of life, smooth coffeed thighs. Sensuous hot skin, subtle curves, the swell of mocha breasts. It was promising stuff but try as I might I couldn't recapture the moment.

"Curse you, Porlock," I said to the empty room.

I saved what I'd written and turned back to what I should have been doing all along: scoping out my next book.

I decided to do some research on the web.

Later I found a note from Genny in the fridge. "I believe in you," it read, with a reminder to make myself some Mormon tea. Beneath her message Chloe had scribbled, "Me too Daddy!" I made a pot of tea, feeling happy, and went back to my desk; but I was restless and jumpy, unable to settle down. I decided to walk to the library to do more research.

*

The days passed. The weeks passed. Then, one morning, there was an email from Peter.

> After receiving rejections on Friday from Spheniscus Canada and Mulroney de Valera in New York, I have this morning dropped a manuscript

into the hands Mulroney de Valera (Canada) while couriering another off to Garfunkel Wayne in New York, after a discussion with a dear friend there, one of long acquaintance and considerable clout, who expressed keen interest in the subject matter. As of this moment, I have not received any reaction from Trafalgar Press in NYC, Sporran & McGonigle in Canada or Holtzbrüken's London affiliate Pequenino to which I dispatched a manuscript a fortnight ago. We are entering the veritable doldrums of summer; these are dead months on the reading front within publishing houses. I expect we shall get what we're looking for in September when publishers and editors read manuscripts at a crisp business-like, post-holiday rate. Summer is a frustrating season, but if it's any consolation, I sold three titles in late spring. Quality does get picked up. Do not be disheartened by an individual house taking a pass. I hope to have good news for you in the fullness of autumn.

Two rejections, but he seemed optimistic. I called him to get the inside scoop.

"Hello!" his voice shouted into the phone.

"Peter. It's me."

He needed a moment to place my voice. "Sorry," he said when he did. "Out last night. Loud music. Can't hear anything today."

"I was wondering about your message."

"Couple rejections. Nothing to sweat. Dust ourselves off. Just keep it moving, what we have to do. Got it in with good houses. Find a good home yet."

"Did they tell you anything? The two that rejected it?"

" 'Not for us'. That's it. Too busy. Clock's ticking. What about you?"

The question caught me flat-footed and I stammered something about keeping busy too—on my next book.

"The spirit! This one about? 'Nother swashbuckler?"

"I, ah, I'm keeping it to myself for now. Till I'm farther along."

"Hah! Mystery! Good! Get out for a few drinks, eh? One of these days. Talk about it. Want to hear. Doing that with one of my writers tonight. Real piss-tank. The hard stuff. Wonder what I'm doing to the old liver. Anyhoo. Be in touch when there's news."

Heartened by his interest, I went back to my research.

CHAPTER SEVENTEEN

"Fool!" said my muse to me, "look in thy heart, and write."

Philip Sidney

Writing is easy. You only need to stare at a piece of blank paper until your forehead bleeds.

Douglas Adams

"So what's all this 'research' about?" Farley said, nudging me with his drink hand. We were at Murray and Darlene's for dinner. Everyone else was in the kitchen. Farley had maneuvered me down the hall into Murray's study.

"Eh?"

"Genny says you're doing research. She collared me while you were talking to Darlene. I think she'll stage an intervention or something if you're not careful. What are you up to, bub, really? Are you still working on your own story? The poioumenon?"

I squinted at a wall of framed sketches. "I'm pretty well up to the present now with that."

I felt his eyes on me. "You look tired, man."

"I am. I didn't sleep well last night."

"Try a hot rum toddy before bed. Easy on the water, hold

the honey, and be generous. Knock you right out."

"Good idea. I'll try that."

"So. Research."

"Yup." I feigned a sudden interest in one of the sketches.

"Research isn't writing, you know. Only writing is writing. Someone said that. Doctorow, I think."

"You're always handy with a quote."

"I strive for relevance. What are you researching, exactly?"

"Ah, well. A lot of things."

He let that ride for a moment. "You don't write a novel about a lot of things. You write an encyclopedia about a lot of things."

I peered intently at the sketch and it worked: he looked to see what had caught my interest. It was ink and pencil, childish, like something Chloe would bring home from school. For a moment we stood side by side, examining it.

Murray walked in with a bottle of Scotch. "You two look like you're plotting something. Or someone just farted."

Farley tapped the wall. "Is this—"

"Yeah. Chagall."

"No shit."

We all stood and looked at the sketch, me thinking I'd done a nice job of changing the subject. But I was wrong.

"Our friend Funk and Wagnalls here was just telling me about his new book."

"Yeah?" Murray looked at me with interest. "How's that going?"

"Right now I'm doing research."

Farley made air quotes around "research." Murray glanced from him to me.

"Okay, okay. I'm spinning my wheels. I'm looking for a big idea, something I can live with for two, three years."

"Like an American car," Farley said softly. "Or a wife."

We all cast glances towards the open doorway and chuckled manfully.

"Listen," he continued, "just sit down and make a list of things that interest you, straight off the top of your head.

Don't stew over it. Give yourself a minute, five minutes even, and don't rule anything out. Your topic's going to be on that list. When you're done, go through it and knock off the crazy stuff. Maybe you can combine some things. Think about it and decide. Then you get down to work. Easy peasy."

It took me a moment to realize why the idea was familiar. "We did something like that at the Firm. It was for team-building."

"There you go. Multiple applications."

"Yeah . . . They brought in a consultant to facilitate. He called it green-hatting or blue-skying, something like that. There was no such thing as a bad idea. Every suggestion had merit. HR and the C-suite loved it. Good for morale, inclusive, that sort of thing. The first time we did it, our topic was 'Growing our Business to Be Number 1'. The second was 'Finding an Appropriate Work-Life Balance'."

"So? How did it work?"

I paused to think. "Both times it was just before we had a big reorg and laid off a bunch of people."

Farley snorted but Murray scowled. "I knew it was time to leave," he said, "when we couldn't decide anything without a circle jerk and some outside quack paving a 'parking lot' with things too hot to handle." He shook his massive head, his expression suddenly wistful. "Whatever happened to dog eat dog?"

In the kitchen, there was a clatter, a burst of female laughter. "Murray," Darlene called. "Come take a look at the brisket."

"Duty calls." Murray said. He put his bottle down and headed for the kitchen.

"I'm just saying it's worth a try," Farley told me. "What've you got to lose? You gotta get yourself on track." His eyes shifted to the Scotch Murray had left. He reached for it and refilled his glass.

"I'll try it. I will."

"A simple story, well told. That's the objective. Winnow it down to the bare bones. Then get cracking."

"On the bones?"

He smiled vaguely and drained his glass. His eyes shifted away, first onto the Chagall, then back to Murray's bottle. He topped his glass again and sniffed at it appreciatively. We stood in companionable silence until Murray called "Yee haw! Come an' git it, fellers!" from the kitchen.

There was more laughter from that direction. I glanced at Farley and pulled a couple of pills from my pocket.

"What're those?"

"This one's a herbal something. This one's lobelia for respiration." I popped them both into my mouth and swallowed them with beer. "Before meals."

"Do they work?"

"Who knows? They're Genny's idea. You remember Cindy?"

CHAPTER EIGHTEEN

I will take any liberty I want with the facts so long as I don't trespass on the truth.

Farley Mowat

Writing is like carrying a fetus.

Edna O'Brien

A setback this morning. Another rejection, this one from Garfunkel Wayne in New York. It follows rejections over the last few weeks by all the original targets and most of those in the second round. Peter seems to have exhausted his New York contacts, and he's lost his inroad at Bertelsberg in London, where his girlfriend Sally rules a publishing empire. Ex-girlfriend, apparently. "Gals!" he explained, omitting the details.

We're now onto the second tier Canadian publishers. Peter has the manuscript out to six of them. He tells me not to get discouraged, that rejections from the big guys don't mean anything. He says he always gives them the first look because of their reach, but the mid-size Canadian houses are usually the best alternative. They're looking for Canadian subjects, and they get grants to promote Canadian authors. If we get published in Canada, he says, we can generate some buzz about the book here, then others will notice and pick it up internationally. He's seen this strategy work time and again.

Or, as he actually put it, "Screw 'em. Means nothing. Little guys, looking for CanCon. Eat it up! Get it out, some buzz, picked up internationally. How it works, oftentimes."

I take solace from his experience.

*

There is more bad news about the spread of the swine flu. There are accounts of sudden death and viral mutations, and inexplicable delays in the production and delivery of the vaccine. Where vaccine is available, clinics are swamped, even though the usual crazies are advising against inoculation.

Even in our household there are grave differences of opinion on the issue.

Genny is a doctor, albeit of social anthropology not medicine; but in matters of health she does not recognize the distinction. She favours naturopathy over technology, and dismisses criticism of herbal remedies (i.e. that they are ungoverned, unregulated, and untested) as competitor-bashing by Big Pharma, which has a vested interest in discrediting alternatives to its patent-protected drugs. Her old friend Cindy is her ally and main source on the subject. One might say Cindy, a high-volume seller of herbal remedies, is as conflicted as Big Pharma in the advice she renders, but Genny will hear none of that.

Cindy is among those who say the risks of the swine flu (what Genny insists on calling "the novel strain of the H1N1 virus") are overblown. Cindy also says the vaccine is unsafe and plumps instead a concoction of herbs mixed with mushroom extract to boost the immune system. At Genny's insistence I have ingested this foul brew myself. It tastes like turd, but what of its efficacy? Genny scoffs when I talk about clinical trials. She requires no proof for anything Cindy says; nor is she swayed by the results of independent trials on the swine flu vaccine.

*

Genny and I were out back yesterday—Sunday afternoon—doing yard work and having a little mister-and-missus spat on this very topic. Chloe was raking leaves in the front, well out of earshot, so our exchange was frank.

"*What* clinical trials?" Genny snorted, looking up at me from a flower bed where she was digging in daffodils. "Everything's short term. Cindy says—"

"But all the scientists say—"

"Cindy's a scientist."

"She's a druggist."

"She has a PhD in pharmacology."

"Yeah, well. You call that science?"

For a moment she stared at me. "Cindy says there are no trials on the long run effects of the vaccine."

"How can there be? The flu's killing people right now. There's no time for long term trials."

"There are better, safer ways to prevent illness," she said, in that tone of hers, the one that says *I have made up my mind based on the facts as I see them.* "Vaccination's just an opiate for the masses."

"Don't do that. Don't make this ideological. There's nothing ideological about it."

She stood up and looked around for more bulbs, saw them on the deck and went for them. "Of course it's ideological. Everything's ideological."

"You're not being consistent."

She stopped to look at me again. "You're one to talk."

Before I could reply Anthony's long face bobbed up over our shared back fence.

"Greetings, neighbours."

Genny and I exchanged glances. She had noticed that Anthony always asked about my work, never about hers. What's more, he never looked her in the eye, but squarely in the chest. She said hello and waited.

Anthony nodded blandly to her breasts and turned to me. "How's the book going, Shakespeare?"

"Good, good." I glanced at my watch. "Did you know the

Roughriders are playing this afternoon? In ten minutes."

"So when can I read it?"

"I've really got to get these leaves—"

"You know, I could read it and give you comments. From the perspective of a published author." He beamed magnanimously. "What do you say?"

He'd made this offer a dozen times, and a dozen times I'd dodged it; but this time I felt a wave of irritation sweep over me. I hadn't slept well again, and I was tired of his published author shtick. I opened my mouth to give him a piece of my mind.

"Not possible," Genny said before I could speak. "His agent's put an embargo on distribution. No one can read it now till it's published. But I've just started working on something new and could really use your perspective on it, Anthony, as an author. It's a comparative study on domestic gender roles among the Basarwa, the Bakgalagadi, and the Bangwaketse of southern Africa."

Anthony's smile faded. "I'm not sure I have much to say on that, Genny." His eyes shifted back to me. "So, the Roughriders, eh? By golly, I haven't watched a basketball game in ages!"

This was a page from my playbook and would never work on Genny. "But have you ever considered," she asked, "the role of Self and selfishness in a traditional, communal society? That's a perspective that needs exploration. I'd really like to hear your ideas."

With an on-the-fly falsehood about a nonexistent embargo, Genny had stopped me from saying something I'd regret, and she persisted now in making Anthony wriggle. I took a Ken Dryden on my rake and pondered her as she ran roughshod over his excuses with the sunny enthusiasm of the late Queen Mum. But just then she looked nothing like a Royal. She was wearing a pair of faded jeans, and because it was sunny and unseasonably warm, she'd taken off her sweater. The pits of her t-shirt were sweaty; she was muddy-kneed and dirty-handed; leaf litter clung to her legs, and she had a smear of dirt across one cheek. I stood in awe and admired the whole package, Genny at forty-something, her passions undiminished, dark-haired still (with help from a bottle), a magnificent rack (securely buttressed against gravity), waist a little thicker, but body still all feminine curves, and a butt that made me want to grab it right then and there, decorum be damned.

I daydream about women. They turn my head on the street. I, like Jimmy Carter, have committed adultery in my heart. I have many faults and am inconsistent on many things. I call myself a humanist, which allows me to chuckle at everyone—male, female, black, white, gay, straight, in-between, confused, and differently-abled. I've been known to laugh at off-colour jokes and tell them myself. I use the F-word too much. I have a quick temper, though my anger blows over and is immediately forgotten (at least by me). I am, in sum, an imperfect schmuck who does not deserve Genny, and after all these years I am still smitten with her; her dazzling blue eyes (now somewhat squinty, endearingly so) still make me giddy. And I have never understood why she is with me. A woman like her could have who she wants—but she, inexplicably, wants me. She loves me, and despite her innate stubbornness, frequent petulant insistence on getting her own way, and unreasonableness on the topic of the swine flu, she is everything to me—and I am terrified of losing her. I am afraid she'll die if she isn't inoculated.

All these thoughts went through my mind as Anthony dangled and dodged on Genny's offer. At last she relented and allowed him to change the subject.

"I couldn't help overhearing your discussion about the swine flu."

"They're calling it the novel strain of the H1N1 virus," I said, feeling I owed Genny one.

"Uh huh. Well, it's interesting to watch the whole issue evolve. I was just doing a thought leadership piece on this yesterday, and I was thinking it's a perfect example of Self empowerment, how embracing the Ish-Ness of Self in the face of a societal crisis, like this epidemic—"

"Pandemic," interrupted Genny.

"—*pandemic* can accelerate achievement of True Self. It's more than ever an individual's obligation to embrace his or her" (he cast an inclusive glance at Genny's chest) "Selfishness to decide on a response to the flu. It's really beyond ideology—"

"See?" I told Genny.

"—and beyond what the authorities say. Selfishness can show the way. An enlightened Self is a necessary condition for True Self. Therein lies the appropriate response. The answer lies in Selfishness." He looked from me to Genny's breasts and nodded. "Check out the piece on my blog. I'm excited about this. Very excited. My next book's going to be on the cris-Ish of Ness-lessness."

Genny and I exchanged glances as he prattled on about Self and Ish and Ness. I knew what she was thinking, and that made me sublimely happy. There were only two people in the world, Chloe and Genny, whose thoughts I could read. Imperfectly, and only sometimes, but still: it made me feel less isolated.

Anthony suddenly fell silent. He turned, and I did too and heard it immediately, a rustling noise from the gap between our houses. It approached, became a rumble, grew thunderous. Its source came into sight. It was a giant brown paper leaf bag wearing red Keds—Chloe, of course, with the bag over her head. She gave out a roar and lumbered into our backyard, broke into a run, guessing at the route, but guessed wrong and ran into a fencepost. There was a sickening thud and she fell like a stone.

A terrible stillness followed. Before I could reach her she began to cry.

*

Now, next day (a bump on the noggin and everything okay) we are still unresolved about the swine flu. I know that vaccination is the way to go but Genny insists on following Cindy's naturopathic approach. So she'll do what she'll do, and I'll do what I'll do, and we'll hope for the best (with me on tenterhooks). But what about Chloe?

CHAPTER NINETEEN

Fundamentally, all writing is about the same thing; it's about dying, about the brief flicker of time we have here, and the frustration that it creates.

Mordecai Richler

The good writing of any age has always been the product of someone's neurosis.

William Styron

I was in a landing craft bound for Normandy. We were the first wave of the attack and many of us would die. And so my senses were finely tuned, my impressions vivid: salt spray, diesel fumes, damp wool, sweat. The motion of the waves, the rapid rolling and twisting of the clumsy vessel, brought a plague of vomiting. There was little room to move in the crowded troop compartment. Overhead flew an armada of bombers. The sea, the sky, the naval guns all roared like frightful—

"Stop it," Genny murmured and poked me in the ribs. "You're snoring." She turned away and was instantly asleep.

I lay in a sweat reliving the dream, then got up and wrote it down. It wasn't surprising I'd dreamt of D-Day. I'd been reading about it. Yes, doing research. But what was disturbing about this dream was that Chloe was there with me in the LC. She was holding my hand.

I finished my notes and took one of Genny's herbal sleep potions. It didn't help; I tossed and turned for ages. Eventually, near dawn, I dropped into a restless slumber.

*

Chloe, Chloe, apple of my eye: she accepted me unconditionally. Writer, father, guy who'd worked downtown. Now she featured in my tortured dreams.

To her it was not unusual that her dad should write a novel. That it had taken years—well, that was just the way things were with books. And because it had taken so long, *Blown to Hell* had been a fixture of her childhood.

When she was six we took a trip to remote Nootka Sound to see where the story was set. One morning, while Genny interviewed Mowachaht elders about gender roles and residential schools, Chloe and I tromped around the site of the long-abandoned Spanish outpost of Santa Cruz. There was nothing left to see. The forest and the Mowachaht had reclaimed the land two centuries before.

"All right," I said, spreading a map out on the ground. "Get your imagination humming."

She made a humming sound and we both laughed. For a moment I studied the map.

"The Spanish commander—his name was Quadra—had his headquarters here, right where we are now. From his balcony, which was just above our heads, he could look out there, into the harbour. Imagine it full of ships, men-of-war and traders, and Indian long canoes bustling back and forth."

Chloe eyes, which are Genny's, shone as she visualized the scene.

"First Nations," she said after a moment.

"Pardon?"

Her dark hair glistened in the morning sun. "Not Indian. First Nations."

"First Nations, then. Over there, on that little island just off the lighthouse, stood Fort San Miguel."

Later, she read some of my historical sources on Broughton's voyage and those of better known explorers like Captains James Cook and George Vancouver; she listened closely as I told her about the hardships of their voyages and their intrepid ignorance of what lay over the horizon. I explained what their ships were like (crowded, uncomfortable, vermin-infested), how they sailed and navigated them; and about the challenge of longitude.

"James Cook used Larcum Kendall's K1 chronometer on two of his voyages to calculate longitude, which saved him all those complicated calculations based on lunar distances. And on George Vancouver's voyage he used—"

"K3, which was never as accurate as K1."

"Exactly."

I was pleased at how she grasped the technique of the lunar method and the importance of the marine chronometer. The child was a whiz with math. Encouraged by her curiosity I explained about coastal navigation and mapmaking and just kept going with various math functions and principles I thought she'd find interesting.

"What are you two tee-heeing about?" Genny asked one day, walking in on us.

"This big happy face. It's called a volatility smile," Chloe said.

Genny looked over our shoulders at the graph on my screen.

"It's something I've been trying to figure out at the office," I told her, rubbing my chin. "It shows the impact of perceived black swan event probability on option pricing. Here, take a look at another expiry date." I flicked to another chart. "You see? It's been that way since the market crash in 1987. There's a flaw in the standard pricing model for options."

Genny waved me off.

Chloe rubbed her own chin. "We're wondering what it means for valuations."

*

The year I left the Firm, the summer before the market crash, we took a celebratory trip to France to mark my change of career. One of our stops was Normandy, for I wanted to see the D-Day beaches. The war had always been an interest of mine, one Genny did not share. So the day I toured Juno Beach, site of the Canadian landings on June 6, 1944, she and Chloe had a beach day of their own in the pretty village of Arromanches. I picked them up late that afternoon and we drove to the Canadian cemetery in Beny-sur-Mer. We walked through a colonnaded entrance, along a tree-lined path to a wide plinth of Portland stone engraved with a simple motto: THEIR NAME LIVETH FOR EVERMORE. Beyond it lay the graves, row after row of markers set amid bucolic greenery peaceful with birdsong.

Two thousand Canadians are buried there. Two thousand souls. Their deaths were theoretical until I walked amongst them. I was struck by the randomness of it all. What if they'd been spared? If a shell hadn't landed where it had, or hadn't exploded? If a bullet from a Mauser hadn't transited at the precise millisecond through the exact geographic coordinates and at the specific elevation above the ground where a young man's beating heart, coursing with life and adrenaline, was also transiting, resulting in a fatal collision of matter, the bursting of consciousness, the end of dreams? What if he and all the others had made it off the beach, over the barricades, through the town and ultimately home? What if they'd lived? What might they have done with the lives they lost that day in France?

If on that September morning in New York I had not made it down the stairs, past the ascending firefighters, out the burning tower and into the noxious, soot-covered street and settling ash, would the world be any different?

Confronted by the graves at Beny-sur-Mer you must question what you are about. You must ask what you have done with your own life.

The sun's rays were lengthening, but those men would

know no succour that night, no hot meal nor glass of wine, no hugs from a beautiful woman nor kisses from a child. They were there for all time, those soldiers, and I could not walk one row and pay homage to a few while ignoring the rest. I could not turn my back on a single one. So I walked down every row.

Genny waited at the entrance but Chloe, with the somber wisdom of a ten year old, took my hand and walked with me the entire way.

*

And now she accompanied me in my feverish dream, in which we travelled inexorably towards that murderous beach. So much horror lay ahead, so much devastation: death in battle, a plague of relentless flu, the scourge of climate change. I had to spare her that. I had to find some way, some hope.

In the days that followed that nightmare I made a surprising connection. An idea took shape in my mind, percolated, brewed and metamorphosized until it burst forth and consumed me with fresh and unexpected enthusiasm.

CHAPTER TWENTY

Novelists are perhaps the last people in the world to be entrusted with opinions. The nature of a novel is that it has no opinions, only the dialectic of contrary views, some of which, all of which, may be untenable and even silly. A novelist should not be too intelligent either, although he may be permitted to be an intellectual.

Anthony Burgess

Every author really wants to have letters printed in the papers. Unable to make the grade, he drops down a rung of the ladder and writes novels.

P.G. Wodehouse

The phone rang: Porlock again. A brisk female voice asked if there was anyone available to participate in a survey about feminine hygiene products.

"Yes, I'll do it," I said.

There was a brief silence on the other end of the phone.

"Excuse me. I thought I was speaking to a . . . um, man."

"Yes."

I heard a rustle of paper as she flipped through the interview protocol.

"Can we move it along? I have a cake in the oven."

That worked. She decided to rush on with her questions rather than lose a willing day-time survey participant. "In the last week, have you used one or more brands of tampon?"

"Personally? No."

A brief silence. "Anyone in the household?"

"I can't say."

"Pardon?"

"Well, I don't think it's any of your business. Actually, have *you* used one or more brands of tampon in the last week?"

"There's no need for that, sir."

"Exactly my point."

Another pause on her end. "I, um, don't think this is going to work—"

"Let's try something else then. Have you had sex in the last forty-eight hours?"

"I beg your pardon?"

"I'm doing my own survey. Would you prefer I call back during lunch or dinner?"

"Sir, I think there's been a mistake."

"One a scale of one to ten, did he, or she—"

"I'm sorry, sir, this isn't working. I'm afraid I'll have to terminate the interview." But, well-trained as she was, she flipped to the last page of her interview protocol. "Thank you for assisting Porlock Polling and Market Research. Goodbye."

I felt fantastic coming off the call. I'd had a spring in my step all day. All my anguish, all my obsessiveness, dead-end striving and "research," had finally borne fruit. The planets had aligned. I'd finally worked it out. And the catalyst was the brainstorming I'd done at Farley's urging—and an idea I got from Genny. One night at dinner she told me about a paper she had written for an upcoming Womyn's Studies conference. It was titled, "Joseph Campbell, Pornographer? Male Power and Sexual Abuse in Myth." She'd enjoyed the research because the topic was a departure from her normal focus. "It's in the way a story's told," she said of what she'd learned. "Allegories and parables are full of meaning and nuance. No storyteller ever out-and-out called the Big Bad Wolf a sexual predator, but everyone knows that's what he is."

I was so startled I dropped my spoon. "What?"

"What's setual?" Chloe asked.

I sprang to my feet. "Chloe, have some more ice cream! Chocolate fudge or butter pecan? Why not some of each? Sprinkles?"

With my inability to grasp nuance I'd never been able to understand what an allegory was, or a parable, but later that evening when we were alone, Genny talked me through both. The distinctions were fuzzy, but what she said resonated. Imagine—delivering a lesson without actually identifying an issue. Here was the perfect device for a lifelong dissembler like me. I felt a tickle of inspiration. And after I finally got around to Farley's brainstorming exercise, the penny dropped.

I went to work, researched and toyed with my idea, refined it, and kicked it around some more. My enthusiasm grew with every day.

*

"Do you remember what we were like in undergrad?" I asked Farley the next time we got together. "We believed in activism then. We believed in getting stuff done, protecting the oceans and the planet, stopping pollution, getting rid of contaminants. I've been thinking a lot about that lately."

"We were kids."

"Yeah, and now we *have* kids, and there's still pollution. And now there's global warming. It's an even bigger problem. That's what I want to focus on."

"Yeah? And how exactly are you going to stop global warming?"

"I'm going to write an allegory," I said.

He gagged on his single malt. Really, sometimes he drank too fast. "What?" he sputtered.

"An allegory. Of hope."

His eyes narrowed as he took this in.

"Or an extended—novel-length—parable, but I think an allegory is the more general form. It's a broader concept. Still, there's a single moral I want to get across. Allude to, that is. I suppose you might call what I want to do, given its length, a parabolic allegory."

For a moment he looked confused. Then I saw his brain go to work on "parabolic allegory." It had word-list potential. Paraboligory. Parabegory. Paragory.

I summarized my plan: I would write about a real-life success over adversity, a victory in the face of peril. It would demonstrate how we could prevail against a seemingly impossible challenge if we committed ourselves. It would be a call to action on the environment—but it wouldn't be based on the environment. "That would be too preachy. Look at Al Gore. Good movie but what changed? I'm going to make the case obliquely, parabolically so to speak."

His expression seemed pained. We were in a place near campus and we'd shared nachos for a snack; a few minutes before he'd swallowed a jalapeno. "As an allegory of hope? For the environment?"

"A parabolic allegory. It's different than a pure allegory. It's going to be about D-Day. After I brainstormed it was obvious. I owe that to you—good idea, man. Thanks. This is how I connect my interests."

"But . . . but . . ." He stammered to a stop. "D-Day?"

"Yup."

"The invasion?"

"The story *behind* the invasion. The logistics."

"A novel?"

I nodded and waited, feeling this was a *ta-dah* moment, but he just stared. "Gee, bud," he said finally. "I dunno."

I explained how the Allies landed a hundred and fifty thousand soldiers in Normandy on a single day. How they deployed seven thousand vessels and twelve thousand aircraft to do it. How in total secrecy they assembled five separate assault forces in twelve ports along the English coast. "Think of all the details, the decisions that had to be made, the plans that had to intermesh. The sheer numbers that had to be juggled. It was a stupendous accomplishment. If that doesn't give people hope . . ."

He remained silent, observing me with an expression I could not read.

"It wasn't enough just to get all those troops to France. They had to be reinforced, and supplies had to be landed and brought up to them as they fought their way inland. Not to mention fuel. The army would grind to a halt without fuel, and they didn't have a port. You know what they did? They landed drums of gas on the beach and poured it out into five gallon jerry cans, then rushed those up to the front."

"Sometimes I tell my students that less is—"

"They needed millions of jerry cans. And if you think of a jerry can as an item of inventory, what we call an SKU today, the Allied supply system had *seven hundred thousand* SKUs. Imagine the challenges that posed in the days before computers, barcodes, databases. And every single item had to be hauled across a beach in a warzone."

I waited for his reaction but he just sat rubbing his temples with his palms. "What's that got to do with global warming?" he said at last.

"It's the challenge met."

He drained his glass.

"I don't know, bub. You think people will get what you're trying to say? About the environment?"

"I know it's complicated. I've always been drawn to complexity."

"Naturally. You're the guy who used to create derivatives."

"See?"

"And how'd that end?"

"What do you mean?"

"Look, I'm just saying, sometimes less is more. Think about that. And what is the allegory, exactly? Can you say it in words?"

"Sure. Here it is. Total inaction on global warming. An

inventory of seven hundred thousand SKUs to invade Europe and liberate it in eleven months. You tell me which story inspires."

There it was in a nutshell, but he seemed doubtful. "Is that even an allegory?"

"It's about commitment. All those SKUs."

He grimaced, tipped his glass and found it empty. He signalled our waitress.

"A parabolic allegory," he said after a moment. "A paragory for the environment about logistics."

I waited for him to continue but instead he massaged his forehead, lost in thought. Finally he looked up. "Your mind's made up. You're going to do it no matter what I say."

"I need to do it."

"Well, then. Break a leg."

We sat in silence. I'd hoped for something more. When he spoke again it was in his academic voice, coolly analytic, thoughtful and professorial. "That link to the environment, that's going to be a challenge for you. Some novels have themes and allegories that are obvious, like *Animal Farm* or *Narnia*. And some have messages that people just don't get. Yours could be one of those. You'll need to work it."

"It'll be a challenge. I know that."

He grimaced again and jiggled his glass. "The service here is crap."

"We should've gone to Gzbrnznkwyc's. Ludwika knows how to look after us."

"Yeah, she's good. But they don't have real Scotch." He caught the server's eye. She held up a finger and mouthed, "One sec." He turned back to me. "You know, you could pitch *Blown to Hell* as an environmental allegory, too."

"How?"

" 'A story set in an unspoiled Eden where despoliation and original sin coincide.' It's a stretch but it could work."

Although everyone on the planet was better at capturing subtlety than me, I doubted anyone would catch *that* message in *Blown*. The waitress was weaving towards us now, navigating between tables. "If you think that'll work, take it on as your mission. You're the deep thinker on literary success. You'd come up with the right angle, one I'd never even see. Besides, all I want to do is write—to be a 'man of letters'." I chuckled to myself and had a sudden absurd idea, one I was sure he'd find funny. "While you're at it, you can be my literary executor too. That is, in the unlikely event *I* kick off before *you*. I'll get this next round, and we'll call you hired. Officially mandated to get the work *and* the message out."

To my surprise, he didn't laugh but flinched as though I'd slapped him. We'd never talked about death before, his or mine, and for a moment he seemed shocked, stricken even, at the thought; then the moment passed and his expression returned to normal. In fact, a sly grin came to the corners of his mouth. "Sure. Okay. One of us has to go first. But you should know, I don't work cheap."

"What can I get you boys?" the waitress asked.

"I'll have a double Macallan," Farley said, eyeing me, now poker faced.

"Let's have menus too," I said, digging in my pocket for a couple of herbal tablets (twice a day, before food, according to Dr Genny). I popped them in my mouth and washed them down with beer.

*

Weeks later, the phone rang.

"Bit of bad news."

"Peter?"

"Turned down."

"Oh."

"Yep."

"Who?"

"Three of them. Trickster House, Broadbent & Linden. Took a pass yesterday. Black Shag, today."

I could think of nothing to say.

"Screw'em. Missing the boat. Get it back out to some more."

"We must be running out of publishers. What do you

think?"

"Not to worry. Leave to me. Find a home, eh?"

"But who's left?"

"Plenty. Smaller guys. Just keep working. But something else . . . might mean we change strategy."

"What is it?"

"Book coming out, same period. Same place."

This didn't make sense.

"Some guy, lives here in T.O. too. Your neighbourhood, I hear. First novel. Spent years on it. Pacific coast, Indians, exploration, diplomacy. 1792."

That was my story! What was going on? "Peter, I don't get it."

"Book's about George Vancouver. *His* voyage."

"George Vancouver?" I exhaled. Thank God it wasn't about Broughton, his number two.

"Yep. Got some marketing behind it." I heard the ruffle of newspaper. " 'Not since Patrick O'Brian has there been a nautical thriller of this ilk.' That's *The New York Times. Quill & Quire* calls it 'a Hornblower for the twenty-first century.' They're talking about a sequel. What else? Let's see . . . Oh, here, in *The Times Literary Supplement*: 'Boney's met his match in Captain George Vancouver!' "

"But Bonaparte wasn't even in power when—"

"True enough—bunch of malarkey, what it is. Hogwash. Still. Problem, for us. Being frank. Hard to push two books about the same guy."

"But mine's not about—"

"Same period."

"Yeah, but—"

"Marketing department at Bertelsberg's really pushing this one. Hundred and fifty thousand copies in hard cover. That's just the States. UK too. Big publicity tour. Release dates in twelve other countries."

"Bertelsberg? That's where your girlfriend Sally—"

"Good riddance! High maintenance. Didn't need it. Dames! Know what I mean? Met someone else last Tuesday. Like her a lot. Might be the one."

By then I wasn't really listening. I didn't care about his new inamorata. I was thinking about the other guy's book and feeling my stomach drop. Had I missed my chance? Had it all been for naught? Would anyone ever read my book?

CHAPTER TWENTYONE

Every writer hopes or boldly assumes that his life is in some sense exemplary, that the particular will turn out to be universal.

Martin Amis

Anybody can write a three-volume novel. It merely requires a complete ignorance of both life and literature.

Oscar Wilde

Peter persuaded me to meet him for a drink. "Buck you up, man. Talk shop," is how he put it. "Invite Farley along, how's about?" Instead of meeting in his office, the bar on Danforth where we usually met, he proposed that we meet in my neighbourhood. I suggested Gzbrnznkwyc's, where I knew it was schnitzel night.

"Don't sweat it," Peter said as we tucked into our first round of drinks. Ludwika had persuaded him to try Polish Scotch. "It's just a novel."

That caught me mid-gulp and I sprayed beer across the table.

He eyed me as he wiped his palm across the rim of his glass. "Didn't mean *your* novel. Meant that guy's. The

Vancouver book. Lucky with timing, is all."

I took another gulp of Żywiec.

"It's not a question of luck or timing," Farley said. "Literature stands the test of time."

"Uh hmm." I drank again, thinking glumly about his novel, the pseudonymously-penned *Möbius's Dick*, now in its sixteenth edition, an established under-the-covers hit at boys schools across the continent and in the United Kingdom.

"What're Genny and Chloe doing tonight?" he asked.

"Dinner at home. Chloe had a ballet lesson that went till six."

Farley took a long swig himself. At Gzbrnznkwyc's he drank Żywiec, although on our last outing Ludwika had gotten him to try Polish Scotch. When she was out of earshot he'd described its taste as "cheese mixed in a toilet with kerosene." He'd christened it Polotch.

"Ballet," he said. "Is that PC?"

"What do you mean?"

"You know . . . tutus, objectification, that sort of thing."

I was used to Farley's mild digs at Genny. "Ballet celebrates the human form. That's how she sees it."

He rolled his eyes.

"Ah, the human form," Peter said. "Speaking of which." His eyes followed Ludwika around the room. He lifted his glass to sniff his Polotch, grimaced and chugged it, then waggled a wrist to draw her attention.

She came straight over. "You want again *Torfowisko?*" she asked, one hand on her hip.

"A round for the table, my sweet," Peter said. "And menus. We are celebrating."

"Do you have any Scotch Scotch?" Farley asked.

"Polish Scotch," Ludwika replied. "Is good. You try last time." Then, turning to Peter: "Celebrate what?"

"Possibility," Peter said, jiggling the ice in his glass. "We're celebrating possibility." He winked and held her eye, then watched her return to the bar for menus. He turned to me. "Been thinking. Good story. Damn good—but competition, now. Other guy's getting a push. Need to think what we can do."

"What do you mean?

"I mean, ride his momentum. Guy's got a best-seller. Writing another. Word is, trilogy. Big advance. Seven figures. So. We do something else. Related. Coat-tails, eh?"

Ludwika arrived with the menus and whiskey. "*Torfowisko* for you, and you," she said, plunking glasses in front of Farley and me. She plunked the last glass down in front of Peter. "And one for horny grandpa."

Farley and I laughed, and Peter took it in stride. Over the years he'd been put in place by many a pretty woman. "Classy broads, dames with gumption, like 'em all," he'd told me once. Now he held his glass up to salute her. "I may appear an aged swain, but my heart yet beats with passion. And I shall ever appreciate a beauteous woman."

The rejoinder has an unsettling effect on Ludwika. She smiled uncertainly and returned to the bar. Peter turned back to me, shelving the elegant banter he used on women for the telegraphic staccato he used with men. "Your book. Talking about. What we'll do."

"Why don't we just keep pushing it? If you can sell it and we can get it into print, it'll stand up fine against the other guy's book."

"The plan, right there. No question."

Farley downed his Polotch in one gulp and took a swig of beer to rinse his palate. Peter watched Ludwika pass by with an order of schnitzel. "Got another idea," he said, turning back to me. "Plan B. You're from Saskatchewan."

"Not a crime, Pete," Farley said. "Lots of perverts come from Saskatchewan."

"Hah! 'Nother joke! Rolling tonight, you guys! Listen. Little press out there, looking for home-grown. Heard they're hungry, got some money. Leave it to me."

"Okay. That sounds good."

"But. Got to be a way . . . something . . . take advantage of the push on th'other guy."

"Like what?"

"Dunno." He fell into a ruminative silence, staring up at the TV behind the bar. The multicultural station was presenting the Polish news. After a moment he wagged his finger at the screen. "Didn't mention. Optioning one of Farley's books. For a movie. The Möbius one. Part of the Hindmost trilogy. Talks anyway."

"Not quite a movie for *theatres*," Farley said, looking uneasy. "More like on the internet, or mail-order."

"The internet?"

"Yeah." He watched me through the corner of his eye. "Nothing'll come of it, probably."

"Still," Peter said, "way we got to think. Outside the box. Different platforms. New channels."

The station broke to a commercial. The theme from a theatrical revival suddenly blared louder than the news. I could hear the lyrics in my head: *Tea, a drink with jam and bread* . . .

"Musical," Peter said.

"What?"

"Musical." He pointed up at the screen. "Your story, adapted. Ties in with their marketing. They're spending the dough, building profile on the period, the characters, the main themes. Ride their coat-tails. Benefit."

"A *musical?*" Farley asked.

"I don't know, Peter . . ."

"Just think about it. Got some potential." He jiggled his glass then poured his *Torfowisko* down his throat. "How's th'other project going? New one?"

I picked up my Polotch and sniffed its peaty aroma. No, it was not an aroma—it was an odour. If imitation is the sincerest form of flattery, the Scots should be proud; but of course, they are—of the real thing, not this swamp water. I tipped the glass up and drained it in one go, feeling Farley's eyes on me, and as the liquid hit my stomach I clenched my teeth and grunted. "Good, real good," I said after a moment. "Doing the research. Hey, we should order. It's schnitzel night. The schnitzel here comes with an egg on top. Ludwika? Ludwika! I think we're ready!"

*

A hammering headache is what I got from my night of bucking up at Gzbrnznkwyc's. I could not remember getting home, but had flash-memories of our table seeming to revolve; of my head swinging on my neck with the weight of an anvil; of struggling to get into my coat, a blast of cold air, a cab rolling by and Peter tumbling into it, Farley and Ludwika helping me walk, all of us helping each other walk, street lights spinning like celestial demons, the sidewalk rolling like an Atlantic swell.

"What time did you get home?" Genny asked next morning as I hid behind the *Globe's* sports page. I was wheezing a bit from the night's punishment. It comes on when I get run down.

"Oh, after midnight. Had a good talk."

I wasn't reading at all, moving slowly to minimize the pain, just keeping up appearances.

"Where'd you go?" Genny was munching on muesli in soymilk, her most normal meal of the day. She'd recently become a raw vegan, which meant a diet of raw fruit, vegetables, nuts and grains. Nothing could be cooked, although it could be dehydrated at low heat.

I burped up a mouthful of bile at the thought and swallowed it while feigning interest in the overnight scores.

"Oh, uhm . . . Gzbrnznkwyc's. We went to Gzbrnznkwyc's."

"Ooh. They have *awful* food. You can't get anything vegetarian there. Even the cabbage rolls have meat. And everything's cooked."

"Yeah, I don't feel so good. Maybe I ate something that was cooked too much."

Genny pulled away the paper to look at my face. "You don't look well, baby." She felt my forehead. "You feel clammy. And I hear you wheezing. Take your lobelia and some ma huang. And some St John's wort to pick you up.

Then just take it easy today."

"Hell no. I've got work to do."

I took what she told me to take and saw Chloe off with some chipper advice for math class, waved goodbye to Genny as I pretended to be engrossed with my laptop, and collapsed into bed when the coast was clear.

*

At one o'clock I took a Xanax and something for my headache, made a pot of Mormon tea, and read the paper. More settlements on the West Bank, more deaths from that novel strain of flu—there was no good news to be had. I flipped pages and stopped at a headline that read "Nazi Victims Fight for Restitution." The report was about a court case between holocaust survivors and a German foundation set up to compensate Second World War slave-labourers. After decades of resistance and denial, the companies had created the foundation to oversee restitution to the victims. But the foundation was refusing to pay interest on wages earned more than sixty years ago.

One name leaped out from the list of foundation members: Heil AG, the maker of those tainted metal water bottles we'd recently banished from our house. The company was taking a lead role in opposing restitution. A senior Heil executive, acting as the foundation's spokesman, questioned the claimants' legitimacy and called their demands "extortionate."

It turned out Heil AG was more than a maker of trendy metal bottles—it was a diversified industrial conglomerate, based in Austria, with investments across Europe. During the war it had been a major producer of steel and armaments for the Nazis. Thousands of Europeans had been conscripted, uprooted, and transported from conquered countries to work in its mills and factories. Thousands of Jews and other *Untermenschen* had been diverted from concentration camps to work alongside them. They were starved, beaten and debased, then murdered when they could no longer work.

Lie, deny, accept no responsibility: Heil has been using the same strategy for decades. It's this kind of capitalist that gives capitalism a bad name.

*

In the following days I ruminated on my future.

It was plain bad luck that some guy wrote a book about George Vancouver while I was writing one about his sidekick Broughton. Who could've imagined that two of us were working on similar themes, using the same historical characters, at the same time? And in the same city—the guy even lives in my neighbourhood! I saw him one night in Gzbrnznkwyc's, playing pool with his cool artist friends. What a phony. His book (I've flipped through it at Chapters) is a turgid read, yet he's just signed a seven-figure deal for two more volumes. I think Peter is right: he's squeezed *Blown* out of the market.

What motivated me in the first place to write about the hapless Broughton? I left a job, a career, threw my life into chaos, to write a novel with (as Anthony once put it) no real preparation. More recently I've pinned everything on an allegory of hope I'll never get around to writing.

Yes, my saga on the logistics of D-Day is going nowhere. Oh, I've got a working title—I've gotten that far. It's *No Bolt Too Small*, a sure winner if ever I produce a manuscript. And I've done plenty of research too. I've scoured libraries, read tomes of history, memoir, and analysis; I've taken hundreds of pages of notes, mapped and remapped a plot, tweaked it, changed it, invented and reinvented characters, then thrown everything out and started over. Always, there was more research to do. As a result, I have become something of an expert on the logistics of D-Day—yet I have not written a single original word. I had a flying start then I lost steam. I was up, now I'm down. Is it the lack of sleep? The disturbing dreams? Whatever the cause I am aground again on a mental reef, marooned on a barren atoll, stranded like William Broughton on the rock of Miyako-jima.

I have to get Broughton out of my mind.

*

It's weeks later now. I've spent the time sitting at my desk, drinking Mormon tea and thinking, trying to work out what to do. And finally I have the answer.

I'd thought Peter crazy when he suggested a musical based on *Blown to Hell*. Now I wonder why I didn't see it before. The story has all the makings: fife and drum, sea shanties, jigs and reels, Spanish fandango, Catalonian folk dances, plenty of Indian drumming and dance. Costumes galore, and a romance across an unbridgeable divide. As a musical, it's got Hit written all over it.

I've got a working title—*North Pacific*—and some tunes in mind already: a ditty about Broughton's ship called "Rinky-Dink Brig"; another about potlatches called "Indian Giver"; one about the trade in sea otter skins called "Doe Eyed and Dead."

I've got the story but I'm not musical myself. I'll need a lyricist and composer. Frankly, the idea of a collaboration excites me. There's respect to be had in musical theatre. Lyrics by *Sir* Tim Rice. Music by *Lord* Andrew Lloyd Webber. Book by *yours truly*. Maybe this is the way it has to be: before I am ever a published novelist I shall be a successful librettist.

CHAPTER TWENTYTWO

At least half the mystery novels published violate the law that the solution, once revealed, must seem to be inevitable.

Raymond Chandler

I will carry on writing, to be sure. But I don't know if I would want to publish again.

JK Rowling

A couple of months later Peter called with good news. His Plan B, the publisher in Saskatchewan, seemed to be working. He'd sent *Blown* to Bunyok Press, which also produced *The Kamsack (Sask.) Literary Review*. They'd responded with interest. They had a government grant and a mandate to support Saskatchewan writers.

"But I haven't lived in Saskatchewan for years."

"'Tsokay. Born there. Good enough. Green and white forever. I know you guys."

"What happens next?"

There was bar noise in the background: the buzz of conversation, glasses and plates clinking. A woman's voice called, "Peter! Everyone's waiting."

Peter's voice, muffled, replied. "In a moment, My Sweet, I'm speaking with a very important client, an emerging writer." Now his voice softened as My Sweet came closer. "You'll know his name soon enough. Will you order me the lamb? And the Veuve Clicquot. We'll celebrate! You *are* a treasure, Pudding. C'mere for a sec. Just a sec." He took his hand off the phone and I heard rustling, then what sounded like lips smacking, a gasp. "Mmm-wwah. I'll be along in a mo'." I heard heels hurry away. "Hey, back. Sorry 'bout that. Real doll, Beth. Love her to death. Listen, going to New York. Business, something else—'nother deal. Iron yours out with Bunyok by phone. Should have the offer when I get back. Sunday morning. Tell you everything then."

Genny asked who was on the phone.

"It's Peter. He's got a deal with a publisher."

She squealed and grabbed me.

"Is that the missus?"

"Yes." To Genny: "He'll have an offer by Sunday."

"Oh, Jack! Maybe things will turn around now!"

"Lovely girl, Genny. Lucky fella, you."

"He says you're a lovely person."

"Tell him to come for dinner on Sunday and bring the offer. We'll celebrate."

I conveyed the invitation while Genny hollered upstairs.

"Chloe! Daddy's book! It's going to get published!"

Chloe screamed, bounded down the stairs and across the room and bowled us both over. I fell backwards into an armchair, unwilling to let either of them go, and they came down on top of me. We squirmed and laughed, everybody talking at once.

Peter listened in benignly until the mayhem subsided. "Okay. Sunday. Handle paperwork then. Just take a jiff. Bring Beth."

For a moment I wondered why I should bring Beth, then realized it was a question. "Sure," I said. "Bring Beth."

We were already having dinner with friends on Sunday. Farley and Paola were coming, along with Murray and

Darlene, and Genny's colleague Andrea. "We'll make it a party," Genny said. "Oh wow! You've got a book deal at last."

"Not so fast," I said. "There are a lot of things that have to fall into place. Let's keep it to ourselves for now."

Next morning, I was out in the back lane where we keep our compost bin, turning its contents with a spade and thinking about the deal with Bunyok. They would have edits for me. That's what I knew about publishers—the work began anew once you had a deal. Editors, publicists, photographers—there'd be cover designs, plans for book tours and media appearances—it was all part of the process. Genny told me to take things easy before the tumult that lay in store, but that morning I was thinking about *North Pacific*. I wanted to get as far as I could on it before I got swept up in the frenzy of a book launch.

I hadn't told anyone I was adapting *Blown* into a musical—officially I was still researching my new project—but fuelled by a new herbal energy booster Genny had received from Cindy, I had already gotten a long way on the libretto. I'd cut things you could include in a 600 page book that would be confusing in a four hour performance. I was pleased with my progress, but at the same time, a voice told me it was a crazy idea, and that I should get back to work on *No Bolt Too Small*. So I did that too—it seemed my energy was boundless. Late at night I reworked *Bolt's* outline then wrote the opening chapters, then began to draft other sections. Improbable as it seemed, my allegory of hope was taking shape simultaneous with my libretto. I wasn't sleeping much, but I didn't feel the need. The fact that I was making progress on both projects kept me invigorated.

I was thinking about this, and grunting away in the compost, when the gate next door squeaked open. At the sound I threw down my spade and grabbed the lid of the bin. Out the corner of my eye I saw a gangly figure enter the lane. I turned away—I could still make it through my own gate—it was open—but the damn lid would not find its thread. The more I hurried the more it missed.

"Hello, Shakespeare," Anthony said. "What're you up to?"

"Research," I replied, feeling the lid slip into place at last. I picked up the spade and made for my gate.

"In the compost?"

"Ah, no. I thought you meant . . . No, I was just mixing it up."

"How's the book coming?"

I sighed, having already anticipated and answered the question. "Why don't you have a composter? Do you know how much stuff you can put in there?"

"Jack!" Genny called from inside our fence, "I'm just going over the list for the party. Can you—" She came through the gate and saw I wasn't alone. "Oh! Hi, Anthony. I didn't know you were here."

Anthony cast a courtly smile at Genny's bust. She turned back to me. "Can I leave you the list, in case you're near the health food store?"

"Sure."

"So," Anthony said, looking from me to Genny. "You're having a party."

"Yes. We're celebrating. Guess who's got a book deal?"

"Weh-eh-ell . . ." he neighed, looking back at me. "That's great news. Congratulations." Then, back to Genny's breasts: "Your husband is far too modest. He didn't let on. Didn't say a thing."

I was going to say something clever about there being an "i" in Selfish, but no "I" in me, but Genny cut me off.

"Anthony, why don't you come too? Sunday, at six. It's going to be a real feast."

I plastered an insincere smile on my face and nodded at the suggestion, thinking, *why, Genny, why?*

*

I had to warn Farley about this "real feast" Genny was planning. Food was a sensitive issue in our house. It was ever thus.

When we first set up house together, Genny was

determined to avoid all traditional gender roles. She insisted on a household prenuptial of sorts, a solemn agreement to share every task straight down the middle. We were in love, we were committed, and the arrangement worked exceeding well—in most areas, for she proved funny about food. Demanding.

Admittedly, my kitchen repertoire was limited. Its highlight was a cuvée of whatever I found in the fridge, mixed with canned tomatoes. She called this delicacy "garbage stew" and suspected I had an agenda. I did not. Frankly, we subscribed to different culinary aesthetics: she believed that each dish should have a distinctive flavour, one which complemented the taste of other dishes comprising a varied meal; and I believed it was easiest to use one pot.

Our approaches were so different, our differences so profound, that we found we couldn't cook together. I could chop and dice for her, but anything else instantly bored me. Measure? Bah! Fold in? Yawn. I watched, fidgeted, and shifted from leg to leg. And when I was chef, Genny seemed mortally offended at everything I did. To hear her tell it, the travesties she witnessed, the indignities I inflicted on innocent food. We evolved into taking turns, she cooking one day, me the next. And she insisted on cooking for company, to vouchsafe what ended up on our table. This was voluntary on her part, but a sore point, for she saw it as creeping chauvinism.

"You shouldn't expect me to cook because I'm a woman," she told me early on.

"I don't. I don't even mind cooking. I just can't follow a recipe. Measure this, time that—it's like following a formula. It stifles creativity. Imagine . . . imagine writing a book that way."

"You should be happy following a formula. You, with all your equations and math!"

This, I think, was as close as Genny could come to spite, an attempt to wound. And as she was wrong, I felt I had to clear the air. "Those aren't the same thing, Genny, not at all.

A *formula* is a statement of general fact or principle, expressed by mathematical symbols. An *equation* is a formal statement of equivalence between mathematical or logical expressions. Technically, an equa—"
 "Warming up leftovers," she interrupted, "is not cooking."
 "A meal's a meal."
 She frowned but let it ride.
 Eventually I saw a way forward, but given her sensitivity I knew it would require guile to effect. I prepared carefully, tweaking the pitch and rehearsing my lines to get it just right. I was ready when the topic came up again. "Maybe I'm just differently-abled," I said, all PC and reasonable. "Maybe we need to look at things more broadly. Who was that guy who said, 'from each according to his ability?'" I knew perfectly well who that guy was, and that Genny would be sympathetic to *his* historic argument. "Maybe we'd benefit from a bit of specialization. You know, to optimize household efficiency."
 This was how I came to do all the shovelling, manage household maintenance, and clean the toilets (which she threw in, gratuitously I thought, to show she was no patsy). Overall I felt it a good deal, because I actually enjoyed clearing snow and wandering around Home Hardware and Canadian Tire, looking at power tools and garden supplies. (I was less keen about the toilet, but there are some fine chemical cleaners I use when Genny is not around, and they work like a charm. When I'm finished I hide the evidence in the basement and wipe the toilet seat with the lemon and eucalyptus oil she prefers in lieu of the good stuff. These are effective for masking chemical odours but not for cleaning. Genny has an uncanny nose, though, and I seldom fool her. "You of all people," she says with a great show of disappointment, "should know what breathing that crap does.")
 I still did my turn in the kitchen, and Genny tempered her expectations accordingly; but she always cooked for company, and as she was then on her raw vegan diet ("It's a *lifestyle choice*, not a diet."), the "real feast" she was planning

for Sunday would be entirely, well, raw.

She had adopted this diet (*"Lifestyle* choice, you, you . . .") with her characteristic rigour and commitment, making no allowances for Chloe or me. "Would a piece of bread kill you?" I asked bitterly, gnawing on a desiccated nut loaf, one of her first forays. She cycled through the raw vegan repertoire but it left me cold. Perpetual salad, nothing cooked. "You can get organic meat, you know," I grumbled early on, to which she responded with a reasoned, principled argument. More energy. Less disease. Longer life, less pollution. No animals will suffer.

"What about my suffering?"

This earned a stern look.

"Who was that guy who said 'to each according to his needs?' "

I tried to remind her who it was by looking a tad crazy, like a dedicated socialist or a *Toronto Star* subscriber.

She looked at me oddly. "You don't need meat," she said. "You need protein."

Despite my wheedling she wouldn't budge. Remember what I told you before, about her being stubborn.

*

So I warned Farley; and he agreed to come over with his family a couple of hours early on Sunday afternoon. When they arrived I made a joke about swine flu and insisted we exchange air kisses instead of real ones, which annoyed Paola, who is Italian and already believes WASPs are distant and anal. "Better safe than sorry," I said, confirming the notion. There was a moment of awkwardness before Chloe took Lucia upstairs to her room. The rest of us lingered in the kitchen. "Genny, let me help you cook," Paola said. "I'm dead curious about raw veganism."

"There's no cooking really, Paola. It's more preparation than cooking."

Preparation indeed. She'd been preparing off and on since Friday.

I met Farley's eye.

"Well, I guess I should show you that thing now," I said.

"Oh, yeah, I want to see it. That thing. It sounds . . . interesting." Our eyes shifted onto our wives, who weren't paying any attention to us. They were into a Q&A on raw veganism.

I cleared my throat.

"Genny?"

They both looked up at me.

"I'm going to take Farley over to the hardware store. There's a thing I want to show him there."

"Sure baby. We'll take care of the women's work."

A claxon sounded in my head. My eyes shifted from Genny to Paola and back to Genny. Her expression was unreadable. The two of them stood silently, watching me. I stood immobile, fighting the urge to swallow. Then they both burst out laughing. "Go, go!" Genny said with a wave. "We've got everything under control."

Farley and I walked over to Roncesvalles Avenue, past the hardware store to Gzbrnznkwyc's. Inside, it was quiet, the late afternoon lull before dinner. A few men sat in ones and twos, drinking beer or vodka. At a back table near the kitchen, Ludwika was lounging over her engineering books, blowing smoke rings at the ceiling. When she saw us she came straight over. "Look what dog choke up."

"What the dog dragged in," Farley said.

"Choke up, drag in. What I can get for you?"

"What we want," I said, "is a little strange. Two schnitzels, but no potato, no dumplings, no bread. No vegetables either."

"And a couple shots of vodka," Farley said. "Each."

I looked at him.

"Undetectable."

I nodded.

Ludwika was unphased. "You want fried egg on top?"

We looked at each other. "Yep," we both said simultaneously.

"Is religious festival? For Canada? Reverse of meatless

Friday?"

I laughed. "No. Not quite."

"Well, what?"

I chuckled and looked at Farley, who grinned. "Well . . . do you know what a *vegan* is, Ludwika?"

"I know this," she said, suddenly angry. "Is part of woman. I not stupid! You make fun of English! I try—"

"No, no, no, no," Farley said. "That's something else. His *wife* is a vegan. It's a kind of vegetarian. They don't eat meat. And also, in her case, they don't cook."

Ludwika's anger vanished. Now she was keenly interested. "I hear of this. Vegetarian. But she's not kook?"

We laughed. "She is a bit," said Farley.

"I thought she no kook."

I realized what she meant. "Oh, no, she doesn't *cook* right now. It's just a recent thing. I'm hoping she'll try it and decide it's no good. But we're having her vegan food tonight. That's why we need a schnitzel now."

She nodded, once again all breezy Baltic efficiency. "Okay understand. You sure want vodka?" This was directed at Farley, with the hint of a smile. "Not *Torfowisko*?"

"No, Ludwika. Never. Again."

She smiled openly now and went to place the order, then picked up the vodka at the bar. When she came back she had a thoughtful look.

"She pale?" she asked me.

"Pardon?"

"Wife. Pale, like vampire?"

"Not really."

"Hmm." She shrugged, perplexed.

Farley watched her as she returned to her texts. "*Na zdrowie*," he said, and shot one of his vodkas.

"Easy, buddy." I shot half of mine.

In the kitchen, something hit the grill with a sizzle. My mouth began to water at the sound. We both looked towards the back just as Ludwika glanced up and found our eyes on her. Farley jiggled his empty glass and grinned. Then his eyes swung onto the big screen over the bar. No one was watching it, and the control was lying on the next table. He stretched across to pick it up. "Got a few bucks on the Seahawks," he said and began to surf channels, looking for the game. "Don't ask me why. They suck."

I sat back and watched images flick across the screen.

"Hey, wait! Go back."

He flicked back a channel, to a studio scene, a panel of trendies dressed in black. It was Kudos!, a specialty channel owned by one of the big media companies, licensed to showcase the best of Canadian culture. The company fulfilled its mandate by recycling Canadian content from its vaults until after 10 pm, when it was permitted to air Canadian-produced soft-porn. The business case, the money, was all in those late night slots, but the network had to go through the motions until then; the CRTC even forced it to produce some original programming as a licence requirement. It was hard to portray *Temagami Tractor Pull* and *Frozen Lake Trucking* as the epitome of Canadian culture, but they got away with it by interspersing those shows with cheap and earnest studio-based talk-fests about the Canadian arts scene. That was what was on now, and I'd recognized one of the panelists. It was Phil Regency, literary agent, man about town, and rejecter of *Blown to Hell*.

The discussion was about new social media. A wild-haired academic was describing how NSM had changed the way artists reached their audiences. Internet forums, blogs, social networking sites like Facebook and MySpace, and micro-blogs like Twitter and Tumblr were creating mass awareness—basically, they were creating demand. The Beatles, he said, had a product that caused a frenzy. Now a frenzy could be manufactured about a product.

Farley belched, crafting it artfully into the roar of the MGM lion at the start of a movie. "Pardon," he said when I glanced his way. "I just had to vent. These guys are empty suits. Bullshit for brains. Yap-yap-yap. There always needs to be *some* substance, some integrity, even if people don't get it."

Suddenly he fell silent. His eyes narrowed. He studied my face. "These guys are just bumsuckling for publicity."

One brow rose in hopeful appeal. I waved him off and turned back to the TV.

"Isn't that the way it's always been?" asked the host.

"To an extent. But today, the potential for viral marketing has no precedent. Millions of users are signing on to NSM every month. The ability to astroturf your product—"

"Wait. Astroturf?"

"Speaking of which . . ." Farley, impatient. His second glass was empty.

I held up a hand to shush him. He shrugged and waved for Ludwika.

"To create an artificial grass roots movement. An appearance of market momentum. That ability simply didn't exist a decade ago—even five years ago. Not on the scale that's possible now."

"So what does it mean for the arts?"

"I'll give you an example," Phil Regency said. "Look at the phenomenon of Infinite Summer. It was an on-line book club set up to read David Foster Wallace's novel, *Infinite Jest*. The book's a masterpiece but it's over a thousand pages—"

"You want again vodka?" Ludwika asked Farley, eyes hooded. They bantered while I tried to focus on Phil Regency.

"—possible for someone, with these media," he said, "to do a Sarah Binks of monumental proportions, to manufacture a market—"

"Another for you too?"

"Huh?" Ludwika was standing slouched, hand on hip, green eyes now fixed on me. "Oh, yeah, sure." I drained my glass. "Why not?"

She looked at Farley and headed for the bar.

"Lemme check the Seahawks now," he said.

"Wait. You see that guy? The weasel in the dark jacket?"

"Yep." I don't think he really looked, because they were all wearing dark jackets.

"He's a dick."

The Seahawks were getting shellacked, which put Farley in a black mood. Ludwika delivered our drinks, doubles again, and he roused himself to kid her about her studying. I stayed out of it, staring at the game but thinking about Phil Regency's idea. Manufacture a market, indeed. The idea had no integrity. There had to be substance underlying the work. It was analogous to . . . I strained for an analogy, which was a literary device, and literary devices were always a challenge for me.

Ludwika laughed at something Farley said and headed for the kitchen. His smile faded and we sat in silence, staring at the game until he switched it off, glowered at the table, and tossed back both glasses. I knew then why he was in a black mood.

"How much did you lose?"

He fiddled with an empty glass.

"It's a mug's game, you know."

"Yeah, sure," he snapped. "Like credit default swaps and mortgage-backed securities."

There it was! A perfect analogy, and from the very field in which I'd toiled! Swaps and derivatives and hybrid securities all had substance and value. They were based on sound concept, and they served a purpose in their own right. But when demand was manipulated—when people were misled about what they were buying (or willingly closed their eyes to the facts)—well, we'd seen the consequences. Surely that would always be the case when a market was "manufactured." The law of unintended consequences would apply, sometimes in spades.

I found myself nodding at that thought—then realized Farley was still looking at me, waiting. I pulled my thoughts back to our conversation. Yes—about his betting, his dig at me. "You can manage default risk," I said. "You can quantify it. But football? They work the probabilities and establish the odds to account for them. *They* manage the risk. You can't build a model that'll beat the house. Not in the long term."

"Lot of good *your* models did, bud. I'm sitting here with Doctor Finanstein, the father of the global credit crisis."

"The models worked. No one listened—"

"Oh yeah. It's human nature to believe what you want to believe."

I didn't respond, wondering if he intended a snarky nuance. I decided he knew better than to snark me after all these years—or, especially, to use nuance. Around us, the place was filling up, the noise was building. Someone turned the TV back on. It was still on the same channel. Farley saw the score and went pale.

"How much did you lose?"

He glared at me. "How're your stocks doing?"

"Geez, those schnitzels are taking a long time."

I glanced towards the kitchen just as Ludwika burst through with a plate in each hand and hurried towards us. "First aid for meat lover," she announced, plunking our platters down. Farley laughed and asked for another couple of shots. She looked at me. I shook my head. He watched her go then tucked into his schnitzel. We ate in silence, ignoring each other. I remembered my supplements and dug them from my pocket and swallowed them with a sip of vodka. He pointedly focused on his cutlet. Ludwika arrived with his fresh shots and he joshed with her and got her laughing. Once more, his eyes followed her as she moved away.

"Don't do it," I said.

He gave me a look and drained one of the shots.

"Up to you, man, but—"

"Don't be a prude. It's just some chemistry we've got going on."

"Even I can see that."

"It doesn't mean anything." He reached for the other shot.

"Take it easy, cowboy. We've got dinner to get through back at my place."

"Hey. You know what? You're not my mommy."

"This thing with Ludwika, I know it's fun, but she doesn't want—"

"You don't know what she wants. It doesn't mean anything. It's just an innocent attraction. A flirtation." He said the word as if it were a rare butterfly. "If you don't savour the moment, you're not living your life."

"Look, she's not going to—"

"No, she's not going to, and I'm not going to, but it wouldn't mean anything if we did. It wouldn't matter. Animal pleasure, that's what it is. No hard feelings, life goes on, and then you die. Look—look at Genny and me, for godsakes, we could still be friends." He chuckled. "Sort of. It's all a lark. Sometimes you've—"

"What?"

"I mean, sometimes you've just got to—"

"No, what about Genny? What about her?"

He looked at me over a forkful of fried pork and egg yolk. "Oh shit," he said.

The fork descended slowly to his plate.

"You didn't know," he said in wonder. His eyes fell onto the table.

I felt the blood draining from my face.

"It was a long time ago," he said, finally looking at me.

I felt numb, with the exception of my stomach, which was falling from a great height. "What are you talking about?" I asked, although I already knew, with a certainty that chilled me to the core.

He looked at me for a long time. "It was before you were together. I would never . . . you know that, I would never do anything to come between the two of you. It was in England, before you got together. We had a, you know, a—it didn't mean anything. I broke it off, when I thought she was getting serious."

I remembered running into her on St Giles, she all teary-eyed and blue. I'd thought it was over the wretched weather. Instead it was over my best friend.

I stared down at my plate, searching for words to match the bitter taste in my mouth. "You couldn't tell me? You couldn't say something? You didn't think it was worth mentioning?"

"I always thought you knew. I thought she told you. I thought you were cool with it."

CHAPTER TWENTYTHREE

The suspense of a novel is not only in the reader, but in the novelist, who is intensely curious about what will happen to the hero.

Mary McCarthy

Writing is a socially acceptable form of schizophrenia.

E. L. Doctorow

We trudged back through a steady rain, Farley trying to engage me, but I floated in a stupor, stunned, distracted, and buzzed by vodka. When we got to the house he stopped me at the door. "Are you okay, buddy?" he asked.

"Never better. Doesn't mean anything. Long time ago."

A long, long time, their little secret, kept from me. All these years.

"It was. It didn't mean anything. Remember that." He pulled a pack of tic tacs out of his pocket and shook some into my hand. I popped them into my mouth and crunched down, not thinking anything until I realized why he'd given them to me. They'd mask the schnitzel on my breath.

A practiced hand, was Farley, at the art of deception.

Peter had arrived with Beth while we were out. They were

in the kitchen, drinks in hand, bantering with Genny and Paola.

"Look, Jack!" Genny said with an exultant smile. "Peter's got the deal!"

I ignored her. Peter grinned and waggled an envelope in his free hand. "Maybe take a few minutes now, if we can." Then he spotted Farley over my shoulder. "Farley, y'old bastard! How's she hanging?" Then, remembering where he was, he cast a sheepish look around. "Please excuse my Latin, ladies," he said, his hand to his heart. He introduced Beth as "my dear, dear friend," and slipped an arm around her waist. She was an energetic-looking woman who bore a striking resemblance to a middle-aged Shirley MacLaine. Beyond that, there was something familiar about her.

*

Peter and I went upstairs to the room I called my office. "Leave these with you," he said, pulling out the papers. "Deal's a bit out of the ordinary. Circumstances. Bunyok's got a government grant. Part of all that infrastructure money—"

"Hold on. How can that be? Since when is a novel 'infrastructure'?"

"Well, when it's 600 pages . . ." He grinned, waiting for a laugh that didn't come. "Bunyok's local MP is a Conservative. Running scared for re-election. Spreading money around like Popeye in a whore house. Got to spend it quick, before the end of the fiscal year. Use it or lose it, eh? Negotiated an advance for you."

"An advance?"

"Yep. Two hundred."

"*Two hundred thousand?*"

"No. Two hundred bucks."

"Two hundred dollars?"

"Cash."

"But I paid you more than that."

"Yep. Advance against earnings. These are your first earnings. You'll keep the whole two hundred."

I normally don't drink much in the afternoon. I was feeling a bit woozy. A lot was going on in my mind. "So, edits? When do we start on that?"

"No time. Real hurry. End of year's coming up. Besides, doesn't need edits, my view. Why waste the effort? Damn good as is."

"What about the marketing plan? And the launch?"

"Nothing for that in the grant. No tour, either—pain in the ass, anyway, what they are." He stopped and peered at me. "Unless you want to take a trip. Up to you. Grant won't cover it. No budget at Bunyok, either. Lean operation. We'll have a launch party here . . . maybe at that place . . . local place. What's it called? Grab-bag-kawitz?"

"Gzbrnznkwyc's."

He jabbed a finger in my direction. "That one! Sounds like a bee. Can't say it sober. They'll do it right! And I'll arrange to get a review. Got connections. *Toronto Star.*"

"Oh my god."

He mistook my reaction and beamed magnanimously.

That schnitzel now sat heavy in my gut. "How many copies will they run?"

"Bunyok? Maybe up to a thousand."

"A thousand?"

"Up to. Big for a poetry run. That's what they usually publish."

"But . . . it's not poetry. It's a novel."

"I know. But remember, it's just the first run. Bigger runs, once it catches on. You'll see. All you have to do is pay for a hundred."

"What?"

"Well, you take a hundred, at wholesale cost. They'll place the rest. No risk to you. The advance is yours. They'll never ask for it back. And you retain all rights. Film, comic books. Characters. Everything."

I'd had dreams of producing a work of literary merit—the Great English-Canadian Novel. Now *Blown to Hell* would emerge in the world as a Tory pork-barrel project at some arty, quasi-vanity press that specialized in *poetry*. It seemed I could descend no lower.

*

The evening went by in a blur. I took charge of filling everyone's glasses and helped carry things out to the table, but I didn't say much, just enough to be polite and register as present. It must be said I had a lot on my mind.

In addition to Farley and Paola, there were Murray and Darlene, and Anthony of course; and Genny's friend Andrea, a vegan of long-standing, the inspiration for Genny's own foray into raw veganism. Andrea was her colleague at the Department of Womyn's Studies. Her specialty was men's studies, an offshoot of womyn's studies focusing on issues of male privilege and various social and historical constructs of men and virility. For the love of Thor I couldn't understand what that meant, or how it justified a place at a university; but on a personal level, Andrea had always struck me as a decent type. Every December at the department's winter solstice and world cuisine potluck party, she played Mother Hera, sweeping into the room in a flowing white gossamer gown to distribute gender-neutral toys to all the one- and two-mothered children. She played the role with zest and maternal good humour.

Dinner began decorously with a conventional green salad, over which we had the usual conversation about the weather. Then Genny proposed a toast to my book deal, and everyone raised a glass to me, which I numbly acknowledged. A lot to absorb, I said. Not really the place to discuss, but thanks.

Genny threw an arm around my shoulders and gave me a kiss on the cheek. "Oh you!" she said. "You're always so modest."

"I have a lot to be modest about."

"Going to make a big splash, that's for sure," Peter said.

"I'm sure that's the case," Anthony said, "But I still think you should self-publish. The whole theory of Self—"

"No, this is the way to go," Farley said. "This is how it happens. This guy's worked hard for this moment. We should celebrate his achievement."

"You don't know the half of it," Genny said. "This is what comes of hard work and inspiration. He's never compromised on anything to get to this point."

My two great defenders, my champions: Genny and Farley.

When it was clear I was not going to take up the subject, the conversation moved on. There was a lot of interest in the meal, which Genny announced would be entirely raw vegan. Beyond Andrea, none of the guests had ever had a raw vegan meal—or even imagined one.

"Daddy calls it rabbit food," Chloe said.

Andrea's presence meant that Genny didn't have to answer every question about raw veganism herself. In fact, Andrea answered most of them with chipper enthusiasm and considerable knowledge. But she did not exactly inspire confidence, for she was thin as a stick, gaunt, and bordering on cadaverous, her elbows sharp as Celine Dion's.

"Looking forward to this," Peter said. "I'll try anything once. Beth and I had ostrich just the other day, in New York. She'd had it before but it was new to me."

Beth told us how she'd once visited a village in Namibia where she was received as an honoured guest. At lunch she was presented with an ostrich omelette; for a moment she'd feared giving offence by not being able to finish it. "An ostrich egg is about the size of a bowling ball," she said, gesturing. "Imagine a forty-eight egg omelette." To her relief, everyone had chipped in and eaten it communally.

As she talked I realized why she looked familiar. I'd seen her on television. She was a print journalist who'd covered politics and out-of-the-way conflicts in Africa. Genny had read her columns and liked her post-colonial perspective. I could see them getting on like a house on fire.

"Ostrich seems to be the It-bird at the moment," Peter said. "The meat, that is. Healthy, good for the heart, that sort of thing. They serve it rare like beef. Fabulous." He beamed happily at the thought and looked around the table. His eyes settled on Andrea and his smile faded. "You eat *poultry*, don't you, Andrea?"

Andrea smiled good-naturedly and explained about the various gradations of vegetarianism.

" 'Pescetarian'," Farley repeated. Since our arrival he'd been subdued, and considering the volume of vodka he'd ingested he was probably drunk, but he perked up now at a word he found worthy.

"It seems pretty complicated," Peter said, counting off on his fingers. "Semi, lacto, ovo, pesco-pollo . . ."

"I like all the options," Anthony said. "You've got plenty of choice, as a vegetarian. You can self-define your veggie-Self."

"But vegan, this raw vegan we're chowing down on tonight—is it *totally* vegetarian?" Murray asked, not hiding his dismay.

"I tried going vegetarian," Darlene confessed, "but I could never stick with it. I always caved when I passed KFC or the chicken stand at Loblaws."

Beside her, his question unanswered, Murray cast a mournful glance towards the kitchen. There were no mouth-watering aromas emanating from there. In fact, there were no aromas at all.

After we'd cleared the salad bowls Genny brought a tureen to the table and began to ladle green soup into bowls. "Oh! What's this?" Paola asked.

"It's called laver chowder," Andrea said. "I brought it. It's one of my favourites."

"Laver is a kind of seaweed," Genny explained.

"Algae, actually," I said, and when she looked at me I added, "technically."

Farley lifted a spoon to his mouth and tasted. I did the same. Cold, salty, lemony, a bit fishy. "Mmm," he said, on his best behaviour. He could really hold his booze. Far better than me.

Anthony slurped loudly. "Andrea, my compliments. This is a delightful summery treat. I've always enjoyed vichyssoise on a nice hot day."

Outside, a November gale was beginning to blow.

"Vichyssoise isn't usually vegan, but you can make it vegan," Andrea said.

Anthony studied her chest with interest. "How long have you been a vegan, Andrea?"

"I've been a vegetarian for twenty years. Since I was an undergrad. I ate dairy in those days, then went vegan ten years ago. I've been a raw vegan for about three years."

"You're on some kind of a quest," Anthony said, flashing a horsy grin. "A journey, in search of Self—"

"Darlene," Genny said, "Murray told me you just won a TV role."

I popped up to clear plates as Darlene described her latest gig, a recurring role in a Canadian series about a woman that goes back in time to relive pivotal incidents and fix her mistakes. As I thought about that possibility and what I'd fix, I met Genny in the kitchen.

"Are you okay?" she whispered.

"Uh huh."

"You're really quiet. Is something wrong?"

"Nope. Nothing at all."

"Then cheer up, baby. This is your big day."

"I'm not your baby. Don't tell me what to do."

I saw her blink, then I was through into the dining room, feeling numb, angry, dead, sad, resentful, remorseful—and an overwhelming desire to be somewhere else. I drained my wine glass then grabbed a bottle of wine in each hand and went around the table. "Red or white, Andrea? What *is* the rule for a raw vegan meal?" Then, raising my voice, "Genny? Are you sure you can have wine? Is it kosher for a raw vegan?"

Genny appeared in the doorway but Andrea spoke first. "Some wines do use animal by-products," she said, "but most are all right. It depends how far you want to take it."

"Right. I guess you can't be too doctrinaire. At the same time," I added, smiling at Genny, "you don't want to be loose with your morals. It's all about principles, I suppose. You have to be true to your principles. Genny! What do you say? Red or white?"

Genny's eyes narrowed. For a moment she nibbled on her lower lip. "Red, I think," she said, looking me in the eye. I could feel Farley's eyes on me too.

"Do you have any more root beer, Shakespeare?" Anthony asked.

"Us too, Daddy," Chloe said on behalf of Lucia.

When Genny announced that the main course was linguini, I watched the reactions around the table. Murray sniffed the air and looked hopefully towards the kitchen. Peter grinned and smacked his lips and stretched an arm across the back of Beth's chair. Farley's eyes met Paola's, and the girls, Chloe and Lucia, both declared linguini was their favourite!

"Genny, I'll give you a hand in the kitchen," Farley said, getting up quickly.

"No, no. Sit, Farley," Paola said, pulling him back into his chair. "I'll do it." Then, to everyone else, "I helped Genny with it this afternoon. I was so curious!"

A look of desperation crossed Farley's face. He drained his wineglass and avoided my eye.

"I like to cook mySelf," Anthony said. "But I confess I like meat. I guess it's my vice. Cooking raw vegetarian would be totally new to me."

"Raw *vegans*," Andrea clarified gently, "don't cook per se. In fact, that's the whole point. We don't heat anything beyond 118 degrees."

"That seems pretty hot."

"Fahrenheit."

"Whoa! No kidding," Peter said. "That . . . that's like a summer day in Calcutta! Hottest place I ever saw. God, it stank." He began relating a story about a business trip he'd taken, years ago, to India.

As he spoke I topped up the glasses around the table, draining my own before filling it to the brim.

Peter finished his anecdote, which involved street defecation and a dead cow. There was a brief silence, then Anthony cleared his throat, but Darlene spoke first to ask why raw vegans didn't cook beyond 118 degrees Fahrenheit.

"Cooking destroys micronutrients and produces carcinogens. So when we prepare raw vegan food, we use low heat, or even the sun, to dehydrate instead of cook."

Farley burped quietly into his fist, a satisfied, meat-eater's postprandial belch. I caught the scent of schnitzel where I sat. "Whoa! I almost forgot the candles," I said, and jumped up.

Genny and Paola were plating linguini in the kitchen. I looked in a cupboard for the scented candles Genny always bought but there were none. I went to check in the basement.

*

Away from the crowd, it was my first chance to think. Why did I feel this way? And what was I feeling, exactly? My rational mind offered a plethora of reasonable arguments. It had been years ago. Water under the bridge. We were all adults. Nobody hurt. Besides, I'd only just met her then—we were nothing to each other. Why shouldn't she fall for him? There was nothing wrong in that. He was *Farley*; seduction was what he did. And why wouldn't he turn it on for Genny? She was beautiful, young, available. And me—what was my problem? I'd never objected to any of Farley's conquests, and Genny was a woman of free will. She was nobody's possession.

Then why was I feeling this way now?

I slumped onto a steamer trunk and held my head in my hands.

Why was I offended by a youthful, decades-old sexual encounter? Why did I feel betrayed, as if my life was built on a false foundation, that it was underpinned by quicksand, that all my assumptions had been wrong?

It wasn't that they'd slept together. That wasn't what hurt. It was being treated like a chump. There was Farley, with his travelling academic road show, his world-renowned expertise on the Welsh bard and literary fame. There was Genny, with her intense principles and serious pursuit of change through knowledge. And there was me, the easy-going floater, ever malleable to the will of others—at best apathetic, never truly engaged. I lived in a world of black and white, unable like a *normal* person to discern shades of grey or hints of hue and texture. Constantly bewildered, I blew with the breeze, this way, that—just like my protagonist, the hapless Broughton. So they'd decided I couldn't be trusted with the truth. They'd kept it to themselves, all these years, their little carnal secret kept from me. How many knowing glances had they exchanged, how many times had one of them rolled eyes at the other, and the other nodded, their signals conveying, *it's just how he is.*

Nothing meant what I'd thought it had. My life, which I'd thought I understood at last, over which I'd finally taken control, had no real meaning. I was a lie, not a man—not someone to be entrusted with a truth, not a husband, not a person with something to say. A nobody.

I was hurt, but I couldn't blame them. I was angry, but not with them. *I* was the problem. It was *me*. I couldn't be trusted. I couldn't be relied upon. I was of no consequence. I'd had no impact, made no inroads, achieved no breakthroughs to make the world a better place. I'd merely floated along, an appendage to substance with none of my own. I'd accomplished nothing with my life. I had not solved Fermat's last theorem, never brokered peace between warring parties, never put myself between whaler and whale. Never, it seemed, had an honest relationship, one in which I could be trusted.

Now I saw the truth of my life, and a stark fact stared me in the face: that September day I'd been spared for no purpose, reprieved for no end. My dream of writing was a delusion. Futility, that was my calling, as it had been all my life. My enduring legacy would not be words that moved a single soul to tears. I would not be remembered for any piece of fiction. I would never be a man of letters, but an anonymous backroom nonentity, some hollow person who dealt with numbers. I was no financial Frankenstein, as Farley had long maintained, but a nameless, faceless, soulless functionary, a conscienceless monster behind a horrible, egregious falsehood: those derivatives I'd created, the ones used to finagle the truth. They would be the full extent of my legacy, the sum total of my contribution to fiction.

Voices now, a chorus sang to my inadequacy, my failure, the inconsequence of my life. And a single voice, a soloist, chipped in from high above.

"Daddy, who are you talking to?" Chloe, halfway down the stairs, was looking at me oddly.

"Nobody, Chloe. I'm just mumbling to myself. I do that sometimes. I've got the candles."

"Daddy, come upstairs. We're ready for the main course."

*

I plunked a sputtering apricot-scented candle on the table in front of Farley just as Genny and Paola delivered the last of the plates to the table. "It's beautiful!" Darlene gushed. It was true. Each plate contained a formed tower of orange- and cream-coloured linguini artfully drizzled with a reddish cream sauce and garnished with a chiffonade of basil. Beth and Peter both made appreciative comments on the presentation; Anthony seemed moved by the very sight.

"Well, you can't go wrong with fresh," Genny replied. "Please, everyone. Bon appétit."

Around the table diners leaned forward, admiring their plates, anticipating their first taste. Cutlery clinked, otherwise there was silence as they sampled initially, then again, as if they couldn't believe the evidence of the first morsel.

Andrea was the first to speak. "This is delicious, Genny."

Instantly there were murmurs of "Oh, yes!" "This is fantastic!" "Mmm . . ." "Lovely!"

Silence fell again.

"Mine's cold," Lucia whispered to her mother.

"This, ah, texture," Murray said, "it's unusual for pasta. It's a bit crunchy."

"It's not actually linguini," Genny said. "What looks like

pasta is actually carrot and parsnip, cut into strands."

"Mmm-mmm," somebody murmured, this time without conviction. The table was quiet but for the clink of silver on dishes. With his fork, Murray poked at the pile on his plate as though it concealed a snake. Chloe and Lucia moved bits of food from one side of their plates to the other in a practiced show of eating. Peter downed his glass and looked hopefully towards the wine bottle.

But Farley, having eaten a schnitzel a bare ninety minutes before, finished his plate with surprising speed. "This is delicious," he said. "I was ravenous. Genny? Could you help me get some more in the kitchen?" He got up to follow her out, and as he passed through the doorway he glanced back at the table. A frown crossed his face when he realized Chloe and Lucia had also gotten up.

"Mommy, can we have some bread?" Chloe said.

Genny looked mildly annoyed when she returned to the table behind the girls. Farley returned a moment later. He'd forgotten his plate in the kitchen.

"Would you ever heat this up?" Anthony asked. "You know, to make it hot?"

"I like it at room temperature," Paola said. "It's a nice change from normal food."

"So . . ." Murray said. "The cheese, or cream, in the sauce. What is that?"

"It's called macadamia mozzarella," Andrea said. "It's not real cheese. It's made from nuts—macadamias and cashews, with a bit of yeast and lemon juice."

"You wouldn't even know!" Paola said. "Would you, Farley?"

"I don't know why there aren't more raw vegan restaurants around," Darlene said. "It'd be a nice healthy alternative for people." She was being kind, like Paola, but she'd drawn everyone's attention just as Murray, sitting beside her, spat something into his napkin.

"Raw vegan for non-vegans," Anthony said. "I know this isn't an easy thing to pull off, Genny, but it's a statement of

True Self. A toast to the cook— ahh . . . to the preparer." He raised his glass and repeated, "To the preparer!"

We all drank to Genny the preparer.

Murray was still struggling with the logic of raw veganism. "This may sound stupid, Genny, but why bother calling it pasta, or mozzarella, when it's carrots and nuts?"

Genny looked at Andrea. "Well . . . People are familiar with those."

"But if you wanted pasta, wouldn't you just eat pasta? Or if you wanted to eat cheese—"

"I realize it's not to everyone's taste," Genny said a bit sharply, forcing a tight smile. "But it is authentic."

A little of my numbness receded as I observed the expression on her face. Genny, dear Genny—Genny at the centre of my soul. Genny, my saving grace, my good fortune, my lucky charm. I couldn't bear to see her hurt. I needed to say something to shore her up. "Genny's right," I said, and all eyes turned on me. "It may not be to all our tastes. It may not be anyone's—Andrea excepted." I swung my glass in her direction, sloshed wine on the tablecloth, and completely lost my chain of thought. I mumbled a whoops then something about authenticity, the real thing, the raw deal, now eat your veggies, trying to lighten the mood. "More wine, anyone, to help with the job?"

"Hear, hear," someone said. I think it was Peter. His glass was certainly the first one extended, a hungry nestling's greedy beak. As I poured I stole a glance at Genny. Her eyes were still on me. There was no gratitude in her expression. She did not look pleased at all.

*

When everybody left we sent Chloe up to have a bath while we did the clean up. We worked in silence, me avoiding her, she avoiding me. She was angry about the dinner, and upset with me. Dishes clanged and clinked carelessly like clay pigeons at a skeet shoot.

"Do you want to talk about what's bothering you?" she asked at last.

"There's nothing bothering me."
"There is."
"No."
"Yes."
Silence.

"Okay. What's bothering me . . . Let me see. I've got a lot on my mind. Oh, yes. I remember now. You fucked Farley is what's bothering me."

She stood very still and studied my face, her blue eyes piercing like lasers. Then she sighed. "Yes," she said matter-of-factly. "I did. A lifetime ago. I was young and lonely and vulnerable. I was a bad judge of character and I slept with him. It was before I was with you."

"And you never told me. All these years, it just slipped your mind? You didn't think I should know?"

"It didn't matter. It's you I love."

"How can it not matter? Twenty years, you keep it a secret."

"It was no secret. It was a fact we didn't discuss because it meant nothing. It's you I love."

"There you were, bawling your eyes out—and you were coming from balling him. And stupid, blind me, not seeing the truth . . ."

"I was such a fool to fall for his line. But it wasn't love. And then I met you. You never broke my heart. You never lied to me. You're not even capable of that. It's you I love. Not him or anyone else. You."

I remained silent. We looked at each other from opposite sides of the room. Her eyes melted.

"I worry about you, baby."

"Don't," I said and turned away.

CHAPTER TWENTYFOUR

The trouble with writing a book about yourself is that you can't fool around. If you write about someone else, you can stretch the truth from here to Finland. If you write about yourself the slightest deviation makes you realize instantly that there may be honour among thieves, but you are just a dirty liar.

Groucho Marx

In writing, you must kill all your darlings.

William Faulkner

It is with heavy heart that I continue my friend's unfinished story, and in preamble to it I profess my narrative limitations. I am not omniscient. I have relied upon the evidentiary trail, the notes he left, along with what I pieced together from my own observations and those of others, primarily Genny. In places the reader may infer that I have implied a thing I have not stated; that is the reader's prerogative, although my friend would be puzzled by it. He was never one to imply anything, not effectively anyway, nor trust an inference, let alone pick one up. Straight talk was what he craved, something of a contradiction in an accomplished dissembler such as him, but there it is. All I will say is that Truth exists in the assemblage of words upon a page; thus the truth lies herein and the truth, after editing, always lies. Such is the conundrum of creative non-fiction.

I will attempt not to intrude but to disappear into the story as it unfolds—as I have attempted thus far, although the fragmentary state of his notes has required me to complete certain parts of the preceding chapters he left unfinished. In doing so I have taken a few liberties, inserting or correcting certain figures of speech where they begged placement or tweak. A picture may be worth a thousand words but my chum, ever challenged by imagery, was no friend of Kodachrome.

*

Factors had conspired to create, for him, a perfect storm, a tempest of arguable scale but undeniable consequence. His world was upended, all his comfortable assumptions pulverised to dust. Beset by doubt, unsure about the merit of anything he had ever done, he reviewed the events of his life and could vouch for only one thing: his love for Genny and Chloe. But had *he* ever been truly loved? Or had he merely been tolerated as an oddity, a charity case, a human project?

He sank deep into depression and questioned everything. What about his career in structured finance? What of his mastery of the notion of risk? He had channelled his energy into a house of cards, thrown his creativity into building an illusion of security in a cosmos of danger. Those grandly-named but toxic "assets" on which he'd toiled—those credit default swaps and mortgage-backed securities, those collateralized, securitized and synthesized debt obligations—had enriched a few but brought their buyers down and the world to the brink of collapse. Where it teetered still; it could yet go.

He had used his acumen, done what was asked of him, raised no objections. He'd shrugged and taken the money, then retreated in search of redemption, turned his back on what he'd wrought and lost himself in the delusion of writing the Great English-Canadian Novel.

He realized that even his crazy literary pretensions were qualified, hyphenated, categorical.

He questioned his choices. Why numbers, not words? Why Broughton, not Vancouver? Why follow, not lead?

He questioned his talent. Him, a writer? What hubris. He knew now he would never incite anyone to say: that story moved me like no other.

He listened to the rasp and rattle of his scarred lungs and believed, without knowing why, that he had no time left, that he had squandered his chances. A heavy certainty settled upon him that he had yet to make his mark and would never do so.

He was the thin stem of a crystal vessel (empty, of course). He felt brittle, like old glass, yet knew he would never crack. That would be too decisive, too definitive for him. Rather than break he would dissolve like overnight ice, without consequence or legacy.

For days, absorbed in self-pity, he moped about the house. Genny tried to bolster his spirits. Eat some soup, get some rest. I love you. Do you want to go for a walk? Do you forgive me? Your book is going to make it. You were coughing last night. Take your ma huang. It's good for your breathing. Where's your puffer? Remember your St John's wort. Drink the tea I bought you. What did the doctor say? Take that too.

Do you forgive me, she asked him again.

He knew he had nothing to forgive; he knew she knew that too. It was a price she was willing to pay, and it broke his heart. He told her she was without fault and hugged her close, wondering again why she was with him. He felt her relax in his arms. It's me, he told her (and felt her tense again). I need to work things out.

He realized he might never do that, but that he had to rouse himself, had to shake himself out of this morbid mood. He took the supplements that Genny recommended; he took his various medications. He forced himself out of the house, knowing exercise would do him good. He spent a day walking in the dreary November rain, felt the sting of sleet on his face, the wind in his tearing eyes. He clumped through puddles, head down, breathing the cold damp air, wrestling with his past, the present, his doubts.

In the days that followed he took more long walks along the shores of Lake Ontario, the banks of the Humber and the Don, through neighbourhoods, crumbling industrial zones, the city's wending and mysterious ravines.

Genny took it as a good sign that he was getting out.

He told himself the darkness would fade, as it had always done before; that he had to endure this endless night until the light returned. Truthfully, he knew no other way—perseverance was deeply ingrained in him. At an early age he'd learned the two principles of prairie survival: work hard, and expect setbacks. When calamity struck (as it inevitably did), you had to persist—until the next hailstorm or tornado, the next drought or flood or autumn blizzard that caught the wheat still standing. Then once more you picked yourself up, cinched your belt a further notch, and carried on. That was the nature of prairie pluck: you made something of a bad hand.

Thus, eventually, he resolved to write. Not his frivolous musical, but something of substance. He would complete *No Bolt Too Small*, his parabolic allegory of hope, even though, just then, it felt false: a story of hope, from a man who felt none himself.

*

Despite his funk he kept informed on his environmental causes. He had to keep up with them—they were relevant to his project. They were the whole point of his paragory.

The situation appalled him. The latest round of global climate talks was heading for failure. Lobbyists and denialists were undermining the science of global warming. Canadian and American oil interests talked about carbon intensity, not emission reductions. A spokesman for European industry, an executive from Heil AG (*quelle surprise*, he thought bitterly) insisted there could be no treaty that did not bind developing nations to the same standards as the developed world.

He felt shame at his country's stance, anger at its being part of the problem not the solution. He thought of the challenges of the past that *had* been overcome. And more recently: it looked now that the scourge of swine flu—the dreaded novel strain of the H1N1 virus—had been avoided. There was a vaccine. People were still getting sick but not in the numbers feared, and far fewer were dying. A serious challenge had been met at great cost. But every challenge had a cost. Every challenge demanded a sacrifice. In his mind's eye he saw the graves at Beny-sur-Mer. Those men and the endeavour they were part of inspired him still.

He tried to write, but there were so many distractions. Chloe, playing the piano. Chloe, asking for help with math. "Daddy, can you show me something on the computer?" He helped her when she asked, and tried to be chipper about it. It wasn't her fault. But his spirits were so low that he could not fake happiness. "What's wrong with Daddy?" he heard Chloe ask from the other room. After a moment's silence he heard Genny's reply. "He's just feeling sad." Did they not know he could hear? How could he work with them chattering back and forth like sparrows? It took him out of the writerly mood. Genny telling him, "I made you some rooibos." Genny asking, "Are you all right?" Genny urging, "Come to bed. You need to sleep," when he needed to work. When he went to the compost bin, Anthony would corner him and prattle on about Self and selfishness, or ask how the book was going. People on the street with cell phones, walking slowly, talking overloud; JW's and charities at the door—distractions were everywhere. He knew he had but little time. He had a lifetime of floating, vacillation, indecision, dissembling, and avoidance for which to make amends. How could he do so if he couldn't concentrate, if he was constantly distracted?

He was edgy, anxious. He stalled on his allegory and started work on his musical again, reasoning a change was as good as a rest.

Fate intervenes in strange ways, shapes destinies on apparent whim, changes lives without a backward glance. So it was that one of those everyday distractions changed his life. One day he was at his computer, not writing but thinking about writing. He felt afterwards that at the moment when fate intervened, in that instant, he was on the brink of a major breakthrough. He could not attribute this belief to any particular thought or inspiration, for he could not recall what was going through his mind, exactly, at that particular moment. He just knew that the ringing sound that had caused him to jump had also caused him to lose the idea forever.

He answered the phone.

It was Porlock Polling and Market Research, inquiring if there was an adult in the household willing to participate in an upcoming focus group.

As annoyed as he was at the loss of an irrecoverable idea, and the fact that it was Porlock (again) responsible for it, he remembered that focus groups paid honoraria and so did not hang up. He answered all the qualifying questions about age, income (a small lie), and a few to test his knowledge of the subject matter. These were general attitudinal queries about "green products" containing phrases like "environmental responsibility," "stewardship," and "corporate citizenship." With an eye to the cash he answered without signalling the strength of his personal views.

"You fit the demographic profile we're looking for," said the researcher. "If you'd like to participate we're offering an honorarium . . ." She described the session: participants would listen to a live presentation by a senior executive of the client, a firm that produced a line of environment-friendly products. They were testing North American reaction to this man, who was known in Europe as Uncle Rolf, a friendly personification of his company.

"Like Gaelan Weston and the ING guy."

"Yes, I suppose," replied the Porlock researcher.

"What's the name of the company?"

The woman referred to her notes—it was the first time

she had been asked the question. "The company is called . . . let's see . . . Heil AG," she said. "It's German."

He felt a sudden rush of adrenalin. "Austrian," he said.

"It says here Mr Heil is coming from Germany. Well, it's definitely European-based. It's good you've heard of it," said the woman from Porlock. "We're looking for informed participants."

*

He contemplated Heil AG: denier of war crimes and product liability, greenwasher extraordinaire. He recalled his anger at the company's BPA-laced bottles; he felt it anew. All thoughts of *Bolt* and *North Pacific* were forgotten now as he listened to a voice in his head, a voice that called on him to act.

No, this was more than a call. He with his preoccupations, his concern about what humans were doing to the planet, to other species, to themselves; he who had ingested toxic dust and paid the price, whose lungs wheezed and rumbled and fought for breath—he felt sure he'd been Chosen.

He was shocked when he learned where Porlock was located. It was on the penthouse floor of a mid-rise tower at the foot of Yonge Street. He knew the building. It stood profiled against Lake Ontario, poised like a solo performer before the city's elite, on stage before the soaring corporate towers to its north. It was grandly named the World Trade Centre.

He'd had two close calls in another World Trade Centre. This combined with the fact that Heil was Porlock's client made him all the more certain that he had been Chosen, and he knew with crystal clarity what he would do. No more sitting on his hands. At long last, he would take direct action.

He had a week to develop a plan.

During those days he felt more alive than he had in weeks. He was focused and energized. He had purpose; he was committed to action. No longer would he vacillate.

His family noticed the difference. "You look good today, Jack," Genny said. "You've got a bounce in your step."

In his first feat of direct action, determined never again to vacillate towards her either, he said, "I love you."

Her jaw dropped open then she got teary and took him in her arms.

"I'll bet your imagination's really humming, Daddy," Chloe said that night. "I can tell when it is."

"It's humming all right," he said and poked her in the tummy. "It's because I love *you*."

She was getting too old for pokes in the tummy, but she didn't object. Instead, happy to see his spirits high, she poked him back.

He made a list of things he needed. Most of them he could get at his favourite hardware store on Roncesvalles—a box cutter, some sturdy rope, duct tape, spray paint—but there were a few other things he needed: an emergency hammer, the kind that can crack a windshield or a safety window; a long swath of cloth, like a tarp with eyelets; the thickest cable ties he could get; and a duffel bag to hold everything. He'd have to make a few trips around town for them. A winter storm was in the forecast; he needed to plan his movements and get everything before it hit.

*

Two months after his death, *Blown to Hell* was released without fanfare by Bunyok Press. It was a small print run, just a thousand copies in trade paperback, yet his friends gathered at Gzbrnznkwyc's to toast his accomplishment: he had become, for all his anguish, and albeit posthumously, a published author.

Bunyok's budget was insufficient to pay for original art work. Thus *Blown*'s cover was a simple design in navy blue (for the British) with red and yellow bars (for the Spanish), superimposed with a photo of the Cree chief Owaktawalawathai (representing the coastal aboriginals) astride his horse. The picture, chosen personally and inexplicably by the widow Patersdotter, was in the public domain and had been ready at hand for Bunyok which, funded by a government grant, had previously published a volume of historical photographs depicting the Plains Indians. Bunyok had intended to produce a series, but there had been no more grants and it had never gotten around to it.

Agent Peter Wannacutt kept his word and arranged a review in the *Toronto Star*, a newspaper the author had hated passionately for its predictably impassioned, knee-jerk sentimentality for the failed, the down on their luck, and the Toronto Maple Leafs. Champion of the second rate—that was his view of the *Star*. The review was positive, even laudatory, recognizing in *Blown* a roundabout ecological allegory, "a story set in an unspoiled Eden where despoliation and original sin coincide." It was written by academic Farley Lictor, whom the *Star* described as an international expert on the poet Dylan Thomas and author of numerous academic volumes and works of fiction. In his conclusion, Lictor declared his long acquaintance with the author and lamented his tragic demise. "He was a man of principle," he said. "and the circumstances of his death epitomize his burden."

The review was reprinted in various Saskatchewan weeklies. Earl Yeares, a retired professor from the author's alma mater who vaguely remembered his former student, added his own tribute in a letter published in the province's two main dailies. He called the author's death "a great loss to the canon, a void in the pantheon of historical maritime fiction authored by Saskatchewan-born writers." When asked to comment on his old professor's assessment, Dr Lictor coined a term, the canontheon, to describe the body that had suffered this loss.

The book did not sell. Bunyok Press failed to place it with booksellers, relying instead on direct internet sales. The strategy puzzled insiders to the author's saga—his widow, his agent, and Farley Lictor. Their enquiries went unanswered, until six weeks after *Blown's* publication, when Bunyok, having exhausted the last of the cash from the grants which had kept it afloat, tumbled into bankruptcy. Its owners, a husband and wife duo, had never physically resided in Kamsack. They'd rented a vacant storefront there for a dollar a month, thus securing a postal code (and tax losses for the building's owner). This scratch-my-back arrangement enabled them to qualify for various cultural grants while actually living in suburban Tucson, from where they ran a virtual publishing house while the money lasted.

The accounts indicated that fewer than a hundred books had been sold on the internet—the publishers had targeted hobbyist historians, but had gained little traction before the bailiffs arrived at their Tucson mansion. The unsold books were in fact not stored in Kamsack, or Tucson, but in a warehouse in Etobicoke, where they'd been shipped directly from their cut-rate printing plant in China. (Bunyok was hip to off-shoring but tragically slow to embrace print-on-demand.) The receiver overseeing the company's liquidation, having taken a hard-eyed look at its assets, deemed the remaining copies of *Blown* to be of no commercial value; they would have been pulped had not the author's widow purchased them for a dollar and the cost of a cube van rental. The eight hundred unsold copies joined the remnants of her husband's hundred, already stored in the basement of her Toronto home. Patersdotter subsequently donated copies to libraries across the country in memory of her late husband who (she said in a touching covering letter) had been her soul mate, a man tortured by his compulsion to write. She appended both the Lictor review and the letter by doddering old Professor Yeares, in case the recipient librarians had not heard of the book.

This seemed to be the end of the late author's quest, a sad and ignominious last chapter to his literary odyssey. By all appearances *Blown to Hell* was destined for oblivion, judged by the world's apathetic response to be without merit, a piece of overlong fiction with a home in a handful of public libraries; a lost and unlamented work.

*

And this would have been the novel's fate but for a strange series of events that revived, or more accurately, created interest in it.

We know now that these events began innocuously enough with a brag session at a chichi bar in the west end of Toronto, an old railroad hotel that had fallen to the status of flophouse before being renovated and socially rehabilitated, the latter by evicting its occupants (a collection of mental patients, addicts, artists, and other down-and-outs) and upping the price of beer to prevent their return. One Thursday night, five urban hipsters were drinking imported suds and arguing over an idea that one of them, an intellectual property agent and man-about-town named Phil Regency, had been batting around for months. His notion was to use electronic social media to create a cultural phenomenon beyond anything yet achieved, just to demonstrate their reach and power. Infinite Summer, the on-line initiative to promote David Foster Wallace's *Infinite Jest*, was a drop in the bucket, he told his friends. Something much bigger was possible.

The rest of the hipsters wanted to talk about beards versus tattoos, the price of E, and where they were going to eat.

"We could mount a pilot to prove it," Phil said. "It would get a lot of publicity."

At this, they perked up. They saw themselves as leaders of the new creative class—media-savvy operators, trend setters, fashion arbiters, social critics, each a man of letters and noted metrosexual in his own right. They all knew the value of self-marketing. Anything that would garner publicity was worth considering.

Over hoppy Leffes and gassy Becks, (both overpriced, but you had to be seen living, and that didn't include anything brewed in Canada) they talked the idea through. Phil maintained that the groundwork had to be meticulous to maximize reach and impact.

"I can see how it's possible," one of them, the latest to join their regular circle, said. "You could build a big tent, metaphorically—an e-tent, hah ha, that draws in hundreds, thousands of people. A niche social network, but with unrivalled reach." He paused, and they all nodded thoughtfully. "But isn't what you want to do, like, manipulative?"

They rest of them gasped. "Certainly not," Phil said coldly. "It's called curation."

The others laughed, and the one who'd asked the question blushed.

"We could start peer-to-peer with 'user-generated content'," one of them suggested. "Seed it, then target some mavens and alpha users, and nudge them towards it. Once they pick it up we're into maintenance mode. It's the power law curve from there." The others nodded, unwilling to admit they didn't know what that meant.

"We'd obviously kickoff astroturfing," the new guy said, trying to recoup some cred, "and rely on a viral expansion loop. Every visitor hit, every 'like' or share or hashtag link attracts more hits, more friends, more fans, and each of those bags more."

"The campaign," Phil said, "would incorporate virality." The others nodded again; they all wanted to be associated with virality. It sounded bleeding edge.

"We could build buzz with social bookmarking and crowdsource demand with collaborative tagging," the new guy continued. "That would build metadata around the content."

The others nodded.

"We could do all of that," the first guy said. "And we could crowdcast on a pull platform and deploy sockpuppets."

The other regulars stared at him with undisguised rancour. He misread their looks and thought they were going to challenge him. "I read that somewhere," he said quickly.

"We don't need to master it all tonight," said Phil Regency, casually looking up from his phone where he was texting himself a note about crowdsourcing, crowdcasting and mavens. "We just need to decide to do it, then get it going."

They sipped their Euro-beer (wishing it was pino noir, which was admittedly passé, or even chardonnay— chardonnay was making a comeback (again!)—but this was their once-a-month downmarket night and beer it had to be. Who knew who might be watching?).

"So what would the pilot be?" one of them asked.

Phil had been sure they would come for the candy. "Not only a pilot. A prank. I've got this idea I've been toying with. Do you know Sarah Binks?"

The others looked uncertain. "The hip hop singer?" one ventured.

"Hardly. 'The Sweet Songstress of Saskatchewan.'" The others looked at him even more uncertainly. They didn't know what he was getting at. Besides, the mere mention of Saskatchewan was un-cool, like galoshes, curling, or long underwear from Stanfield's. "She's not a real person. She's a fictional poet. Years ago, a guy wrote a fake biography about her, as if she were real. It was a hoax, but some people didn't get it. They thought she was legit."

"But Phil," one of his companions said. "Poetry is last century. It's all spoken word now."

The others didn't get it, either. Phil could see they were losing interest. It was that mention of Saskatchewan. "Look, here's what we do. We pick a dud of a novel by a dud novelist. Then we plug both of them. Use Facebook and Twitter and other platforms to incite interest and direct people to our site. We'll manufacture buzz. We'll make it the It thing. We'll create a phenomenon and keep feeding it. Then once it's underway, once it's big, really big, we'll tell everybody what we've done."

The others considered the idea.

It'll take too long, one of them said. Too much work. Besides, shouldn't we choose something cool? What if it doesn't take off? another asked, checking his phone for messages. We'd have wasted our time. They were all marketing types, into buzz, mostly about themselves. Putting effort into plugging someone else with no sure payoff, well ...

A waiter interrupted to offer them menus.

"No, no," someone said, waving him off. "Let's do sushi! I know a place around here that does *amazing* sushi!"

"Ahch—sushi!" another said. "That is *so* 2006. Let's do sashimi. There's nothing like blue fin tuna. It's *the* rarest endangered species on the *planet*."

"We could be the *last* people on Earth to eat blue fish tuna—"

"We could be the *first* of the last."

"Tuna. Japan," one of them sniffed. "That's so eighties. Think China. Bird's nest soup—now *that's* rare. I know where we can get the best in all Chinatown. It's a little hole in the wall you wouldn't—"

"Oh come on. China's so last September now . . ."

Phil saw that he'd lost them, but the conversation had served its purpose. He had their ideas, and as slapdash as they were, they showed promise. He'd research them on his own. None of these guys had the big picture, a clear concept of the prize. He could already see himself alone before the cameras as he disclosed the hoax. Imagine the publicity, the impact on his reputation—the far-sighted genius behind the biggest marketing prank of the decade, engineered for and delivered via new social media. He'd be set for life.

He needed a product to plug—a certifiable dud—and he already had something in mind. A short while before he had seen a book review in the *Star*. He'd recognized the title because he'd rejected the book himself. Sweet and sweeter! That would gain him a delicious degree of notoriety. No, he didn't need the others—who were putting on their coats now, intent on some Creole-Lithuanian fusion at a new place on Ossington. Phil was feeling hungry himself. He reached for his own coat.

He would get on this in the morning. The research, to refine a plan (he wouldn't do it himself—he had an unpaid intern at the office), then a few calls. He knew people who could set up the e-frastructure and help out with the viral buzz to implement the scheme. He could trust them to be discrete. They were techies, anyway. He wouldn't let them in on the big picture.

Online booksellers and librarians across the country began to receive queries about *Blown to Hell*. The Toronto Public Library soon had a backlog of more than two hundred requests for its single copy. Librarians in other cities reported similar demand. Many tried to place orders for the book on the basis of the interest they were registering, but their distributors drew a blank. Messages to the publisher went unanswered.

Fortunately, the receiver working on the Bunyok Press bankruptcy hadn't quite finished its work. The sole accountant remaining on the job had been incommunicado for several days; he'd been at a *Star Trek* convention in Las Vegas. On his return, Byron Bennett received the accumulated queries and orders, and wondered how to respond—for he no longer had the books. They'd been deemed of no commercial value, even as remainders. The author's family had taken them away, saving him the disposal costs. Byron remembered it well, because a very attractive lady had shown up at the warehouse to cart them off. He'd had time on his hands, the job was winding down, and she was a good-looking woman. Too old for him, but obviously a looker in her prime. Nice tits. And she had these eyes—blue eyes that pierced to the soul. Byron Bennett found them more intense, more seductive even, than those of Tasha Yar, security officer on the Enterprise (*TNG*, Season 1), who was his all-time blue-eyed fantasy lover. There were things that went on behind his daytime accountant's facade, if people only knew. It was lonely in the receivership business. He spent weeks in drafty, dark warehouses, at shuttered workshops and factories, winding up failed businesses and dealing with their detritus. He missed human contact. Female contact.

Byron Bennett had been so taken with the blue-eyed woman that he'd helped her load her van. A pretty, dark-haired girl, maybe twelve, the spitting image of her mother, had also helped. She slogged boxes wordlessly, looking so morose it was touching. And those eyes—they were just like the woman's. He'd felt compelled to make conversation, just to engage the sombre pair. "*Blown to Hell*," he said, reading the label on a box. "Is it about some explosion? A disaster?"

"It was a disaster, certainly," the woman replied. "Here." She handed him a book from an open box. "I won't give away the ending." But she wasn't in the mood to talk, and the girl said nothing at all. When the books were loaded, Blue Eyes thanked him and signed the appropriate form and drove away.

As Byron Bennett read the inquiries that flooded his screen the morning after his return from Las Vegas, he remembered the two of them, the beautiful mother, the pretty, sad-eyed girl, and thought longingly of women. There'd been a few at the *Star Trek* convention, but they'd all been dressed as Vulcans. Why didn't the genre appeal to women? Why didn't *he* appeal to women? He didn't get it. To boldly go, these days. A lot of women boldly went, just not with him. He retrieved the *Blown to Hell* file (proud that every transaction, even for a dollar, and every item of inventory, even the worthless stuff, was traceable). He found the woman's contact details and dialled her number.

She sounded surprised to hear from him, and about the number of inquiries he'd received about the book. He offered to forward them to her and explained how she'd need to work out payment details and arrange shipping to buyers. He told her how this was done. He'd learned a great deal in that drafty warehouse in Etobicoke, picking over the bones of Bunyok Press, and he was happy to share the lessons with an attractive woman.

Later, once he'd dealt with all the email, once he'd caught up on everything, he found his copy of the book. It would be a quiet week in the warehouse, probably his last before he was dispatched to his next bankruptcy. He kicked his feet up on the desk and began to read.

*

For several days, orders came in to Genny through the accommodating Byron Bennett, but they remained unfilled as she haggled with a credit card company over billing arrangements. There was sales tax, too. The minutiae bewildered her. It was all percentages and flat fees and gross versus net. Her dead husband had handled all the numbery-things. She became frustrated, then angry. But Chloe, who was good with numbers (Genny had never realized how good), explained it to her then gently took over to make the on-line arrangements they needed with PayBuddy, the bank, and the tax people. She mastered the details quickly and seemed to enjoy negotiating solutions. She was good with computers, too.

Over a hectic weekend they caught up on the backlog. Over the next week they received more orders and worked together every night billing and packaging books from the pile in the basement. Chloe addressed the courier envelopes and arranged for pick-up. They were amazed to find a number of international buyers among the orders they shipped.

The following Monday, Byron Bennett called to say he was forwarding more orders. It was an excuse, a pretext so he could tell Genny how much he'd enjoyed the book. "If you're thinking about doing a reprint," he told her, "I can recommend a distributor. They'll do all the shipping and billing for you. And the way the orders have been coming ..."

The books were half-gone, then only a couple hundred remained; after ten days the basement was nearly empty.

It was then that Genny received a call from the head buyer at the biggest book chain in Canada. He was receiving inquiries about *Blown*. Many inquiries. The interest warranted getting the book into stores.

"How many do you want?" Genny asked. There were about twenty left in the basement.

"Two thousand," came the answer. "We're seeing a lot of on-line interest too. Unusually strong."

"We're doing a reprint. I'll check on its status and get back to you."

Genny hung up and called Peter and Farley for advice.

That evening they met around her dining room table to talk it out. They agreed they had to get more copies, fast.

"So how do I do that? What do you think I should do?"

"Before we get into that," Peter said, "I'm trying to understand what's going on here. What's behind all this sudden interest."

Genny turned her cold laser gaze on him.

"Not that it's not a fine book. A fine book, an accomplishment, worthy of all the—"

"I've been wondering the same thing," Farley said. "The book's been out for months. There was no interest at all, now suddenly there is. There's something behind this."

"Exactly!" Peter said. "Something we can use to our advantage, if we can figure it out."

They fell silent, wondering how to figure it out.

"I know what it is," Chloe said.

Until then she'd been sitting quietly at the end of the table, listening. Now she pulled her chair closer to theirs. "I was curious about all those orders, so I did some basic reverse off-site web analytics—you know, deep-link tracking, but working backwards by isolating IP addresses and temporal signatures. I learned how to do it for a project at school. Daddy showed me. I just followed the timing of weblog link creation. When you track back you can get to the original source. Then I looked for a model or theory to explain it. It's a viral expansion loop. It expands according to a power law curve."

They all stared at her.

"What?" she asked.

"Go on, go on," they all urged at once.

They sat in silence when she finished. Finally Farley asked, "Are you sure? About the source?"

Chloe looked disappointed in her Uncle Farley. "I used a temporal link sequence algorithm."

"Ah."

The girl's eyes moved from face to face. A look of wonder spread across her own as she realized they did not understand what she was talking about.

"It's like triangulating a position fix from multiple observations. That's used for pilotage. You know, navigation? I've got all the data if you want to look at it. You can see the connections that triangulate that address."

Farley waved a hand. Genny's eyes were fixed on Chloe.

"Dammed if I understood any of that," Peter said, "but with all this interest I know I can find a mainstream publisher now." He began to rhyme off ideas and names to Genny, and Farley got up to stretch. He stood in a window and looked out at his old friend's backyard. It was spring, and the tulips were out, lilies were springing from the earth; a saskatoon bush was in full snowy bloom, and his dead friend's rhubarb, in a patch by the fence, was at its sour peak.

On the other side of the fence stood a barefooted figure in white pyjamas: Anthony, poised like a tai chi master with hands pressed together, one leg bent midair. He held Namaste, pointed his airborne foot down at the grass and slowly brought it to its mate. He bowed, straightened, stood stock-still, and abruptly leapt into the air. When he landed he skipped and circled his yard, flapping his arms like a man-sized bird. He did a round of figure eights, then another complete circle before stopping in his original spot to execute a surprisingly competent pirouette.

Farley was struck speechless, unable to call the others to the window.

Anthony tottered to catch his balance, breathing hard, then bowed slowly to an object in the centre of the lawn which Farley, absorbed in the spectacle, had not noticed. At a distance, it looked like a framed photograph of—could it be?—Anthony himself.

Anthony held the bow, straightened, and launched into a slow motion reprise of his initial dance, this time in the opposite direction.

Farley realized what he was witnessing; he'd heard about it from his dead friend. It was one of Anthony's rituals, a self-actualization ceremony called the Dance of the Spring Self.

He turned away from the spectacle beyond the window. Genny and Peter were still discussing mainstream publishers. Chloe was listening, eyes narrowed in concentration.

"Genny."

Everyone at the table looked up.

"Publish it yourself."

"Eh?"

That was Peter, suddenly unsettled.

"Look at all the buzz. Publish it yourself and take control of what happens. Look how it's flying out of the basement. We'll build on the buzz and keep it flying. I think Chloe can help with that."

His eyes returned to Anthony, who seemed on the verge of taking flight himself.

*

The second edition of *Blown to Hell* came out in hard copy, a rare reversal of the normal publishing sequence. Its publisher, Indiana-based Eitelkeit Press, was best known for the eclecticism of its catalogue, which included a series by Toronto self-fulfillment consultant and commentator Anthony B. Bliss. The print run was two thousand copies, which retailed at $37.95. In parallel with the hard cover edition, Eitelkeit produced another soft cover edition (retailing at $24.99) in a run of five thousand. When both versions sold out in a couple of weeks (by this time on-line sales to US and international buyers were taking off) another larger run was ordered for both the hard and soft cover versions. The scarcity of physical books seemed to drive demand for the e-book version, which was priced competitively with the latest Dan Brown.

*

It was Phil Regency's clever viral campaign, of course, that had engendered the phenomenal interest in *Blown to Hell*. It had taken off among tech-savvy first adapters and hipsters who received the tweets and read the feeds, saw the tags and touts and raves, and followed the links on blogs and Twitter and Facebook; they caught the buzz and *HAD* to have the book. Some of them even read it, then joined the on-line forums and fan pages that Phil had established. He'd created several (or rather, his intern had) in order to hide his cyber tracks—the whole happening had to seem spontaneous. Phil knew any sign of contrivance or manipulation would be the death of his campaign.

His forums took off, and spontaneously, surprisingly, new sites, new forums like Friends of B2H, and B2H-4EVR sprang up and took off, too, with enthusiastic commentary and reviews. A "brilliant and ironic study of mediocrity," someone called *Blown*, "a fascinating take on life in the shadow of a more interesting person." The debate was wide ranging, both among those who'd read the book, and those who said they had. More said than had, for as a rule most of those opining never read beyond 140 characters, and *Blown* weighed in at more than 600 pages.

Many tried reading the book and decided it was not for them, concluding it was wandering, overlong and dull; and so they gave it to their older relatives, who knew something about the period in which it was set. It had been the subject of a recent best-seller, a first novel by another Canadian writer. Among this older demographic, word of mouth still mattered, and they'd heard about this phenomenon all the young people were twittering about. *Blown* became de rigueur for the book clubs popular among middle-aged women and homosexual men. As a percentage, no more of the oldsters read it than had the hipsters, but they kept it in a conspicuous spot on their bookshelves. At social gatherings, they talked about it like they'd read it cover to cover. Implausibly, many claimed to have read it in one sitting.

*

With all that buzz it was inevitable that *Blown to Hell* slipped onto and then climbed to the top of the Canadian bestseller lists, where it camped for months, recognized now as a come-from-nowhere phenomenon, the book equivalent of the Little Engine That Could. It was unusual for the book to be re-reviewed, but several new and glowing reviews followed the unexpected sales surge. "An English-Canadian masterpiece," declared reclusive novelist Basil Letherman in an exclusive *Toronto Star* commentary to mark the release of the fourth edition. Letherman considered it THE notable book of the year. "Get *Blown* for Christmas!" he urged the *Star's* readers. In the *National Post* and related Post-Media papers, the normally publicity-shy Cynthia Powell Ducat, writing from her castle in the south of France, called it "a stunning achievement, a must-read swash-buckling bodice-ripper for all ages." In the *Sun*, Pussy Hindmost declared it sexy. (Known for three volumes of rollicking cult erotica, Ms Hindmost was perhaps an odd choice for a reviewer of historical fiction, but it was the *Sun* after all. Ms Hindmost declined the paper's offer of a Sunshine Girl shoot, citing her privacy policy. "Because of my pornotoriety," she told the editor via email, "I never appear in anything but blacked-out profile—and a negligee of the same colour.")

The tone of the *Globe's* coverage was more restrained than that of the other papers. It printed no independent author commentaries or reviews, but in light of the book's popularity it ran a short assessment of the author by the director of the writing school from which he'd taken courses. "His characters are cardboard, his similes laboured, his predilection for the semi-colon a distraction; yet his book is an undeniable success." He concluded by describing the author as "seemingly, the Susan Boyle of Canadian letters" and his untimely death "a loss of un-measurable impact." Meanwhile, recognizing the phenomenon that had created a bestseller—and fearing new media itself—the *Globe's* editorial board commissioned a story on the role of social media in popularizing the book, intending to publish an exposé on the making of a bestseller in the digital age. And it resolved to secure an interview with the author's widow, the noted academic and feminist thinker Genny Patersdotter, who had declined all media requests (as agent Peter Wannacutt explained) "because of her ongoing desolation over the loss of her husband and the unfortunate circumstances of his death."

*

The book continued to garner attention. A French translation, *Coup Vers le Bas*, prepared with the aid of a Canada Council grant, was released to the francophone market. "A story about the English during the period of Quebec's subjugation," said the review in the journal *De Souche*, "it represents yet another historical humiliation. In its entire six hundred pages (translated by Ottawa) there is no mention at all of Quebec!" However, francophone *trendistes* soon caught the viral bug for what became known on *le web* as CVB, and forums dedicated exclusively to it multiplied like fake ballots in a sovereignty referendum. Back in English Canada, the *Star* followed-up on its latest commentary with a sympathetic profile of the author, describing once more the circumstances of his death in a feature called "*Blown*: the GTA Connection." Out west there were features on the author's prairie origins. And none other than Lord Black championed *Blown to Hell* on CTV's annual "Come On and Read, Eh?" competition, describing it as "loquacious, verbose and occasionally pompous—in short, a delightful read and, at a mere six hundred pages, hardly a prolix tome. Its perspicacious perspective and historical quiddity are sufficient to exculpate its exanimate author from the scurrilous yet spavined criticisms of my opponents on this panel, who will undoubtedly speak with insipid velleity as champions of authors of greater brevity and lesser merit." His Lordship's comments elicited an uncertain silence from the other panellists; host Lloyd Robertson appeared to have dozed off.

(On discussion forum B2H-4EVR, it was felt that the exanimate author, had he been able to choose his own champion, would have picked his home-boy Brent Butt over Mr Crossharbour but—something of a sesquipedalian himself—he would have appreciated the old windbag's gasconading summation.)

Stories featuring Broughton, Vancouver and the sea otter

began to appear on various fan fiction websites. Tweets, Facebook posts, and comments on the popular B2H discussion forums helpfully directed users and followers to these sites. The initial story trickle became a torrent. Soon there were crossover stories featuring Broughton and characters from *Harry Potter* and *Twilight*. The latter was also set in the Pacific north-west.

*

Phil Regency considered what he had wrought.

There would be a furor when he disclosed the scam. He would be at the centre of a firestorm.

He smiled. That was just where he wanted to be: at the centre of a firestorm. Publicity was what he thrived on. Buzz was his business. Oh, he would make a splash with this.

He chuckled at the way things had snowballed. It had gone even better than he'd anticipated. It was almost as though someone were manipulating his masterpiece, amplifying what he'd created. Oh, it would be delicious when he went public. The moment for the Big Reveal was fast approaching, but it wasn't quite time. Not yet.

Near what he thought *must* be the climax of the frenzy, he received a request from the *Globe* for an interview. The reporter was known to Phil by reputation, a former foreign correspondent who wrote occasional weekend features and specials for the *Globe*. She said she was preparing a story on the phenomenon of *Blown to Hell* and wanted to talk to him for an industry perspective. Phil was flattered but wondered, why him? Perhaps it was his man-of-the-arts reputation, carefully nurtured and projected to the world via his regular gig on Kudos! Dividends, that's what his appearances were generating. Profile!

He agreed to meet her in a downtown wine bar. (Why not let the *Globe* buy him a drink? Or two.) For a woman in her forties, Reporter Girl was hot. He'd seen her on TV, where she was a regular panellist on a CBC news program. (He'd only been channel surfing—he would never dream of watching CBC.) True, she was a bit old for him, but he wouldn't be averse to a roll in the hay. He liked the thought of doing it with another celebrity. And she bore a striking resemblance to Shirley MacLaine in her prime.

When they met it was clear she'd done her research. She had the statistics on *Blown's* sales, and she was exceedingly well informed on the web's role in creating a publishing sensation. She'd even interviewed the late author's widow, which Phil recognized as a scoop for the *Globe*. Genny Patersdotter had long declined media interviews. Probably embarrassed, Phil thought, by her husband's book.

He asked the cougar-reporter how she got the Patersdotter interview.

"I was an acquaintance." She held Phil's eye for a moment before continuing. "I want to talk about the phenomenon of *Blown to Hell*. There's a theory doing the rounds that it was engineered. That public opinion—that people—have been manipulated."

"That's possible," he replied carefully, suddenly alert. This was not the way he intended to go public. He wanted a bigger forum than one paper. Besides, it was *his* story, not hers. He pictured a packed news conference, live streaming video feed, a top trending topic on Twitter.

"Who could do that?" she asked. "Who could manipulate all these people? I mean, it would be extremely difficult to pull off. And risky, too, for an insider."

"Why's that?" he asked, sipping his wine, a terrific Bordeaux, the 1998 Chateau Léoville-Barton at $29 a glass. She'd ordered an unremarkable red, which she hadn't touched.

"Well, say it was a publicity stunt. Someone did it to prove a point, or to play a practical joke. If that's the case, it's a brilliant hoax, one for the ages. Did you know that the Olympic torch relay is a manufactured event? Totally made up. No tradition at all. The Nazis invented it in 1936. Today it's huge, but it's just a marketing event, kind of a hoax on all of us when you think of it, but it's accepted because there aren't any victims. It doesn't embarrass anybody. So it's not really comparable to *Blown* . . . if *Blown* were a hoax."

He thought moodily that if she would only take a drink, he'd have a chance for a roll in the hay with a war correspondent. That was kind of a turn-on. But she was all business, damn it. Where was she going with this Olympic torch nonsense, anyway?

"No, if *Blown* were a hoax, it would be dynamite. Look at the sales numbers. Look at all the luminaries who bought in and praised it. Everyone's joined the parade. They've all gone on the record, too. That's the thing about the web. What you say stays on the record forever. So many people would be embarrassed. Humiliated. It would be way beyond a prank. You couldn't get more punk'd than this."

"I suppose," Phil said modestly, "it would make the person who did it famous."

"Not famous. Infamous. I'm sure it would be delicious for the hoaxster, but if it was someone with a stake in the business, well just imagine. He or she—let's call him he—he goes to the same parties, the same receptions for good causes and visiting writers, the same awards ceremonies. After humiliating all his peers, he'd be shunned. He'd never be forgiven. He'd be Ben Johnson, Mel Gibson and Charlie Manson all rolled into one. He'd be a pariah. And if the target of the hoax was *this* guy, it would be even worse. Did you know he survived 9/11? He was in the North Tower. I never knew until Genny Patersdotter told me. He didn't want it known. He didn't like the way the media created a myth around it. You know, everyone a hero. I guess he saw things that day . . .

"But that's what they've become, isn't it, in the popular mind. Everyone who died, whatever they did, they're all heroes now, the victims. And he definitely was a victim. His lungs were damaged, he was deeply affected. He probably had PTSD, though he refused to be treated or even assessed . . . and now he's dead. From complications, many would say. So he's a 'hero' too, I suppose, by that reckoning. And a hoax directed at a genuine hero . . . well. The person who did that would be a monster." Her eyes went from Phil to the table. "Oh, I forgot my machine. I'm so sorry." She leaned over and clicked on her digital recorder. "Phil Regency, this story's pretty well in the bag. I've just got some loose ends to tie up, and then it goes to print tonight. So I just wanted to ask you—Phil Regency, any comment on that possibility? That the phenomenon of *Blown to Hell* could possibly be the product of an elaborate hoax, a hoax intended to embarrass the Canadian literary establishment?"

Phil Regency sat very still. He studied the reporter's face for a moment. His eyes dropped to the recorder on the table.

"I'd find that hard to countenance," he said.

"One final question, Phil, if I may. Is it true you turned him down?"

Again he studied her face, thinking what a bitch she was, and ugly, too. She was typical of the old media and their notions of narrative and truth. He drained his glass, thinking what plonk it was. Since when did vinegar come with an *appellation*? "Yes," he allowed at last.

"Why?"

He swallowed but said nothing. At last he cleared his throat. "Well, I missed him, I guess. It's a . . ." He paused and thought carefully about his next words, staring now at the recorder. He'd not read the book himself, but he had to say something about it now. "What he wrote . . . it, ah . . . boggles the mind."

She reached for her recorder. "Thank you, Phil Regency," she said. "I think I've got what I needed."

*

Eventually *Blown to Hell* was issued in a full-colour gift edition that shared with readers the many photos, works of art and documents that had inspired its late author to create a new Canadian classic. It included more than 150 images, including early maps and documents, archival photos, period paintings, and extracts from the original handwritten journal of William Broughton, the novel's epic second-rate protagonist. It was hailed as an historic keepsake, a holiday gift to treasure, an essential addition to any booklover's collection; it sold out in weeks. A second, expanded gift edition soon appeared, this with lost scenes from *Blown*, including an interior monologue by the novel's beloved sea otter character. Many who had bought the first gift edition bought the expanded one as well.

On eBay, the homely, ink-smudged, cheaply-bound Bunyok Press first edition paperback sold at a handsome premium over its original price. Like an inverted postage stamp, the first edition of an historic bestseller set in the Pacific north-west but adorned with a photo of a Plains Indian on a horse was a curiosity that screamed "COLLECTIBLE!" The author would have shaken his head at this, for with all his mathematical logic he had never understood the psychology of markets. He'd always wondered what sustained the demand for gold and diamonds, who would buy Napoleon's socks, and what would drive a person to speculate in derivatives. No financial psychologist, he: his tastes had always run to the utilitarian. Perhaps this was because of his lifelong inability to capture nuance.

*

The unexpected success of *Blown* created enduring interest in its author. As edition after edition was issued and absorbed by the market, the public clamoured for more; but it was unclear if any other works, finished or unfinished, existed. Rumours circulated on the web about an unfinished opus, but they were never substantiated by the author's literary co-executors, his widow Genny Patersdotter and his friend Dr Farley Lictor. For two years, speculation ran rampant amongst Blownies, as they came to be known, until agent Peter Wannacutt called a press conference to announce that the executors had discovered several unfinished works among the author's papers. They were studying the collection to determine if any could be released to scholars or completed and published in their own right. Wannacutt's main purpose in calling the press conference was to announce that the author had been planning a musical adaptation of *Blown to Hell*. He had been working on it at the time of his death, and now his executors planned to fulfill his wishes and finish it. Dr Lictor would complete the libretto for *North Pacific* himself, and a well known British composer-lyricist duo had been commissioned to work with him on the score. The author's heirs had joined with legendary financier Murray Rothstein to form a company, B2H Productions, and retained former theatre impresario Garth Drabinsky to advise them on production matters. Wannacutt emphasized that Drabinsky, fresh out of prison after swindling investors on past megamusicals, would have nothing to do with finances. A young accountant of impeccable reputation, Byron Bennett his name, had been hired to head the venture and oversee all financial arrangements. Bennett was a former employee of a prominent accounting firm specializing in receivership; he had been introduced to *Blown to Hell* by Genny Patersdotter herself before it became a publishing sensation. He had been an instant enthusiast of the book; independently, he had founded the William Broughton Voyage Re-enactment Society. He'd served as trusted advisor to the author's heirs from the earliest days of *Blown's* rediscovery.

Immediately upon this news, two competing impresarios, one with a fedora, the other without, both bald and with capacious theatres to fill in Toronto, began vying for the right to premiere *North Pacific*. B2H Productions chose the one with the track record.

For months, as the production came together, the Toronto theatre world and Blownies everywhere were abuzz with anticipation. The book and score were completed, directors were hired, financings proceeded, work on staging commenced, casting calls were made, rehearsals began. One of the key casting decisions proved controversial, and speculation was rife as to why a thirty-something actress, blonde to boot—one Darlene Monroe—was cast as a teenaged aboriginal, the romantic interest for the Broughton character. Monroe's resume was slim: roles in alternative theatre in Toronto, a season at Stratford, and a supporting role on a Canadian TV series, a fantasy about a woman who travels back in time to fix her mistakes. B2H discussion forums and Broughton-bloggers went wild; rumour had it that Monroe had been the author's mistress. Or his widow's. The furor added to the buzz surrounding the production, just as the box office opened for advance sales. "Trust me," Drabinsky told the press, "we've got a runaway on our hands." (At his next meeting with his probation officer, the impresario, still wearing an ankle monitor, was quizzed on what he'd meant by "runaway.")

North Pacific, paired down to a lithe two and a half hours from the author's original four, premiered to mixed reviews. "A world-class musical tsunami," gushed the *Toronto Star*, "mounted first, right here in Toronto!" "Darlene Monroe shines, but Broughton's breeches steal the show!" shouted *Xtra!*, ever a fan of musicals and tight pants. For its part, the *Globe* was not impressed. "Pocahontas with totems," it sniffed. Other reviews were nuanced. "A complex narrative, successfully dumbed down for musical theatre," Maclean's said. "One to endure," said the *Post*, likening it to *Lion King* and *Cats*. (The *Post* reviewer's connotation was the subject of heated debate on B2H-4EVR, where the final vote was four to one for "enduring" over "unendurable.")

Reviews notwithstanding, it soon became clear that Drabinsky had been right. Wearied by the longest recession in eighty years, and by never-ending forecasts of environmental doom, audiences responded with enthusiasm to a simple love story from a pristine bygone era, when there were no concerns about environmental degradation or global warming. *North Pacific* became the feel-good hit of the year, a runaway success that sold out night after night. As it settled in for a long run at the Princess of Wales Theatre, plans were launched for productions in New York and London as well as for a tour of secondary Canadian markets like Gander and Montreal.

In an interview, co-protolibrettist (a term he seems to have coined himself) Farley Lictor expressed regret that audiences did not recognize *North Pacific's* (and *Blown's*) setting in the unspoiled Pacific north-west as the late author's wake-up call on environmental despoliation. "While he struggled with nuance himself," he said, "he'd be disappointed that people don't get his meta-message about the environment. As everyone knows, he was a staunch environmentalist. He abhorred what he saw happening and was determined to make a difference." He went on to stun his interviewer by acknowledging for the first time the existence of an unfinished manuscript, the author's final work. "He was working on it when he died. He intended it as an extended, novel-length parable cum allegory of hope. We called it his paragory. If the circumstances of his last days had been different . . ." he left off without finishing, leaving his interviewer to ask breathlessly if there were plans to release the unfinished masterpiece to the waiting world.

*

"I don't call it vanity publishing or even Self-publishing," Anthony B. Bliss told the moderator. He was discussing his dear dead friend's success on the arts and soft-porn cable channel Kudos! "I call it taking Self control of the intellectual and production processes at the creative/market interface."

*

Close on the box office success of *North Pacific* and the ongoing strength of *Blown's* sales, the co-executors of the author's estate, along with the president of their production company, Byron Bennett, announced that a William Broughton action figure would arrive in stores in time for the next Christmas season. It would be made in Canada, and would contain no bisphenol-A whatsoever.

*

Speculation continued about a film adaptation of *Blown to Hell*. Fans agreed that the casting for the Broughton character would be crucial to its successful transition to the Big Screen. The consensus on B2H-4EVR and other dedicated on-line forums was that the actor ultimately selected to play Broughton had to be a B-movie veteran; and that William Shatner was too old for the role.

*

Genny Patersdotter endowed numerous environmental causes in her dead husband's memory. They were causes close to his heart, groups fighting to ban harmful chemicals or to publicize the risk of global warming. Otherwise she kept a low profile. She only ever granted a single interview on the strange phenomenon of *Blown to Hell*. It was for the *Globe & Mail*, which had a personal In with the reclusive widow. The reporter it assigned to the piece was an acquaintance of both Patersdotter and her late husband.

The audio of the interview is widely available to this day. (It was bundled, for example, with newly-released lost scenes, additional historical content, and sundry musings by the author on global warming and toxic chemicals, on the latest, full-colour holiday gift *Blown to Hell* e-book, and with the *Blown*-themed video game.) There are numerous clicks on the recording; evidently the digital recorder was giving the reporter some difficulty. Several times she is heard to say mildly, "Oh this darn machine!"—an oddly helpless exclamation for a seasoned correspondent used to problem-solving in the field.

Frankly, there is nothing exceptional about the interview. The reporter concludes their session with the soft bromides typical of interviews about the dead. "What would your husband have said about all this?" she asks.

It is clear from the voice of Genny Patersdotter that she is smiling. "He would have been pleased at how his work was received. A bit mystified by it all, but pleased."

"And what of his legacy? How would he have liked to be remembered?"

On the recording there is a long pause. At last the widow finds her voice. "He would want to be remembered," she says softly, "as a person of letters."

A pause. A rustle. *Click. Click.*

"He had many passions."

"Oh yes. History. He drew inspiration from history. Heroes. He was passionate about real heroes, the unsung ones who sought no glory for themselves but did the job. And the environment, of course. Everyone knows now what he felt about the environment. I don't need to go into *that*. It's a shame he . . . he died how and when he did, that he didn't finish his allegory. It would have linked his interests . . ." A pause, but the recording continues. "And writing was a passion. I guess that's clear to everyone. He regretted not pursuing it earlier. When he finally took it up, he pursued it without a backward glance . . . until the end." Pause, and now she can be heard smiling. "Numbers. It's how his mind worked; he saw patterns in numbers. He saw equations everywhere. He loved underdogs. He loved veterans. He loved football, and you know what that meant, where he came from."

"He was passionately *against* some things."

"He didn't like phonies—"

"This darn machine! I'm sorry, Dr Patersdotter." *Click.* They sit looking at each other. "Genny, don't say anything on tape about the viral loop. Or Phil Regency. I'll keep both of them out of this piece, and we'll deal with him. I'll do another article on viral marketing to satisfy my editor, but this story stays with us."

"I know."

"Go on, from the phonies."

Click.

"Ah, he didn't like politicians who lie or deny science. Or separatists. Same reason – the selective lies. He didn't much like political correctness" (her voice smiles again) "and he was sceptical about a lot of things . . . But history and the environment, those were his passions to the very end."

Click.

"And you."

Tears well in Genny's eyes.

"Tell me what happened, Genny. At the end. You know we're off the record."

*

They were able to piece together something about his

intentions from what he wrote in the days leading up to the focus group—and the contents of the duffel bag. But there would always be uncertainty about his specific plan. "Direct action" can mean many things, and many things were possible based on what he took with him. He had the cutters and the hammer; he had enough rope, duct tape, and heavy-duty cable ties for handcuffs; he had spray paint for the security cameras. It's possible that taking a hostage was his first and only priority. The presence of an executive from the carbon-spewing, green-washing, Jew-exploiting Heil AG had infuriated him. Perhaps this unfortunate German (or Austrian), would have been his only victim. Or perhaps he intended to take Porlock down with him. He'd long suffered Porlock's annoying interruptions and he'd been, well . . . emotional lately. Once he was on their premises . . .

Or maybe he was only going to banner Toronto's World Trade Centre with an eco-message, as Greenpeace had bannered Big Ben during the Copenhagen summit. He'd admired that accomplishment, and he had a golden opportunity to do it himself: on that day he'd be on the top floor of a prominent building facing the city. He could easily access the roof from there. He had the spray paint; he had the tarp for the banner; and he had the ties and rope to secure it. They found numerous slogans scribbled in his notebooks, phrases like "Stop Global Warming!", and "Deny THIS." (They also found "Go Riders," but that was probably an unrelated doodle, made during the team's plucky playoff run that fall.)

If it was his intention to festoon the WTC with an environmental message, it seems incongruous that such a methodical person didn't make the banner in advance—until you consider the state of his lungs. The propellants used in spray paint are composed of volatile hydrocarbons and organic compounds, dangerous to inhale, especially for a man with reduced respiratory capacity. He would surely have waited until he was on the roof before endangering his mission by exposing himself to debilitating chemicals.

Or perhaps he was planning something else. It will never be known for certain. What happened, happened.

*

A blizzard hit on the day of the focus group. Schools closed down, the airport was in chaos, and snow clogged the roads. Streetcars ploughed through drifts until they stalled. It was difficult to get anywhere in the city but he would not be denied. He hauled his heavy duffel bag to the subway, then rode underground to Union Station, then trudged to the World Trade Centre on Queen's Quay. He slipped through the lobby and into the elevator where he pressed the button for the top floor.

The doors stayed open. And stayed open. It seemed they would never shut. His stomach tightened. Doubt seeped into his mind. What of this plan of his? There was still time to change his mind. He was sweating heavily. The weight of the bag dug into his shoulder; he hiked it up and pushed the button again, and again, until the doors finally began to close, but slowly, with attitude, as if programmed by an anarchist on work-to-rule. And when they were almost shut, when their glacial journey towards closure was near its end, a hand appeared in the ever shrinking gap. The rubber edges of the doors closed on its wrist like toothless jaws. The doors froze instantly.

He stared at the hand. Its fingers waggled experimentally. Its nails were dirty. A buzzer jangled. The doors began to inch open, still on grudging work-to-rule. He stood with his heart pounding in his chest, his eyes fixed on the expanding gap. There were surveillance cameras in the lobby, and he'd walked right past a security desk. Had he done something to draw attention?

A man squeezed through the doors. But he was not a security guard or policeman, at least one on duty. He was dressed in a long parka—a *civilian* parka—from which he brushed snow impatiently. The doors continued to spread open, the buzzer continued to blare. The man glanced at his watch and shook his head. He looked at the floor buttons and saw the top one lit. He pressed it anyway. "You here for that focus group?" he asked the shaken author. His face was gray, his nose runny.

"Yes."

"Me, too." He stomped snow off his boots. "What a crappy day. I'm just here for the honorarium." He pressed the Close button repeatedly until the doors finally rolled shut and the elevator began its slow ascent. The buzzer, mercifully, fell silent.

Between the 10th and 11th floors, the man in the parka sneezed. He made no effort to contain it. "Cats," he said. "Always happens."

There were no cats in the elevator, just the two of them, one fidgeting and shifting his duffel bag from shoulder to shoulder, the other pale and sniffling.

These days, everyone sneezes into his armpit, the eco-warrior thought randomly. It's because of SARS and the swine flu.

No, it's *not* the swine flu, he corrected himself loyally, thinking of his wife. It's the novel strain of H1N1, or the novel flu; she calls it that to avoid casting blame on innocent swine farmers. She hasn't eaten pork in years, and she's got a beef with their farm practices (ha hah, a beef with swine producers!) but she's on their side—as she is for all the down-trodden, the dispossessed, the oppressed, the have-nots, the can't-save-themselves-for-trying second-stringers and B-teamers. And me.

His thoughts were rambling—it was as though he was babbling in his mind. Babbling was one of his perennial ways of coping with stress. So was changing the subject. The elevator really was on a lackadaisical schedule. He should have taken the stairs. He'd popped a Xanax that morning—another way to cope with stress. And Genny had insisted on St John's wort and ma huang, which she said expanded the bronchial tubes. Ma huang was one of her Chinese herbal medications, from a plant called *ephedra*—he'd looked it up on the web one day. He'd meant to read more but he'd been rushed. (He was in the middle then of his research.) He was always curious about what she suggested, even though he inevitably took it. After all, she hadn't poisoned him yet! Ha hah ha! He felt sweat trickling down his back. He hadn't slept the night before, or much the night before that; he was jumpy, like he was coffeed up, but all he'd had before bed was herbal tea, that Mormon stuff that was good for you. The thought of Mormon tea made him think of Cindy. Well, Cindy, he told her in his mind, you haven't poisoned me either—yet! Ha hah ha! Ha hah ha! Suddenly he felt magnanimous towards Cindy and her rank herbal remedies, her Tea Party politics, her undying crush on Genny . . .

The other man snorted and sniffed and cleared his throat. Somewhere between the 25th and 30th floors he sneezed again.

The elevator stopped with a bump; the doors rolled open, and the two of them stepped onto the penthouse floor. At one end of the hall was a reception area where, on a good day, floor-to-ceiling windows provided a magnificent view of Toronto harbour, the Islands, and Lake Ontario beyond. But it was not a good day, and the blizzard had obscured the view completely. Snow blew hard against the windows, ice crystals ticked the glass—everything outside was white and pure. They had arrived, it seemed, in heaven's antechamber, and God's receptionist was on the phone. They stood in front of her desk, gazing out at the storm. She finished her call and hung up. "Are you here for the eleven o'clock focus group?"

The cat man affirmed they were.

"Can I have your names?" She checked them off a list as the author's heart thudded in his chest. "I'm sorry, gentlemen, I appreciate you coming all this way, but this blizzard's really messed things up. The consultant who was going to lead the focus group couldn't even get in from Richmond Hill this morning. We've sent all our staff who did make it in home already. We're closing down. They say on the news the mayor's calling in the army."

"What about the German?" asked the writer. "The one who was coming in to make a presentation?"

"He's Austrian, actually," she said. "He was flying in from New York this morning but they couldn't land. They diverted his plane to Montreal."

"Oh man!" said the man with the cat allergy. "I just came for the honorarium. I should've just stayed in bed. I feel like crap."

"We'll reschedule," the receptionist said. "I'll give you both taxi chits to go home *and* your honorarium, for your trouble."

The cat man felt a sneeze brewing, and out of delicacy he turned away from Porlock's capable receptionist to deliver it upon his elevator companion.

Our writer, thwarted focus-group participant, and would-be direct actionist rode home in a taxi, feeling somewhat mollified by the fifty dollars in his pocket.

Within a day he felt fluish. He was badly congested; he had a cough and fever. Over the next two days the infection spread deep into his lungs, which were already damaged from a previous incident of direct action (not one of his). He was rushed to hospital, where he worsened, then stabilized. For days he clung tenaciously to life, fighting with what his doctors called extraordinary pluck. It was not enough. The virus, in his case, proved deadly.

As much as he'd insisted that inoculation was necessary, as ardently as he'd debated the point with his wife, what with the shortage of vaccine, and then with the flu scare blowing over, he'd never bothered to get the shot.

*

"Oh, Genny . . ."

"Then when we got the first hundred books, we were clearing space in the basement, and Chloe found the duffel bag. I didn't make a fuss about it in front of her. I called Farley as soon as I could, and we tried to piece things together. I don't even know if he took it with him to Porlock that day. I don't know what he intended. We went through what he'd written—there was a lot about direct action. So maybe . . ." Her voice trails off.

Beth looks at her without speaking. She can think of nothing to say. Finally, she finds her voice and utters a single word: "Tragic."

"Yes."

They sit in silence, lost in their own thoughts.

"But don't you think it's ironic, too?" Genny asks, brightening suddenly. "Even appropriate? If it had to be?"

Beth's face shows her surprise. She had not expected a comment like this from Genny, who has become a friend since they met months before over a raw vegan meal. "Ironic, Genny? 'If it had to be?' What do you mean?"

Genny looks away. A smile forms on her lips but there are tears in her eyes. Finally she looks at Beth. "He wouldn't care about the sensation it became. He wouldn't understand it, really. Marketing wasn't his thing. He would've gladly left that to others. He just wanted to write, and to get what he wrote into print. It was a way for him to connect with others. That's what he wanted, more than anything, to connect with others, because he always felt . . . he always felt . . ." She stopped and brushed a finger beneath both eyes. "He worked hard to overcome what I thought made him special. He was so determined, in those final years. And after all he went through, everything he put up with, all those years of wanting to do it, he did it. He did what he set out to do. He became a novelist. So, you see, Beth—this is the ironic bit. Even he would have thought this was funny. He was, I guess you could say, a literalist, you know, but he'd been working on irony. He'd been working really hard on it, and I think he was getting it, too. Metaphor and analogy were still beyond him, but he was making real progress on irony. Well, the irony of it is—he had no immunity to *that* virus. To the novel strain of H1N1. It turned out to be a second-rate virus, not the scourge we feared it would be, but that name . . . For him, it was a fitting, ironic way to go. In the end, he was a true novelist: he died of the novel flu."

Genny snorts at the punch line to her husband's life. The snort blossoms into a giggle and then a laugh, a laugh that renews itself in great unstoppable gales. She is bent double in her chair, holding her sides; and then her face is in her hands. Manically, uncontrollably, she laughs, yet she weeps too. Sad, happy, ecstatic, lonely and resigned—she cannot help herself. Tears stream down her cheeks, cheeks her husband, the late novelist and incipient ironist, once and ever deemed perfect.

EPILOGUE

> I wrote in this way for a couple of reasons: First, I knew I wanted the ending of the story to be poignant and heartfelt, and second, because I didn't know if I would be able to do that, since my previous novels hadn't been good enough to publish.
>
> Nicholas Sparks

> I should love to do a novel . . . about one abnormal character seeing present-day life, very ordinary life, yet arresting through it, abnormality, until at the end the reader sees, and with little reluctance, that he is not abnormal at all, and that the main character might as well be himself.
>
> Patricia Highsmith

Over our shared back fence, or standing beside me at the compost bin, Anthony frequently advises that I must write my own eulogy. This is one of the Self-love exercises he uses in his seminars, poached off the internet from some other quack. Recently he's been extolling a corollary venture, that of the on-line memorial. For a fee you can leave a Self-eulogy on the internet, along with your life story, pictures and video, or some doggerel you wrote after abusing yourSelf in the shower. It will survive on the web (in the e-ther, so to speak), and so you will too—even though you are dead. As part of the service you can leave special messages for friends, deliver an email from the grave, or post a periodic update on a dedicated URL. "With my buddy John Lennon at a bistro on the River Styx. Fabulous prosciutto. Risotto to die for!" There is no way (yet) to post a selfie, but you could pre-pay a licence fee and upload a stock photo of your meal; and there is nothing to stop you from leaving a taunt for an enemy or a zinger to set the record straight. Best to keep these short. "I always loved you" has a timeless quality; tacking on "more than my wife" is a tad too much. So too is "I bonked Christine while you were skiing in Whistler," or "The man you call Dad is not your father," though I suppose it depends on the kind of immortality you seek. That's worth some thought; your eternal brand hinges on what you choose to say.

But truly, for us mere mortals, the notion of eternal is false. It is impossible to cast your brand in concrete. Reappraisals will happen as mores and fashions change. And your heirs and executors may fiddle with your legacy after you are gone. They may do it to burnish your reputation or ensure your point is made—or to maintain a lifestyle they've come to enjoy. It doesn't matter. You have no control over what comes After. Just assume they'll pull things out of context and place it out of sequence; they'll twist your words around and make people wonder what you really wrote—or if you even existed. That's just the way it is. *Que sera, sera.* After all, what is "Truth" in a postmodern world?

Anthony says that in the digital age (which is surely postmodern) you need never leave anything unsaid. He says that as if it's a good thing.

He has already registered several domain names for his on-line memorial scheme, and paid to link certain keyword searches to them. Business, he asserts, is good. It seems everyone wants a legacy. And I will concede this to him: take away all his Self nonsense, and there is something concrete at the heart of his obsession. It *is* important to consider your life in perspective, and to do it *now*, because you cannot know how long you may have left.

Writing your own eulogy is entirely Self serving. To Anthony that's the whole point. Far more interesting, in my view, is to write your own ending. That way you can put what you've accomplished (or tried to accomplish) in perspective, and admire those you loved (or tried to love) one last time. That's what I would do. I'd tell them how I felt.

In the fullness of time what you write may seem prophetic, wise, or foolish. It doesn't matter. Just do it—write your own ending and don't get hung up on it. Write it and get back to work, remembering that the time you have is finite and precious. Your days are numbered. It's the work, The Work, that is important, and you need to get on with it—as I must get on now with my own.

But first . . .

The phone is ringing, and I must answer—although it's likely just another person from Porlock.

Note to Reader:
As Samuel Taylor Coleridge composed *Kubla Khan* he was interrupted by "a person from Porlock." He never completed the poem.

ACKNOWLEDGMENTS

Thanks to the many readers who provided gentle feedback and input on successive whole drafts or particular sections of this novel: Lorna Clark, Kathryn Shailer, Beverley Trull, Laurie Leclair, Nancy Clark, Richard Smith, Mark Hume, Linda Maddaford, Aaron Badgley, Steve Garrett, Andrew Judd, Bill McCutcheon; and anyone I have inadvertently omitted Thanks also to Jana Pavlasek and Andrew Judd whose design concept and illustration, respectively, are featured on the cover, and to Adriana Soudek for her support on cover layout.

ABOUT THE AUTHOR

Ron Thompson was born in Saskatchewan. After training as a naval officer on Canada's Pacific coast and backpacking across Europe, he spent two years working as a CUSO volunteer on the margins of the Kalahari Desert. He subsequently pursued a career in Canada and internationally as an economist, investment banker and consultant. He lives in Toronto.

Ron is a Chartered Financial Analyst and a graduate of the University of Saskatchewan, the University of Toronto, the London School of Economics, and the Humber School for Writers. *A Person of Letters* is his first novel. His second, *Poplar Lake*, will be published by Martin Scribler Media in 2016.

Made in the USA
Charleston, SC
16 September 2015